THREE DAGGERS DRIPPING

BOOKS IN THE
DONALD YOUNGBLOOD MYSTERY SERIES

Three Deuces Down (2008)
Three Days Dead (2009)
Three Devils Dancing (2011)
Three Deadly Drops (2012)
Three Dragons Doomed (2014)
Three Daggers Dripping (2016)

A DONALD YOUNGBLOOD MYSTERY

THREE DAGGERS DRIPPING

KEITH DONNELLY

HUMMINGBIRD BOOKS

Gatlinburg, Tennessee

Hummingbird Books
A division of Harrison Mountain Press
P.O. Box 1386
Gatlinburg, TN 37738

Designed by Todd Lape / Lape Designs

Library of Congress Cataloging-in-Publication Data

Names: Donnelly, Keith.
Title: Three daggers dripping : a Donald Youngblood mystery / Keith
Donnelly.
Description: Gatlinburg, Tennessee : Hummingbird Books, 2016.
Identifiers: LCCN 2015039914 | ISBN 9780895876645 (alk. paper)
Subjects: LCSH: Private investigators—Tennessee—Fiction. |
Terrorism—Prevention—Fiction. | Missing persons—Fiction. | Mystery
fiction.
Classification: LCC PS3604.O56325 T45 2016 | DDC 813/.6—dc23 LC record
available at http://lccn.loc.gov/2015039914

Printed in the United States of America
by Maple Press, York, Pennsylvania

To Tessa,
The farther we go, the better it gets.

Prologue

This time, he drove the van. He had not driven the van before because the commander did not want him seen in it. Night came quickly, aided by the thick gray canopy of clouds and the light rain. All for the best—fewer people out to possibly see them and cause a problem.

Badger had set it up. It was Badger's first outside assignment, and in a few minutes Adams would find out if Badger had been successful. Badger was twelve and had been in training for two years. Badger was a nickname given to him by the commander because he was tough and smart. Adams was betting Badger would bring the target home.

The target had been well researched, as all the targets were. The commander was meticulous in choosing them. In the eight years Adams had been with the organization, there had not been one failure. A 100 percent success rate—now, there was a number to be proud of.

Badger had spent three weeks befriending the target—a carefully chosen ten-year-old boy named Michael—during the summer camp for underprivileged kids. He had asked immediately if Michael would be his roommate. Michael was thrilled that an older boy wanted him as a roommate and said yes at once. Then the carefully planned manipulation began. In three weeks, Michael thought Badger was his best friend on earth. Badger convinced Michael to "run away" to a special place where other boys their age lived. It would be a better life, Badger told Michael. Michael agreed that it sounded good. His home life was nothing to brag about—a distracted working mom, a dead father, and a near-poverty existence. His mother owned a house, but that was about all.

"If you don't like it, you can leave," Badger said an hour before they were supposed to slip out of their dorm room. That, of course, was a lie.

There was no leaving. Once you were in, you were in for life, or death. That was a well-kept secret that only the commander and Adams knew. "But you'll love it. I've been there two years now," Badger continued.

"Well, okay," Michael said. He would feel like a chicken if he backed out now, after he promised he would go.

The order for lights out came at ten o'clock. Fifteen minutes later, Badger whispered to Michael, "Let's go."

"How are we getting out?" Michael asked, keeping his voice low.

"The window," Badger said softly.

Getting through the window should be simple, except for the fact that the first-floor windows were supposed to be locked inside and out—nobody in and nobody out.

"The windows are locked from the outside," Michael whispered.

"Don't worry," Badger said. "That's been taken care of. Get your duffel."

The boys dragged their duffel bags to the window. Badger unlocked the window from the inside, placed the heel of his hand against the top, and pushed. It slid easily upward.

"Adams," Badger whispered into the darkness.

"I'm here," Adams said, coming out of the shadows.

Badger tossed his duffel bag out the window and then Michael's. Then Michael went out the window, and finally Badger. Badger turned and pulled the window back down and locked the outside lock. Adams hoisted the duffel bags as if he were carrying a couple of feather pillows.

"Let's go," he said. "Step lively."

They hurried through the woods to where the van was parked. Less than five minutes from the time the boys went through the window, Michael was on his way to a brand-new life.

The authorities would be notified; an investigation would take place.

Michael, like Badger, would never be found.

1

Gretchen arrived at ten o'clock, as she always did. Gretchen was my Girl Friday, although she would probably beat me with a stick if I verbalized that thought. Officially, she was office manager, which meant she did everything that needed to be done to keep the office running at top efficiency. The office is Cherokee Investigations. She made her job look easy and rarely complained. Gretchen was well paid.

Donald Youngblood, private investigator, that's me. After a brief stint in training with the FBI, I had spent my early years after college in the Big Apple on Wall Street. I got a good taste of the big city and decided I wanted to do something different. So I moved back to my hometown and opened Cherokee Investigations with my partner, Billy Two-Feathers. Billy is a Cherokee Indian I met in college. He has since married, fathered a child, and become a full-time deputy sheriff in Swain County, North Carolina. Life happens; things change.

I was reading the *Wall Street Journal* when I heard the faint sound of the outer office door opening and closing, followed by muted voices. My intercom buzzed twice, a signal that Gretchen was about to enter my inner sanctum. Seconds later, she came in and shut the door behind her.

"There's a lady here to see you," Gretchen said. "She won't tell me why, only that it's very personal."

"Did you at least get her name?"

"I did."

"And?"

"Buckworth," Gretchen said. "Sheila Buckworth. And if I might add, it fits her to a *T*."

"Send her in," I said.

◆　◆　◆　◆

Sheila Buckworth was an eyeful. She sat across from me in one of my oversized chairs looking around my office as if it were a local tourist attraction. She was a tall, auburn-haired, well-dressed, well-built, attractive woman around forty years of age who had sad eyes and a smile to match. An expensive briefcase sat at her feet.

"What can I do for you, Miss Buckworth?" I asked.

"Mrs. Buckworth," she said. "I'm married."

"Okay," I said. "What can I do for you, Mrs. Buckworth?"

She took a deep breath and did some more looking around. "Is everything we discuss confidential?" she asked.

"Unless you confess to a crime," I said.

"No, I haven't committed a crime."

"Then this conversation is between me and you unless you hire me and I need to share it with other people."

She nodded. "I don't quite know where to begin," she said.

"Just begin anywhere," I said.

"Did you read or hear about the bombing of the federal courthouse in Dallas last week?" she asked.

"Sure," I said. "It was the third courthouse bombing in about three months, always on a weekend and at night."

"The suspected bomber died in the blast," Sheila Buckworth said. "His picture was in the paper. They guessed his age at eighteen to twenty years."

"Yes," I said. "I read that."

"Did you see his picture?"

"No, I did not."

She paused and looked out the window. "My son disappeared over eight years ago," she said. "I haven't heard from him since."

"I'm sorry to hear that," I said.

"The police say he ran away," Sheila Buckworth said. "But I don't think so."

What mother would want to think her son ran away and hasn't been in touch for eight years? I wondered. I waited for the punch line. I knew it was coming soon.

"I wasn't a good mother," she said, trying to put her thoughts together. "My husband was a long-haul trucker who was killed in an accident. My son, Michael, took it hard. We lived near Amarillo, Texas. I decided to move soon after the accident. I thought it might do Michael some good. I grew up in Provo, Utah, so I decided to go back. I worked a lot to make ends meet. It was tough. Michael was distant and withdrawn. The summer Michael went missing, I thought things were improving. He was excited about going to summer camp. Then he and another boy disappeared on the last day of camp. Michael was ten years old. His disappearance has haunted me every day since."

"And you think the Dallas bomber is your son," I said.

"Maybe."

"Why?"

"A few years after Michael's disappearance, I remarried," she said. "My husband has money, lots of money. He hired a private investigator to look for Michael. He had someone run one of those facial recognition programs that ages faces. He had pictures of Michael projected all the way up to age thirty."

Sheila Buckworth picked up her briefcase, set it in her lap, and opened it. She reached in and handed me a shot of a young man with the number 18 on it and an article from a Salt Lake City newspaper. The resemblance between the facial recognition picture and the newspaper photo of the bomber was startling.

"This is your son aged to eighteen years?"

"Yes," she said.

"Could just be a coincidence," I said.

"I would like to know for sure," she said, handing me a sealed test tube with a swab inside. "This is my DNA."

"If I agree to look into this, I'll need more information," I said.

Sheila Buckworth went back into her briefcase and handed me a worn manila file folder. "This is everything I know about my son's disappearance, including personal notes from me in a diary. If you decide to read the diary, I expect that to be confidential unless I say otherwise."

"Agreed," I said. I set the file on my desk.

"If you decide to take my case, you must be discreet," she said. "My husband is a prominent businessman throughout the West, and any connection to a federal courthouse bomber would be disastrous."

"I understand," I said. "I'll need some time to look over the file and make a decision. Can you come back tomorrow afternoon?"

"Certainly," she said. "If you need to get in touch sooner, call my cell phone."

She handed me an engraved business card. Her cell-phone number was handwritten on the back. The front of the card read,

Sheila Buckworth
Vice President
Buckworth Enterprises

"Do you currently live in Utah, Mrs. Buckworth?" I asked.

"Salt Lake City area," she said. "I moved back to Provo but grew tired of it—too many acquaintances asking too many questions. My second husband had a house in Salt Lake City when we married. We sold both houses and bought a new house on 'the Benches.'"

Houses on the Benches were prime real estate overlooking downtown Salt Lake.

"Why did you come all the way to Tennessee to hire a private investigator?"

"Well," she said, "I did not want to hire anyone local, so I went online to search out well-known private investigators, and your name came up. I remembered you from that case you worked on with the FBI in Salt Lake City, the one that involved the boy who killed himself. I also have relatives in Kingsport who I wanted to visit, so I thought I'd mix business with pleasure. I didn't make up my mind to come see you until the last minute."

Lucky me, I thought. *The Three Devils case is still haunting me.*

◆   ◆   ◆   ◆

That night after dinner, Mary and I sat at the kitchen bar enjoying a second glass of old-vine red zin and discussing our day. Mary is my wife and the love of my life. She is also a detective for the Mountain Center police. Our adopted daughter, Lacy, and her boyfriend, Biker McBride, were downstairs watching TV; they were high-school seniors. Jake and Junior, our two black standard poodles, were downstairs chaperoning—probably doing it with their eyes closed.

"I had an interesting visitor today," I said.

"Do I smell a big case on the horizon?" Mary asked.

"Maybe," I said. "If I decide to take it."

"Tell me," Mary said.

I told her about my visit with Sheila Buckworth.

"It would be quite a coincidence if it was her son," Mary said.

"It would. But the resemblance between the facial aging program and the newspaper picture was really close."

"What are you going to do?"

"I don't know," I said. "Guess I'll sleep on it."

"Maybe you need to know more about the mother," Mary said. "And her husband."

"Gretchen is already working on it," I said.

"Well, here's to Gretchen," Mary said, taking a drink of wine.

2

I was in the office early the next day with a cup of Dunkin' Donuts coffee and a poppy seed bagel with cream cheese, reading the Michael Brand file. John Brand was Sheila Buckworth's first husband.

Michael had disappeared from a three-week summer camp in Provo, Utah, with another boy, Danny Marshall. The missing boys were classified as runaways and not kidnap victims. An Amber Alert went out on the runaways, but there were no reports that they had been seen. Michael was attending the summer camp on a scholarship for underprivileged children from a local Methodist church. There was no mention if Danny Marshall was attending on a scholarship.

The file contained a decent-length newspaper article on the runaways and a shorter one a week later. A copy of the initial police report offered information about Michael and Danny, including the clothes they might have been wearing and a picture of Michael from the chest up. The investigating officer was Jock Smithson.

There was a five-year diary kept by Sheila Buckworth, mostly about her feelings for her missing son and her conversations with Detective Smithson. It contained a few references to her marriage to her second husband, Marlin Buckworth, and a mention that Jock Smithson had been promoted to chief of detectives. The tone of the diary was that Smithson had not done enough to find her son. That did not surprise me. As long as her son was missing, enough could never be done.

Also included was a later report from a local private investigator, a retired Salt Lake City detective hired by Sheila's second husband. The PI's name was Abraham Webb. His business card was attached to the report. Webb concluded that Michael Brand was probably not in the state. A computer-generated picture of a fourteen-year-old Michael had been run in many Utah papers, along with an offer of a substantial reward for his location. Numerous leads were pursued and dismissed.

I had just finished my first pass through the file when my intercom buzzed.

"I'm in," Gretchen said. "Whenever you're ready, I have the information you wanted."

"Make yourself a cup of coffee and come on in," I said.

◆   ◆   ◆   ◆

To help with her search, Gretchen had copied the Buckworth file before going home, but I had not given her the diary. Her file looked noticeably larger than the original.

"Sheila Brand was married to John Brand for ten years," Gretchen said. "He was twenty and she was eighteen when they got married. Michael was born a couple of years later, so he was eight when his dad was killed."

I was in college when I lost my parents, and for a while I was in a dark place. I knew how it affected me. I could only imagine the effect on an eight-year-old.

"Did you find any details on how he died?"

"Yes, in an Amarillo newspaper," Gretchen said. "He apparently fell asleep at the wheel and ran off the road. No reason to think it was anything other than an accident."

"Insurance money?" I asked.

Gretchen smiled. I knew that smile. She delighted in anticipating what I would want and staying one step ahead.

"Don't know for sure," Gretchen said. "Walker Trucking says they carry a twenty-five-thousand-dollar life-insurance policy on their drivers as part of their benefit package. It triples if death is accidental. So Michael Brand's father probably had insurance."

"You called Troy Walker?"

"I did, just for background on the industry," she said. "He was glad to help even though it was not one of his drivers. And he said to tell you hello."

I had once taken a case for Troy Walker to investigate the death of his college-age daughter. It had turned into the nationally known Tattoo Killers case, otherwise known as the Three Devils case. Out of all the cases I had ever worked on, it haunted me the most.

On my notepad, I wrote, "Insurance?"

"Go on," I said.

"She bought a house in Provo six months after the accident and went to work as a waitress at the Slate Restaurant in the local Marriott. A couple of years later, she married Marlin Buckworth. He owns the Destiny Hotel chain."

"So she married money," I said.

"Millions."

"Nothing wrong with that."

"Not a thing," Gretchen said.

Some people might think Mary married me for my money. I didn't care what they thought, since I knew better. Likewise, on the surface, it could look as if Sheila Brand was a fortune hunter. But looks could be deceiving, so I would give the lady the benefit of the doubt.

"Her business card says she's a VP at Buckworth Enterprises. Is that title honorary or real?"

"It looks real," Gretchen said. "She's in charge of food services. An ex-waitress would know a thing or two about that, especially if she worked at a Marriott."

"What else?"

"That's all I could find," she said.

◆   ◆   ◆   ◆

That afternoon, Sheila Buckworth was back. She sat in front of my desk with a cup of fresh black coffee that Gretchen had brewed for her in the office Keurig.

"This is very good," she said. "What is it?"

I held up one finger and pushed the button on my intercom. "Gretchen," I said. "Mrs. Buckworth would like to know what kind of coffee she's drinking."

"Gevalia Signature Blend," Gretchen said over the intercom.

"I'll make a mental note," Sheila Buckworth said. "We have a couple of high-end hotels, and I might consider this for our restaurants."

"Never hurts to look at alternatives," I said.

She took a deep breath. "Have you made a decision?"

"I have a few questions first," I said. "Did you receive insurance money from the death of your first husband?"

"Why would you want to know that?"

"I suspect you did, so I'm curious why your son was on scholarship to the camp," I said. "If I take this case, I may have to ask some personal questions."

"I see," Sheila Buckworth said. "Yes, I did receive insurance money, and I used all of it as a down payment on a house in Provo. The scholarship was based on annual income and other factors. I was a waitress with no husband and minimal income, so Michael was chosen by the church for a scholarship."

I let that settle for a moment, then moved on. "Would it surprise you if you found out that Michael did run away?"

"Yes," she said, "it would. But I need to know the truth, and I need to know if he is alive or dead. I'm not sure why, but I think you can find the truth."

The gauntlet is down, Youngblood, I thought. Well, I had been bored the last couple of months, and the last time I thought something was nothing it turned out to be a whole lot of something. I could hear T. Elbert Brown in my head: *Better to know than not to know.*

"I'll see what I can find out," I said.

Sheila Buckworth exhaled a sign of relief. "Thank you."

"But if I pursue the DNA thing, the FBI or Homeland Security might get involved. Are you ready for that?"

"I am," she said. "But I would expect you to do everything you could to keep it out of the press."

"I would," I said.

She nodded and was silent for a minute. "How much of a retainer will you require?"

"Gretchen will take care of the details," I said. "You can see her on your way out."

"How soon will you start?"

"Today," I said."

"Good." Shelia Buckworth stood and extended her hand, and we shook, the deal confirmed. "Thank you again, Mr. Youngblood." She turned and disappeared into the outer office.

◆   ◆   ◆   ◆

Lacy's senior basketball season had been memorable so far. The Mountain Center girls team was still undefeated, coming off a big holiday tournament win in Johnson City against a number of highly regarded teams from as far away as Florida, New York, and California.

A number of teams from Knoxville were on the regular season schedule, and so that night Mary, Billy, and I went to Knoxville and watched as Lacy and her teammates systematically took apart another opponent. Lacy led all scorers and sat out the fourth quarter of a twenty-five-point win.

"That team is going to be hard to beat," Billy said as we were driving home. "Lacy is the real deal. Has she beaten you one-on-one yet?"

"Not yet," I said. "But it's going to happen. We'll start playing again once the season is over. If she got hurt playing one-on-one with me, a whole bunch of people would want my head."

"Including me," Billy said.

And he wasn't smiling when he said it.

◆   ◆   ◆   ◆

Late that night, Mary and I were in bed reading. She hadn't been home long from her girls' night out with Wanda Jones. Wanda was the county medical examiner and my best female friend other than Mary. Mary and Wanda had become good buddies and went out to dinner every week or so. Mary had few friends, and they were mostly male, so I encouraged the relationship.

"Do you ever wonder if I'm really out with Wanda?" Mary asked out of the blue. She loved to rattle my cage every now and again.

I almost laughed out loud but contained myself. I had an idea where this was leading. I played along. "No," I said.

"I could be out shacking up with another guy," she said.

"No," I said, "you couldn't."

"You're awfully sure of yourself, Cowboy," Mary said.

"No," I said. "I'm sure of you."

Mary smiled and returned to her book.

"I really was out with Wanda," she said a few minutes later.

"I never doubted it," I said.

"You're very trusting."

"Naïve," I said.

We read for a while.

"Are you going to take that case we discussed?" Mary asked, closing her book.

"Yes," I said, closing mine. "I'll have to go to Utah for a few days."

"When?"

"Soon."

"How soon?"

"In a day or two," I said.

"We'd better get to work on your send-off," Mary said, pulling her nightshirt over her head. "But we'll have to be quiet."

"As church mice," I whispered, chucking my T-shirt.

3

I was in the office early, but I waited until I knew he was in before I called his private line.

"Glass," he answered on the second ring.

"Hey, Professor," I said. "What's happening?"

Scott Glass, college friend and fellow FBI trainee, was now the special agent in charge of the Salt Lake City FBI office. We had worked together on a few cases, to the point that I had received consultant status in the bureau and credentials to prove it. I also had a federal gun-carry permit.

"I wouldn't know where to start," Scott said. "The bad guys never seem to go on vacation."

"Maybe that's their problem," I said.

"Among many," Scott said. "I'm thinking this is not a social call. It's been only a few weeks since you were here."

Mary, Lacy, and I had flown out for a week of skiing after Christmas.

"I need a favor," I said. "I'm thinking either you or Deena can help."

Deena, Scott's love interest, had recently moved in with him. She was a Salt Lake City cop.

"Tell me what you need," Scott said. "I'll help if I can."

"I need to talk to the chief of detectives on the Provo police force," I said. "His name is Jock Smithson. I looked at their website, and he's still there. I don't want to go in cold. I need someone to open the door for me."

"I'll talk to Deena," Scott said. "Most local police think FBI agents are a bunch of spoiled hotshots."

"Which in your case is absolutely true."

"Funny, Blood," Scott said. "That's the pot calling the kettle black, for sure."

"Guilty," I said.

"What's this about?" Scott asked.

"An eight-year-old cold case concerning a runaway boy," I said.

"And the mother asked you to take another look," Scott said.

"How'd you know?"

"It's always the mothers," Scott said. "Mothers never give up hope."

◆　　◆　　◆　　◆

Since I still kept my nose in the investment world, I went online that afternoon and did some research on a few stocks I thought might be worth investing in. As it turned out, only one had the potential I was looking for. I made a note for Gretchen to have our clients take a look. Then the phone rang.

"Jock Smithson will see you as soon as you get here," Scott said without preamble. "I told him you would spring for an expensive lunch."

"Not a problem," I said. "Thank Deena for the fast response."

"How'd you know it was Deena and not me?"

"Dumb question, Professor."

"Yeah, I guess it was," Scott said.

◆　　◆　　◆　　◆

I closed down soon after Gretchen left and went to Moto's Gym. Moto was his usual surly Asian self. It didn't work with me. I had known him too long and understood he was just an old softie.

"I got new dog," Moto said when I walked in.

"Is Karate okay?" I asked.

Karate was Moto's beautiful Siberian husky, a friend and playmate of my older standard poodle, Jake.

"Karate fine," Moto said. "But won't live forever. I wanted another dog before Karate pass."

I understood. I felt the same way about Jake. That was the reason we had decided to get another standard poodle, Junior. Jake was Junior's father.

"What did you name the new dog?" I asked.

"Kid," Moto said. "Get it? Karate and Kid."

Moto laughed at his own cleverness. I smiled politely, shaking my head, and went to work out. I went through my full routine.

An hour and a half later, sufficiently worn out, I went to the condo and took the dogs for a walk. Jake was doing well for his age. He was pushing fifteen. He had gray in his muzzle and was moving slower, but still better than expected for an aging Poodle. I was convinced that Junior was partly responsible. I dreaded the day when I would no longer have Jake around. We had spent a lot of time together over the years.

I pushed those melancholy thoughts away and headed back to the condo. Mary and Lacy were still out, so I took a minute to call Roy Husky. Roy was someone I had met on my first big case, and we had become unlikely friends. He was an ex-con who had put his past behind him and with the help and guidance of Joseph Fleet had risen to the position of president of Fleet Industries. Fleet, now chairman of the board, had taken off on a sabbatical, promoted Roy, and left him in charge.

"It's your favorite private investigator," I said when he answered.

"I guess you're right," Roy said, "since I know only one. What's up, Gumshoe?"

"I need to go to Utah," I said.

"When?"

"Tomorrow."

"Hang on," he said.

I was on hold while Roy checked the schedules for the two Fleet Industries private jets. Joseph Fleet had made them available to me if my schedule did not conflict with theirs.

"No can do," Roy said. "We can get you to Memphis tomorrow, and you can fly direct from there."

"Okay," I said. "It's a deal."

4

Out the window of the Delta Airbus A320, I looked at the snow-capped Rockies. I had booked a first-class ticket out of Memphis on a flight that left after lunch and would arrive before dinner. I had checked my ski boots, in case I found the time to do a few runs at one of the local resorts. I would have to rent skis.

I called Scott Glass on his private line as soon as we were given permission to use our cell phones.

"I'm here," I said when he answered. "We're taxiing to the gate."

"Want to get together for dinner?"

"I'm beat," I said. "Maybe tomorrow night."

"Can't," he said. "I'll be out of town for a day or two."

"Okay, how about breakfast Sunday morning?"

"My office at seven," Scott said.

"I'll be there."

By the time I retrieved my luggage, found my rented SUV, and drove to the Cottonwood Residence Inn, night had enveloped the city. I checked in and called Mary. We talked for a while about nothing in particular.

"Be careful skiing," Mary said.

"Yes, Mother."

"Well, you are a bit of a mad bomber," she said. "And you're getting older."

"An oldie but still a goodie."

Mary laughed. "Don't forget where you live."

"Not likely," I said.

"I miss you."

"I just left."

"I'm incomplete without you," she said seductively, trying to sound like Marilyn Monroe.

It took me a second to realize she was messing with me. "Knock it off, doll," I said, doing a pretty good Bogie.

She laughed. "Have fun, Cowboy."

◆   ◆   ◆   ◆

I was tired and hungry. I ordered takeout from a local Asian restaurant and picked up a six-pack of beer at a convenience store. I ate in front of the TV watching a *M*A*S*H* rerun and went to bed early. Sometime in the early hours of the morning, I dreamed I was on skis roaring down a long, steep groomer, spraying powder behind me. I could feel the snow biting my face. I stopped before I reached the edge of a bottomless precipice.

A moment later, another skier roared by, seeming not to notice me. He had a determined look on his face. I realized it was Michael Brand seconds before he flew over the edge and disappeared into the darkness below.

I woke with a start and looked at the red, glowing face of the bedside clock: 2:07 A.M. I tossed and turned for an hour and finally dozed off.

5

The next morning, after a rigorous workout and a hot shower, I was in the lobby early with my laptop, drinking coffee and catching up on all the news from the worlds of sports and finance. Six o'clock Mountain Center time was four o'clock Utah time, and at that hour I had the place to myself.

The Dow continued to bounce around seventeen thousand, a head-scratching number screaming for a correction. I maintained my holding pattern with both eyes wide open. The sports world was preparing for the Super Bowl. Sadly, the Titans had finished out of the playoffs.

I emailed T. Elbert to tell him I was working on a case that could turn into something. T. Elbert was a close friend and a semi-retired TBI agent who had been wounded in the line of duty. The bullet in his back had done enough damage to permanently put him in a wheelchair. Since we first met, he had been at different times my mentor, my confidant, and my cheerleader. Over the years, his front porch had become a "Little Switzerland"—neutral and confidential. We had planned multiple strategies there, most of them successful. I promised a visit soon.

I logged off the Internet and helped myself to the complimentary breakfast, watching my portions, as I anticipated a generous lunch. I ate slowly and read *USA Today*, still enjoying the look and feel of a real newspaper, a species slowly fading into extinction.

When I finished, I called the private cell-phone number Scott Glass had given me for Jock Smithson.

"Smithson," he answered in a soft voice with a lot of depth.

"Donald Youngblood," I said. "Thank you for agreeing to see me, chief detective."

"No need for formality, Donald," he said. "Just call me Jock."

"Okay, Jock," I said. "Call me Don. Are you free for lunch?"

"Sure," he said. "Where are you staying?"

"The Cottonwood Residence Inn."

"Great," he said. "I have to be near there anyway, so it will work out just fine. Let's say Ruby River Steakhouse in Sandy at one-thirty. That won't be too far for you. You got a GPS?"

"I do," I said. *A very annoying one*, I thought. "I'll see you then. How will I know you?"

He laughed: a low rumble. "Just ask for Jock," he said. "I'm well known there."

◆   ◆   ◆   ◆

"I'm meeting Jock," I said to the attractive greeter- seater at the station just inside the door.

"Right this way," she said.

I followed. The curvy figure poured into tight black slacks made the trip more enjoyable. It ended at a corner booth. Jock Smithson stood. His handshake was firm but not aggressive. He was a big man, six-four or -five and probably on the high side of 250 pounds. Not fat, just thick.

"Sit," he said. "Would you prefer the corner?"

"Actually, I would," I said.

"Let me know if anyone is sneaking up behind me," he said, motioning me to the corner seat.

"I will be ever vigilant in covering your back," I said.

Jock laughed.

We ordered drinks. Jock ordered scotch whiskey, and I went for an Evolution Amber Ale on tap. We made small talk until the drinks arrived.

"Welcome to Utah," Jock said, raising his scotch. "In case you're wondering, I'm not drinking on duty. You're paying, and they have great steaks and scotch, so I'm taking the afternoon off."

"Enjoy," I said.

We both ordered steak. Jock had the biggest on the menu. I was more conservative. We ate and talked. Jock ordered a second scotch, and I ordered my second ale.

"What can you tell me about the Michael Brand missing person case?" I asked.

He reached down, picked up a manila envelope, and handed it to me. "I made you a copy of the file," he said. "Our little secret."

I nodded. "I'll look at it later. Right now, tell me what you remember."

"Not much to it," Jock said. "No indication that it wasn't anything more than a runaway."

"Don't runaways usually turn up in a few days?"

"Not always," he said. "But most of the time."

"Any hits off the Amber Alert?"

"Plenty," Jock said. "We ran them all down, and they were all dead ends. Michael Brand's mother was on me constantly about finding her son. I really wanted to locate him and get her off my back, but there were no leads."

Jock ordered a third scotch. "Two or three years later, she married a rich hotel guy and sometime after that hired a private investigator. Once the PI was on board, I didn't hear from her much. I guess he finally told her that finding her son was a dead end."

I took a sip of my second beer. "What about the other boy's mother?"

"What about her?" Jock asked.

"Did she bug you?"

"A few times," he said. "Then I never heard from her again."

"Is she still in town?"

"No," he said. "She moved. No forwarding address. It was like she didn't care if her kid ran away or not."

"How old was her son?"

"Twelve," Jock said.

"So, old enough to influence a ten-year-old," I said.

"Yeah," Jock said. "My thoughts exactly."

We sat in silence. Jock seemed to be accessing distant memories.

"Did anything in particular about this case not make sense?" I asked.

Jock smiled. "I see why you came all the way out here to talk to me. You can always learn things face to face that are not in the file."

"That and the skiing," I said.

"Yeah, we locals seem to take the skiing for granted," he said, taking another drink. "Anyway, the thing was, I tried to keep in touch with Danny Marshall's mother to find out if she had heard anything from her son. I'd call her once a week. Then, about a month later, she's gone. She had rented a house in a low-end neighborhood and signed a one-year lease, but didn't even claim the deposit. So I did some asking around. She didn't appear to have a job, and she paid cash for the summer camp. I couldn't find a bank account or a credit card in her name."

"Driver's license?" I asked.

"Not in Utah," Jock said.

"The private investigator Sheila Buckworth's husband hired was Abraham Webb," I said. "Do you know him?"

"Retired cop," Jock said. "I knew him to say hello, that's about it. He died last year."

"I wonder if his files are still around."

"Should be," Jock said. "He had a partner. I'll be glad to check."

"I would appreciate it," I said.

The waitress came with the check, and I paid cash, leaving a generous tip. We left our booth and walked out into a cold afternoon with a light snow meandering downward.

"Supposed to get a storm tonight," Jock said.

"Think I'll try to ski tomorrow," I said.

"Should be good," Jock said, looking up at the pale gray sky.

"Do you ski?"

"Not anymore," he said. "Bad knees."

A gust of wind urged me to seek sanctuary in my rented SUV. "Thanks for your time," I said. "Keep an eye out for pairs of missing boys in Utah. If anything pops up, let me know."

"Will do," he said.

We shook hands.

"Thanks for lunch," he said. "If I think of anything else, I'll give you a call. And I'll check on Webb's file. If you happen to find anything interesting, let me know."

"When it's over," I said. "If there's anything to tell, I'll be in touch."

◆   ◆   ◆   ◆

On my way back, I stopped at Utah Golf and Ski, rented a pair of high-end powder skis and purchased a lift ticket for Brighton Ski Resort. Returning to my suite at the Residence Inn, I spent two hours online, then another hour in the workout room. I showered and walked to a nearby restaurant and picked up a pizza. I sat in front of the TV, ate pizza, drank beer, and watched a basketball game.

Near halftime, my phone beeped with a text message from Mary:

> **Girls won by 20. Lacy had 18 and 5 assists.**
> **No need to call. We'll talk tomorrow. Love you.**

I had forgotten about the time change. It was already past ten o'clock in Mountain Center. I smiled as I reread the text. The Mountain Center girls basketball team was ranked number two in Division 1-AAA in Tennessee. Lacy, its best player, was leading the team in scoring and assists.

This could be a dream season, I thought.

6

Early the next morning, I drove into Big Cottonwood Canyon. I climbed steadily, watching the temperature on my outside monitor drop from thirty-five to twenty in about fifteen minutes. A few miles from my destination, I stopped at the Silver Fork Lodge and had breakfast. The Silver Fork was one of my favorite Utah hangouts, and during my many visits I had gotten to know the staff.

"Sit anywhere," Beth said when I walked into the dining room after giving me a hug.

As soon as I was seated, she poured a mug of coffee for me and took my order. Out the window, I watched the snow. Six inches had fallen overnight, and there was a promise of another six during the day.

Breakfast arrived, and I devoured the generous portions of scrambled eggs, hash browns, ham steak, and rye toast.

About the time I finished, Dan, the owner, came in and spotted me. He walked over to my table and sat.

"Hey, Don," he said, shaking my hand. "Weren't you just here in the last couple of weeks?"

"Sure was," I said. "Just can't stay away from all this good food and Utah powder."

"You should buy a house out here and come for the entire winter," Dan said.

"Believe me, I'm seriously considering it."

Dan was a self-made man who had come to Utah at a young age with a few dollars in his pocket and a willingness to work. He had become a successful entrepreneur.

"I didn't think I'd see you," I said. "I figured you'd be out plowing somewhere."

"I started at four this morning," he said. "Looks like I'll have to go out again later."

29

Beth poured Dan a mug of coffee.

"You alone this trip?" he asked.

"I am," I said. "Quick trip. I'm working a case that brought me to Provo, so I thought I'd take a day or two and ski my legs off."

"Well, your timing is impeccable," Dan said. "This may be a big one."

"I sure hope so," I said, draining my mug.

♦   ♦   ♦   ♦

Brighton Ski Resort sits at the end of Big Cottonwood Canyon. Brighton shares the canyon with Solitude Ski Resort, and you can ski both on an upgraded ticket. I chose to ski only Brighton.

I parked near the high-speed Great Western lift, unloaded my skis and poles, and went inside the lower lodge to change into my boots. I was waiting at Great Western when it opened promptly at nine o'clock. I skied from the top of Great Western down to the Snake Creek lift in six inches of the lightest powder in the world, making fresh tracks as I went. Even though it was a Saturday on a powder day, the mountain did not seem crowded. I skied six runs off the Snake Creek lift, making fresh tracks most of the morning. I had an early lunch at the main lodge and then did six more runs off the Crest lift before heading to the Millicent side of the mountain. In early afternoon, I took a hot chocolate break, then skied seven runs off Milly, another high-speed quad that got me up the mountain in a hurry. I quit at three o'clock, exhausted. Snow continued to fall steadily. I made a slow, cautious descent down Cottonwood Canyon to the Residence Inn.

♦   ♦   ♦   ♦

"How was it?" Mary asked that night when I called after dinner.

"As good as it gets," I said. "The only thing that could have made it better would be if you were here."

"You're such a sweet-talker," Mary said.

"I try."

There was a pause. For a second or two, I thought I had lost her.

"I have some bad news," Mary said.

A wave of fear swept over me. I waited.

"We're all okay in the Youngblood household, but Mountain Center has had a tragedy."

"What?" I managed to ask through a cold chill.

"Clay Carr had a bad car wreck late last night. His girlfriend, Julie James, was killed," Mary said. "He's in the hospital in a coma. They don't know if he's going to make it. The whole senior class is really shook up, Lacy and Biker included. They were all at the after-basketball-game party. I guess Clay was taking Julie home."

"I'm really sorry to hear that," I said.

Clay Carr was Mountain Center's senior all-state tailback, who had led the Bears to the Division 1-AAA state football title, the first in school history. He had committed to play football at the University of Tennessee.

"Drinking?" I asked.

"Don't think so," Mary said. "They were trying to save his life. Nobody thought about running an immediate tox screen. They ran one a few hours later. I was told it showed no trace of alcohol."

"Who's investigating?"

"Big Bob is handling this one personally," Mary said.

We moved away from the bad news and talked for another half-hour—easy, uncomplicated conversation, less about what was said than about the sound of one another's voice.

"When are you coming home?" Mary asked.

"I'll be in late tomorrow afternoon," I said. "I need to see Scott about this case. I have a few ideas."

"Don't stay a minute longer that you have to, Don," Mary urged. "We need you home."

"Tomorrow night, for sure," I said. "You can count on it."

There was something she was not telling me, something she didn't want to talk about over the phone. I was sure of it.

7

Early Sunday morning, I met Scott at the Salt Lake City FBI offices on West Amelia Earhart Drive. The door was locked. I knocked. Scott opened it.

"They actually gave you your own key?" I said.

"I stole it from the janitor," he said. "Come on back."

I followed Scott to the conference room. The offices were empty except for the two of us. Scott had brought coffee. Two medium-sized cups sat on the conference table—Dunkin' Donuts, no less. I was surprised. I didn't think Dunkin' Donuts had made it to Utah.

"This is a nice surprise," I said. "How did you know?"

Scott smiled. "We're the FBI. We know all."

"Nearly all."

"Meaning you're about to tell me something I don't know," Scott said.

"How would you like a possible lead on the federal courthouse bombing in Dallas?"

Scott sat up straighter in his chair. "How would you know anything about that?"

"Not sure I do," I said. "It's just a possibility."

"I'm listening."

"I assume you did a DNA profile on the bomber," I said.

"We did," Scott said.

"And came up empty," I said.

"Right."

"If I give you a DNA sample, can you run it for a familial match to the bomber?" I asked. "Off the record, of course."

Scott stared at me for a few seconds. "What the hell have you stumbled onto this time?"

"It may be nothing," I said.

"You think it's something or you wouldn't be here," he said.

"I think it's worth checking out."

"If I try to sneak a DNA test through and tie it to the federal courthouse bombing, I'll be grilled from here to Sunday," Scott said. "You need more juice than I have."

"Like maybe David Steele?"

FBI agent David Steele had been my chief instructor at Quantico when, fresh out of college, Scott and I had joined the bureau, a memory I'd shoved into a far corner of my brain. At Quantico, my relationship with David Steele was rocky, but we reconnected when I was working the Tattoo Killers case. David Steele and I formed an unfriendly alliance that became considerably friendlier as the case progressed. Later, we again worked together, on the CJK case. Soon afterward, David Steele had been promoted to associate deputy director of the FBI. He had given me some of the credit for his promotion.

"Maybe," Scott said. "But David Steele has never been a big fan of bending the rules."

"He seems to be mellowing in his old age," I said.

"I wouldn't be too sure about that," Scott said. "Anyway, tell me what you've got—off the record, of course."

I trusted Scott completely, so I told him all of it.

"Do you really think the bomber is her missing son?" Scott asked.

"It's possible," I said. "She believes it is. And some things about her son's disappearance just don't add up."

"It's probably best not to ignore a mother's instincts."

"Sound advice, Professor," I said.

◆　　◆　　◆　　◆

I was at the lake house in time for dinner. A changeover in Atlanta had given me a new appreciation for Fleet Industries' private jets. How could an airport get so big that you had to take a train from terminal to terminal?

Mary had prepared a pot roast with mashed potatoes, gravy, green beans, and homemade biscuits. I ate like a recruit who had been on

C-rations for a month. Biker joined us for dinner. He ate almost as much as I did. The conversation was casual but subdued. Clay Carr had yet to be mentioned.

Lacy cleared the bar top and returned with a plate filled with brownies. Mary had added black walnuts and a light sprinkle of powdered sugar. I ate one. Then I ate another and had to stop myself from reaching for a third.

"Don," Lacy said, turning a serious gaze on me. "The senior class wants to hire you."

I nearly fell off my barstool. I had not seen that one coming. "To do what?"

There was only one possibility. I waited for confirmation.

"To find out who or what was responsible for the death of Julie James and for putting Clay Carr in the hospital," she said.

"That's the job of the Mountain Center Police Department," I said. I looked at Mary for support. "You told them that, didn't you?"

"I'm staying out of this," Mary said.

"We want a second opinion," Lacy said. "We refuse to believe that Clay just fell asleep at the wheel."

Biker said nothing.

"Who says he did?"

"Mary said that was Big Bob's conclusion," Lacy said.

I looked at Mary. She shrugged.

I said nothing. I wanted no part of this. But it didn't matter what I wanted. All eyes were on me.

"Is Clay still in a coma?"

"Yes," Lacy and Biker said almost simultaneously.

I paused to think how I could wiggle my way out. "I'm working a big case with the FBI," I said. "It's really keeping me busy."

Lacy was having none of it. "You've worked two cases at the same time before. You need to do this for us."

I looked at Mary. She said nothing.

I looked at Biker. "Say something."

"You need to do this," Biker said. "If there's something to be found, you'll find it."

I knew a hopeless cause when I saw one. I remained silent long enough to let the suspense build.

"Okay," I said. "On one condition."

"Name it," Lacy said.

"I might need you-all to question some of your classmates. I don't have time to talk to all of them. You two can probably find out more than I could. But don't do anything until I have a chance to think about this. Agreed?"

Lacy looked at Biker. He nodded.

"We can live with that," Lacy said. "When do we start?"

"I'll let you know," I said. "But soon."

"Your retainer," she said, seemingly pulling an envelope out of thin air and handing it to me.

Inside was a check from the Mountain Center class of 2015 for five hundred dollars. I didn't like this at all, but that didn't matter. I was in it now.

8

"What's so important that you couldn't just make a phone call?" David Steele asked when he sat down at my table late the next morning. "And why are we meeting here and not in my office?"

We were in Chesapeake, a restaurant in the Baltimore-Washington International Airport Marriott. Jim Doak had flown me up early that morning in Fleet Industries' jet number one. Jim had flown me around the country on many occasions. He was not in my inner circle, but I knew

I could count on him. Jim had a good sense of humor and treated jet number one as if it were his child.

"To start with, all your phones are probably bugged, and I want this conversation to be off the record," I said. "If anyone asks, I'm just an old friend buying you lunch."

"Or maybe I'm talking with an FBI consultant about a confidential case I might want him to work on," David Steele said.

"Could be. We'll see."

We ordered club sandwiches. I asked for an Amber Bock on tap. David Steele grimaced and ordered an iced tea.

"Do you know why I have a feeling I'm not going to like this?" David Steele asked. "Because trouble finds you like a heat-seeking missile."

I shrugged. "It's a gift."

"So tell me," he said.

"It has to be off the record."

"No," he said. "I can't make that promise. The fact that you asked means it's something I'll want to know."

"Okay," I said. "What else is new?"

He stared at me for a while. "You're not going to tell me," he said.

"Nope."

I knew curiosity would finally get the best of him. I waited. He stared. We said nothing. Our dead period seemed longer than it actually was. He was searching for another angle.

"Maybe I can bring you in as a consultant on whatever it is you've uncovered," David Steele said. "Your track record is pretty good."

"My track record is excellent."

He ignored me and pushed on. "So, if I have you working an angle no one else knows about, there might be a good reason for me to keep it confidential."

I thought about that for a few seconds. "Like maybe an angle on the federal courthouse bombings," I said.

"Good God," he said. "What have you stumbled onto?"

"I'm not sure yet," I said. "Maybe nothing."

"And maybe something," David Steele said.

"Maybe."

Our food arrived. We quit talking and started eating. I took a long drink of Amber Bock as David Steele watched. He looked forlorn.

"What do we need to do?" he asked.

I had been thinking about that for a couple of days. I was developing a theory based on the premise that the dead Texas bomber was indeed Sheila Buckworth's son.

"You need to develop a list of boys around ten years of age who have gone missing in the last ten years, especially if they went missing with another boy," I said. "If you can find an instance that occurred in the last month or so, that will be perfect."

"How are missing boys connected to the Dallas bombing?" David Steele asked.

"Might not be," I said. "I'm working on a theory. If it looks promising, I'll share it. I'll need the Dallas bomber's DNA profile."

"You think you know who he is," he said flatly. It was a statement, not a question.

"Maybe," I said. "But I need to confirm it one way or the other."

"I can get results faster," he said.

"Yeah, but do you want it in your system?"

"It will never show up in our system," he said.

I smiled, reached into my jacket pocket, and handed him the sealed test tube with the swab inside that Sheila Buckworth had given me.

"How long?" I asked.

"Tomorrow," he said. "Next day, latest."

"Wow," I said. "You guys are good."

"Shut up," David Steele said. But he was smiling when he said it. The smile disappeared. He held up the test tube. "If this is a familial match, I'll want to know a lot more."

"Let's don't get ahead of ourselves," I said.

But I knew that if it was a match, there was no way to avoid telling him all of it.

9

We sat on his front porch under overhead heaters drinking coffee from you know where. T. Elbert was eating a toasted poppy seed bagel with cream cheese. The day was clear and brisk. The wind was calm. The sun was making progress against the morning darkness.

"You know that eating that bagel in some countries could get you arrested," I said.

"So I've heard," T. Elbert said. "Quit stalling and tell me what you've been up to."

"I was in Utah skiing."

"And working a case, I'll bet," T. Elbert said.

"That, too."

"Tell me all," he said. "I want details."

"You always want details."

"The devil is in the details," T. Elbert said, wiping cream cheese off his mouth.

I didn't have to say it was confidential. That was understood. So I told him all of it. T. Elbert listened like a priest in the confessional.

"You can't seem to get away from the feds," T. Elbert said.

"Lucky me."

"Maybe not." T. Elbert regarded most of the FBI as prima donnas. He paused to eat more of his bagel. "You're not eating," he said.

"I'm meeting Big Bob later at the diner," I said. "I need to talk to him about Clay Carr. Lacy and Biker think it was not an accident."

"Yeah, I read about that," T. Elbert said. "Terrible thing."

We were silent as we ate our bagels and drank our coffee. I didn't tell T. Elbert about the senior class hiring me. I'd save that one for another day.

"You have a theory about the bomber?" T. Elbert asked.

"I do."

"Care to share?"

I laid it out for him.

"So," I said when I had exhausted my theory, "what do you think?"

"Makes sense in a weird sort of way," he said. "But it's going to require some tricky research."

"True," I said. "That's where the feds come in."

"Well, if I can help, let me know. It meant something to me to be able to help on that CJK thing."

"I'm sure I can find something for you to do," I said.

◆   ◆   ◆   ◆

The Mountain Center Diner was the social hub of downtown. It served breakfast and lunch—terrific food at a reasonable price. Certain things on the menu had risen to legendary status: the omelets, the home fries, and the biscuits and gravy at breakfast, the cheeseburger with fries and the meatloaf special at lunch.

I was at my usual table in the back of the diner when the big man came in. As usual, the place got noticeably quieter when he arrived, then returned to its normal buzz when he sat and tossed his cowboy hat on a nearby chair.

Doris arrived with coffee and took our order. Doris Black, the owner, held me in such high esteem that I had my own table. Maybe it was the stock tips, or maybe it was my fifteen seconds of fame on CNN during one of my big cases. No matter. I humbly accepted the perk and enjoyed the fact I did not have to scramble to find a place to sit. I ordered my usual: a feta cheese omelet, home fries, and rye toast. Big Bob ordered half the breakfast menu.

"So you're buying me breakfast, which means you want something or you're going to tell me something I'm not going to like," Big Bob said. Big Bob Wilson was a lifelong friend who was now the Mountain Center chief of police. He was as big as his name suggested and could really fill up a room.

"So cynical," I said.

"Which is it?"

"I don't want anything," I said.

"So tell me," he said, picking up his coffee and taking a drink.

"I've been hired to look into the Clay Carr accident," I said.

"Hired by whom?"

Normally, I kept my clients confidential when I could, but I was looking for the big man's cooperation.

"The Mountain Center High School class of 2015," I said. "Complete with retainer."

He smiled. "Really?"

I nodded.

"Well, good for them," he said. "That certainly speaks well for Clay Carr."

"So you won't mind if I look into this?"

"Hell no," Big Bob said. "If you find anything, let me know."

"What can you tell me?"

"Nothing much," Big Bob said. "It looks like he just fell asleep, drove off the road, and hit a tree. They had their seat belts on, but they didn't have airbags, and seat belts alone are sometimes not enough."

"Was the car totaled?"

"Well, I'm not an insurance adjuster," he said, "but I'd think so."

"What about getting run off the road or avoiding an animal?"

"No evidence of skid marks or swerve marks," Big Bob said. "It looked as if he didn't make a curve and drove straight into a tree."

I took a deep breath and asked the question no one wanted to ask: "What if it was on purpose?"

The big man shook his head. "I don't even want to think about that."

◆   ◆   ◆   ◆

At five o'clock that afternoon, my phone rang as I was closing down the office. I started to ignore it, but caller ID read, "Private caller."

"Cherokee Investigations," I said in my I'm-trying-to-get-out-of-here voice.

"We need to talk," David Steele said, ignoring my annoyance.

"You got a match."

"We did," he said. "I cannot believe this. We've been breaking our butts trying to find any lead on these bombings, and one falls right into your lap. Why is that, Youngblood?"

"Divine providence," I said. "Or I'm cursed. I don't know which. I would just as soon they didn't fall into my lap."

"Well, I really don't care one way or the other, but I do need to know the details."

"I planned on telling you if you got a match," I said.

"Not on the phone. I need to be in Knoxville anyway, so I'm coming down and bringing the file on these bombings. Meet me at the Knoxville airport tomorrow morning. This time, *I'll* be the one in a private jet."

Rank does have its privileges, I thought.

◆　　◆　　◆　　◆

Mary, Lacy, Biker, and I had dinner at the condo—tortellini Alfredo, Caesar salad, and Parmesan garlic toast. Mary and I shared a bottle of Chateau Ste. Michelle Chardonnay. Lacy and Biker shared a bottle of Diet Coke. The only mention of their classmates was that Clay Carr was still in a coma and Julie James's funeral was tomorrow afternoon.

When we finished dinner, the young people disappeared downstairs into the den to watch TV, leaving Mary and me alone for the first time since I arrived from the office.

"What do you think they're doing down there?" I asked.

"What would *you* be doing down there at their age?" Mary said, smiling wickedly.

"I'd better check," I said, and feigned getting up.

"Stay right where you are, Cowboy," Mary said. "Lacy can take care of herself and make good decisions."

"Right," I said.

"Tell me about your day," Mary said. "You were out of here before I got up."

"Let's see," I said. "I had coffee with T. Elbert."

"How is he?"

"Same as always."

"What else?"

"Then I took Big Bob to breakfast to tell him about my newest case."

"How did he react?"

"He surprised me," I said. "He was impressed that I was hired by the senior class and gave his blessing."

"Well, that's good," Mary said. "What about the rest of your day?"

"It was fairly uneventful until David Steele called," I said.

"Tell me."

"He got a familial DNA match to the sample I gave him," I said. "Apparently, the Dallas bomber is Sheila Buckworth's long-missing son."

"Holy shit," Mary said.

Really!

10

Midmorning of the next day, I was standing outside security at Knoxville's McGhee Tyson Airport waiting for David Steele. I was carrying my briefcase. *Professionalism is all.*

As I waited, I saw a familiar face. Buckley Clarke was on the other side of the checkpoint talking to a security guard. He turned, saw me, and waved me forward through the passenger exit. We shook hands.

"I should have known I'd run into you," I said.

"Good to see you again, Mr. Youngblood," Buckley said.

Buckley Clarke was an FBI agent assigned to the Knoxville office and had reported to David Steele before Dave was promoted to his current position. I had worked with Buckley on the CJK case.

"Sir," the security guard interrupted, "could I see some ID?"

I handed him my FBI consultant credentials.

He looked at them, nodded, and handed them back. "Sir, are you carrying a sidearm?"

"No," I said. "I'm relying on Agent Clarke to protect me."

He smiled. "Carry on," he said, turning away from us.

"This way," Buckley said.

I followed him to the end of the north terminal. He punched a series of numbers on a keypad beside a door. I heard a click. Buckley opened the door, and we went through it, down a flight of stairs, and out another door onto the tarmac. A jet with the stairs down waited a hundred yards away. Emblazoned on the side of the jet were the letters FBI in red, white and blue with a small American flag underneath the letters. The same logo was also on the nose of the jet.

◆　◆　◆　◆

"I see that being associate deputy director has its perks, Dave," I said.

I sat across from David Steele at a table for four inside the luxurious Gulfstream V jet that had flown him in from Washington.

"I'm pretty far down the pecking order," he said. "I was lucky it wasn't in use. We have to justify its existence, so if it's available I can use it."

"Lucky you," I said.

"I'm on a tight schedule," David Steele said. "Tell me what you know, and then you can read the file."

I told him all of it.

"So a boy goes missing and ends up dying in a terrorist bomb blast eight years later," David Steele mused. "Maybe he was just a runaway who fell in with the wrong crowd."

"Maybe," I said.

"Any reason to think he was kidnapped?"

"Not yet," I said.

David Steele looked thoughtful and said nothing.

"I'd like to keep the Buckworths out of it," I said.

"I'll do my best to keep the family name confidential, but we'll need to interview the mother," David Steele said. "Talk to her as soon as you can and pave the way. I don't want her stonewalling us."

"I understand," I said. "I'll call her as soon as we're done here." I handed him the business card Sheila Buckworth had given me. "Her cell-phone number is on the back."

He wrote the information in his notebook and handed the card back to me. Then he reached into his briefcase and handed me a thick folder. It was marked, "Level 3 Security Clearance Required."

"I've got Level 3 security clearance?" I asked. I didn't know how many levels there were, but I was guessing a heck of a lot more than three.

"Don't let it go to your head," David Steele said. "Take your time. I'm going forward to make some calls. You can take notes if you wish."

There was a lot to read. Over the past two years, six courthouse bombings were tied together. All had occurred at midnight. Three had been state courthouses and three federal. Only three made the national news. The other bombings had been managed by the FBI to look like something else: one, a natural gas explosion; another, a lightning strike during a thunderstorm; and the third, arson. The FBI had linked them all to a group who called themselves the Midnight Riders. Their manifesto was in the file. I read it. Their mission was to bring down our fascist government and give control back to the people. They were tired of liberal politics in which criminals had more rights than upstanding citizens, a society that embraced un-Christian behavior, and a media that distorted the truth. The manifesto rambled on for pages. It even contained a reference to Paul Revere, in honor of whom the group's name was chosen: "Like Paul Revere, we strike at midnight to warn of the evil that exists and to rally like-minded citizens to our cause."

When I finished reading, my head was spinning. How had Sheila Buckworth's son become part of a fanatical conservative group of homegrown terrorists? I was working on my theory when David Steele returned from the forward cabin.

"Interesting reading, isn't it?" he said.

"Very interesting."

"There's one more thing," he said. "I didn't show you before because I didn't want you distracted." He handed me a single sheet in a protective plastic sleeve. "This is the title page of the manifesto."

At the top of the page was what I guessed the Midnight Riders considered their symbol or logo or trademark. In a typeface I had never seen before were the words, *The Midnight Riders.* Each lowercase *i* had been replaced by a dagger with blood dripping from the tip, with a human eye over the handle representing the dot. The three daggers dripping blood had a chilling effect after my reading of the manifesto.

"They have a flair for theatrics," I said. "How did you get the manifesto?"

"They sent it to us," David Steele said.

"Cocky bastards, aren't they?"

"Very," David Steele said. "I want to find their leader and shove this manifesto where the sun doesn't shine."

"Good luck," I said.

"There's more, something that's not in the file. At every bombing site, the three daggers are painted somewhere on the building in a place not consumed by the blast."

"Their way of claiming responsibility," I said. "Which begs the question, why haven't they gone to the press?"

"We don't know," David Steele said. "Maybe because it would make them look more like terrorists than freedom fighters."

"Sooner or later, they'll go to the press," I said. "Why hasn't the FBI?"

"Because we don't want to encourage copycat fanatics to take up their cause," he said. "A lot of disillusioned people are out there right now. Just look at all the shootings."

We seemed to have a mass shooting or two a week. It was as if our nation were on the verge of anarchy, as if a virus were going around infecting on-the-edge potential killers. I made no comment.

"Will you officially sign on to this case as a consultant?" David Steele asked.

"Why not?" I said. "I *am* getting a little bored."

"Any final thoughts before I get airborne?"

"A big, scary one," I said.

"Which is?"

I unleashed my theory. "This group places an insider in a school or youth camp to look for candidates. I'm guessing an older kid targeting a younger kid. The younger kids are told about this great new life. They probably don't realize they are being recruited as freedom fighters. It sounds exciting and romantic. It's easier to convince the younger ones since they'll have an older friend to run away with. Then they're brainwashed and trained to go into the field when they're ready—say, eighteen years old."

"That's scary," David Steele said.

And then some, I thought.

◆   ◆   ◆   ◆

Buckley and I stood at a window in an empty passenger departure area and watched the Gulfstream V lift off the tarmac and disappear into the distance.

"I've got to get back to the office," Buckley said. "Are you leaving now?"

"No," I said. "I'm going to sit awhile and do some thinking about this case. And I have to make a phone call to Sheila Buckworth."

"Well," Buckley said, "I'm sure we'll be talking soon, Mr. Youngblood. Safe travels to Mountain Center. Say hello to Gretchen for me." He turned and walked away.

I sat near a window and dialed Sheila Buckworth's cell phone. She answered on the third ring.

"Mr. Youngblood?"

"Yes," I said.

"You have news?"

"I do."

"Tell me," she said.

"Your DNA sample was a familial match," I said. "You're going to get a call from the FBI."

"My God," she whispered.

I waited for what seemed a long time. It actually wasn't.

"How does my son go missing and then eight years later end up dying while bombing a federal courthouse?" She seemed confused, like a person trying to sort out news that didn't quite make sense.

"Good question," I said. "I have no idea."

"I want you to find out," she said, steel in her voice. "Whatever it costs, I don't care. You're on retainer until further notice. Let's see if you're as good as your press clippings."

She hung up before I could respond. Another gauntlet was down.

◆　　◆　　◆　　◆

On my way home, I started my investigation of the Clay Carr case with a trip to Proffit's Garage. Proffit's had been a Mountain Center institution for as long as I could remember. It was started more than fifty years ago by George Proffit's grandfather. If your car had a problem, you took it to Proffit's. If your car needed to be towed, you called Proffit's. If your car was totaled, it went to Proffit's junkyard, directly in back of the garage.

I parked and went in one of the open garage doors. George was in the back talking to another mechanic. He saw me and came forward, wiping his hand on a dirty rag. He was a big, beefy man with dark hair showing some gray; he was taller than I was, but not by much.

"Mr. Youngblood," he said. "I haven't seen you in a while. Your wife came in recently for an oil change. How can I help you?"

"Can we talk privately?"

He nodded.

I followed George to his office and closed the door. All of a sudden, he looked concerned.

"What is it?" he asked.

"George," I said, "I'm working a case, and I have to ask you not to discuss this conversation with anyone."

"Sure," he said.

"You can talk about it when it's over, but not now."

"Sure," he said again.

"Is Clay Carr's car in your junkyard?"

"Sure is," he said. "Towed it in early Saturday morning. Terrible thing, that."

"I need you to give it a good going over," I said.

"To see if I can find any reason for the accident," George said. "Brakes, steering, and such."

"Exactly," I said. "I'll pay you for your time."

"No you won't," he said. "You and your family are loyal customers. So are the Carrs and the Jameses. I'll take a look this evening after everyone's gone."

"Look for things you might not normally look for," I said, "like bullet holes or a small explosive device."

"Bullet holes? Explosive device?" George looked a bit afraid.

"I wouldn't expect that," I said. "But I have to cover all the bases and think the worst."

"Sure," he said. "I understand."

"Call me when you're done," I said.

◆　　◆　　◆　　◆

That night, the Mountain Center girls played at home in front of a full gym and a boisterous crowd. *There's nothing like being the number-two team in the state*, I thought. The usual suspects were there: Billy, Roy, T. Elbert, Mary, and me. We watched a rather boring thirty-point blowout.

As usual after the game, we went to a late dinner at The Brewery. Lacy and Biker met us there.

I said quietly to Lacy, "I could take the whole team out sometime."

Her reply: "That's a nice thought, but don't do it. That would make us look like we're showing off how much money you have, and it might make some of the other parents feel inferior."

"You're right," I said. "I wasn't thinking."

"No, you were just trying to be nice," Mary said, leaning in on the conversation. "And we love you for it."

"We do," Lacy said.

No one else seemed to notice the exchange. I swallowed hard and said nothing.

Toughness is all.

11

The next day, I was in the office early when the phone rang. Caller ID read, "Proffit's Garage."

"Youngblood," I answered.

"Mr. Youngblood, it's George Proffit. Long story short, I didn't find anything suspicious. Brakes, steering, and everything else looked fine."

"I didn't think you would, George," I said. "But it needed to be checked."

"I understand," he said. "And I'll keep it confidential."

◆   ◆   ◆   ◆

Later that morning as I was enjoying my second cup of coffee, I had another phone call. I waited for Gretchen's voice on the intercom. I waited at least a minute.

"Buckley on line one," Gretchen said.

"You mean FBI agent Buckley Clarke?" I asked.

"How many other Buckleys do you know?"

I picked up the phone. "Sorry, I forgot to tell Gretchen hello for you."

"I know," he said.

"Are you and Gretchen dating?" No beating around the bush with me.

"Classified," Buckley said.

"I have Level 3 security clearance," I said.

"You would need at least Level 5," Buckley said. "But you have my permission to ask Gretchen."

"On second thought, I don't want to know." I said. "What's up?"

"Associate Deputy Director Steele wants me to work with you on this Midnight Riders case," Buckley said. "I await your instructions."

I had anticipated that David Steele might assign Buckley to me and had thought about the direction we should take. "We need to start running down missing boys around ten to twelve years of age," I said. "The more recent, the better. I'm really interested in ones who went missing in pairs, and in cases where at least one mother is no longer on the radar."

"That won't be as easy as it sounds," Buckley said.

"But not impossible," I said.

"Probably not," Buckley said. "It will take awhile. We have a database of kidnapped and missing kids, and ours is only the tip of the iceberg. Many runaway and missing-children cases are handled by local authorities. Many times, we don't get called in. And other times, they're never reported."

"Do what you can. Start with the Western states."

"As good a place as any," Buckley said.

"Time's a-wastin'," I said.

"I'm on it right now," he said.

◆   ◆   ◆   ◆

Right after lunch, my intercom buzzed.

"Sheila Buckworth on line one," Gretchen said.

"Mrs. Buckworth," I said. "How may I help you?"

"I wanted to apologize for my behavior yesterday," she said. "Although he looked like the software aging picture, I didn't really think the bomber in the paper could be my son. It was quite a shock. I'm having a hard time processing all of it."

"I understand," I said. "You don't owe me an apology."

"Thank you," she said. "Will you continue to look into this for me?"

"I will. What happened to your son will be part of an ongoing investigation by the FBI. They have asked me to participate. Have they contacted you?"

"The FBI?" she said. "No, not yet."

"You will probably hear from Associate Deputy Director David Steele, or maybe Special Agent Buckley Clarke," I said. "Director Steele has promised to keep your interview confidential. Once the match was confirmed, I had no choice but to tell him where the sample came from."

"Well," she said, "you did warn me."

◆　　◆　　◆　　◆

UPS showed up in the early afternoon with a package from Provo, Utah. I opened it to find Abraham Webb's file on the Michael Brand case. A note from Jock read, "Return to me when you are finished." I left it on my desk as a reminder to read the file later. I doubted there was anything in it that could help, but you never know.

◆　　◆　　◆　　◆

I wanted to put the Clay Carr case behind me as quickly as possible so I could concentrate on the courthouse bomber. I buzzed Gretchen.

"Yes, my liege," Gretchen said.

"Very funny," I said, stifling a laugh. "Please find out the whereabouts of Dr. Evan Smith. Start with the ER at Mountain Center Medical."

"As you command, sire," Gretchen said.

"You're watching way too much *Game of Thrones*," I said.

Fifteen minutes later, Gretchen tracked down Dr. Evan Smith. He was working at a free clinic in Johnson City. She left a message for him to call me.

That afternoon, he called back. I had met Dr. Evan Smith on several occasions, none of them good. Most involved my getting shot or beat up. One involved Mary. Dr. Smith had been much more attentive to Mary than to me, even when I was the one being treated.

"Thanks for returning my call."

"No problem," he said. "Anytime our paths cross, it proves to be interesting. Is this about Clay Carr and Julie James?"

"How did you know?"

"Only reason I could think of that you would call," he said.

"I understand you ran a tox screen for alcohol on Clay," I said.

"And Julie James," Evan Smith said.

"Did you check for anything else?"

"Is this confidential?"

"Unless it turns into something more than it appears to be," I said.

"Let me put it another way," he said. "Is this off the record? Technically, medical records are confidential, and you would need a court order to get this on the record."

"Off the record," I said.

"I ran a tox screen for alcohol, marijuana, and cocaine on both. Clay was completely clean." He paused.

"Julie wasn't?"

"Not exactly," he said. "Traces of alcohol. She had been drinking. Not a lot. Nowhere near the legal limit."

"And you kept it to yourself," I said.

"She was gone, and she wasn't driving. I didn't want to add any more grief for the family. Was that wrong?"

"No, not that I can see. I would have done the same thing."

"Thanks for that," he said. "Anything else?"

"Do you still have blood samples?"

"Yes," he said. "I was going to keep them awhile in case there were any questions."

"I want you to run a complete blood toxicology on both Clay and Julie," I said.

"On whose authority?"

"The FBI's," I said.

"Is this an FBI case?"

"Not really," I said. "But it covers you. If it comes up, you were asked by an FBI consultant to run the tox screens. I can fax you a copy of my credentials with my request, if you need it."

"Please do," Evan Smith said.

"Have the bill sent to me," I said. "And hide the fax unless you need it."

"Will do."

"How long do I have to wait for the results?"

"I'll have to send the samples off," he said. "A week to ten days. Depends on how backed up they are."

"Let me know the minute you have anything," I said.

◆　　◆　　◆　　◆

I went back to the office, brewed a cup of coffee and sat at my desk going through the Alexander Webb file. Webb kept very detailed notes, probably because he was billing Sheila Buckworth a pretty penny and he had to justify the bill. Reading the file I had no epiphanies but there was a notebook page of random thoughts, one of which I found very interesting: *other boys missing in pairs?* It seemed private investigator Webb had come to the same conclusion I had. I wondered if he had ever shared that thought with Sheila Buckworth.

I put the file back in the envelope, made a note for Gretchen to send it back to Jock Smithson and placed the file on her desk.

◆　　◆　　◆　　◆

Later that afternoon, Lacy and Biker sat in the oversized chairs on the other side of my desk, wondering why I had texted them to come to my office after school. *Yes, on rare occasions, I do text.*

"Whatever we say here doesn't leave this room," I said.

Lacy looked at Biker, then back to me. "Sure," she said.

Biker said nothing. I stared hard at him.

"No problem," he said.

"I mean it," I said.

"We get it," Lacy said, sounding exactly like Mary.

Biker nodded.

"I need some straight answers," I said.

"Ask," Lacy said.

"Was there alcohol at the party?"

"Probably," Lacy said, not hesitating. "Did I see any? No."

"You see any?" I asked Biker.

"Some kids had beer in the parking lot."

"Was one of those kids Julie James?"

"No," Biker said, looking surprised.

"Either one of you see Julie James drinking?"

"No," they said almost simultaneously.

"Julie was drinking?" Lacy said.

"Not much, but some," I said.

"Clay?" Biker asked.

"Apparently not," I said.

"Want us to ask around about who had alcohol at the party?" Lacy asked.

"No," I said. "Not yet."

I paused. They were quiet.

"What I really want you to do is find out who saw Clay and Julie leave," I said. "Be casual about it. Don't come on like junior private eyes."

"We're seniors," Lacy said.

"Cute," I said. "But you know what I mean."

"Don't worry," Lacy said. "We'll find out."

"We will," Biker said.

12

That Friday morning, I was in my office on my computer searching out missing children websites. They were numerous. I picked one and started making a list of boys ages ten through twelve who went missing. I had three possible leads when the phone rang.

"This is a bigger job than I thought," Buckley said. "I have twelve leads already, and I've only scratched the surface. Furthermore, a number of websites not associated with the FBI list missing children. We need more manpower, and it's not going to come from us. You've got me full time for now, but I'm all you get."

"I'll handle the websites and funnel my list to you," I said. "You can cross-check for duplications. I think a dozen names are enough for you to start with. Make some calls and get more details. If any of them went missing with other boys near their age, get as much information as you can."

"Will do," Buckley said.

"I'll email some names later for you to follow up on," I said. "Call me in the morning and give me an update—or sooner, if something promising turns up."

◆　◆　◆　◆

By noon, I had a list of ten possible leads. I emailed them to Buckley and got off the web. Seeing the faces of hundreds of missing kids was depressing. I wanted to know their stories. I wanted to know why they went missing. I wanted to know that they were all okay.

I called T. Elbert.

"A telephone call," T. Elbert said when he answered. "This must be important."

"You busy?"

"Hell no," he said. "I'm rarely busy."

"What say I come by your place and you get the Black Beauty out and we go to lunch at the country club?" The Black Beauty was T. Elbert's custom-equipped Hummer that allowed him to drive.

"Sounds like a plan," T. Elbert said. I could hear the excitement in his voice. "Come ahead."

♦   ♦   ♦   ♦

We sat at my usual table in the corner overlooking the eighteenth green. We placed our order: club sandwiches with fries and sweet iced tea.

The eighteenth green was devoid of golfers; there was no flagstick and no cup to put it in. Its grass, splendid in spring, summer, and fall, was the dull dark green of winter. The golf course was closed.

Only four tables in the large room were occupied. No one was near us. We could talk freely without being overheard.

"I'm working on something I'd like your help on," I said.

"Sure," T. Elbert said. "What is it, and what can I do?"

"I need you to do some web research on the Midnight Riders case," I said. "There are a number of websites for missing children. We need leads. I'll email you the parameters."

"Glad to," T. Elbert said. "You concentrate on other things and let me handle the web work."

"Glad to," I mimicked. "I spent the morning on one site and found ten leads, but it was a real downer."

"Missing kids," T. Elbert said, taking a drink of iced tea. "They'll break your heart."

♦   ♦   ♦   ♦

Friday night, Lacy had another road game in Knoxville. We sat in the bleachers on the visitors' side in a half-empty gym and watched as the

Lady Bears ran their record to 25–0. Lacy scored seventeen points and dished out six assists in a nineteen-point win. Billy was there with his wife, Maggie, a tall, attractive Cherokee woman. They had one son, Donald Roy Youngblood Two-Feathers. They called him "Little D." I asked Billy once why he had chosen such a long name, thinking the *Youngblood* could have been omitted. His response was, "Donald Roy Blood Two-Feathers just didn't sound right."

Lacy and Billy had a special relationship. Maybe it was because they were both adopted. Maybe it was because of basketball; Billy saw almost every game Lacy played. Maybe it was because sometimes people just connected somehow, and age, race, and sex made no difference. All of the above, I suspected.

Biker McBride sat a few rows down from us with Lacy's best friend, Hannah, and Al, Hannah's boyfriend, who used to be called Alfred before Biker, Lacy, and Hannah had transformed him from a geek into a fairly cool dude. Alfred's nickname was "the Brain"—no explanation needed.

Afterward, the young crowd went back to Mountain Center for a party, and we old folks went to Calhoun's on the River for a late dinner. We were in the middle of it when Billy asked, "Working on anything interesting, Blood?"

"Two things," I said. "One with the FBI and one local."

"The FBI," Billy said. "Again?"

"I can't seem to stay away."

"Can you tell us about it?" Billy said.

"Depends," I said with a straight face. "Can I trust you to keep quiet about it?"

That was like asking if the sun was going to come up in the morning. Billy smiled. He knew I was messing with him, as he sometimes did with me. We enjoyed it.

"I will take it to the grave untold," Billy said with all the seriousness he could muster.

"What about her?" I nodded toward Maggie.

"Don!" Mary said.

"Her, too," Billy said. "My woman doesn't speak unless I give her permission."

"Lucky you," I said.

Maggie laughed.

Mary kicked my foot under the table. "Stop kidding around and tell them."

So I did.

"So what are you thinking?" Billy asked.

"I'll let you know when I have more information," I said. "Something's not right about a ten-year-old runaway turning out to be a courthouse bomber for the Midnight Riders."

"I think you're right," Billy said. "So what are you doing about it?"

"Buckley, T. Elbert, and I are looking for pairs of boys who went missing together," I said. "If we find any, I want to check out the parents. If I can find a pattern, I may be able to develop a lead."

"If you need backup, I can always get away for a day or two," Billy said.

"If I need backup," I said, "you'll be the first one I call."

13

Winters in East Tennessee are unpredictable. I've lived through East Tennessee winters with mild temperatures and little snow, and I've lived through East Tennessee winters with below-freezing temperatures and snow every week. This winter was shaping up as the latter. So far, it had been a cold one with a few days approaching zero. We had counted at least six decent snowfalls in January, and the month wasn't over yet. Saturday, we awoke to yet another snow. An inch or two was already on the ground, and the light snow that was falling promised to continue through the day, according to my calculations after a quick check of Doppler radar.

We were at the lake house: Mary, the dogs, and I. Lacy had stayed in Mountain Center with Hannah. Mary and Hannah's mother, Suzanne, were wise to the ways of teenage girls, having gone through the experience themselves. Still, they couldn't cover everything.

I got up early and took the dogs out. They loved the snow and the cold weather. They ran around the fenced-in area like they'd been inside for a month. Even old man Jake showed more enthusiasm than normal. I let them stay out while I swept the walk and cleaned snow off my SUV and Mary's truck. I knew it was a waste of time, but it was exhilarating to be out in the cold.

Back in the house, all was quiet. The dogs lay down in front of the freestanding gas stove in the kitchen to take a nap. I made coffee and went to the bar in the den and turned on my computer. I had two interesting emails, both saying almost exactly the same thing: *Found something. Call me.* The emails were from Buckley and T. Elbert.

I called T. Elbert first.

"You're up early," he said when he answered.

"I'm most always up early," I said. "Do you have snow?"

"We do," he said. "An inch, maybe. Are you at the lake house?"

"Yeah, we probably have two inches," I said.

"I found something interesting in an old local newspaper article while doing my missing kids research," he said.

"Let's hear it."

"About ten years ago, there was a camp for troubled youth in the middle of nowhere in Arizona. I guess 'troubled youth' was the terminology for juvenile delinquents. Anyway, the whole camp disappeared without a trace. As far as I can tell, it was never found."

"How many kids?"

"Doesn't say." T. Elbert paused, as if I should say something.

"Go on," I said. "I'm sure there's more."

"There is," T. Elbert said. "It was rumored, but never confirmed, that the camp superintendent, the supervisors, the counselors, and even the cook were all ex-military. I'll bet some of them were Native Americans."

"Sweet Jesus," I said. "Are you thinking what I'm thinking?"

"You tell me," T. Elbert said.

"It would be a hell of a way to start a domestic terrorist movement if you brainwashed a bunch of discarded, impressionable kids and then disappeared to parts unknown, then trained them and waited for them to grow up to do your bidding."

"My thoughts exactly," he said.

"What else?"

"Half of the kids attending the camp were thought to be Native Americans."

"Sounds like a pretty loose article," I said.

"All rumor and conjecture," T. Elbert said. "But it's something."

"It is, but how can it help us now?"

"Don't know," T. Elbert said. "Other than this article, I couldn't find any coverage in the press."

"Did you find a follow-up? Do you know if they ever were found?"

"I did not, and I do not," T. Elbert said.

"Was the camp on a reservation?"

"It was. The Tohono O'Odham Reservation. It's in south-central Arizona. The south end borders Mexico."

"That's the reason it didn't make the national press," I said. "The whole thing was handled by tribal police. They might know what really happened."

"That would be a secret well kept," T. Elbert said. "Probably one that would never be told to a white man."

But maybe to a full-blooded six-foot-six deputy sheriff Cherokee Indian, I thought. I knew I'd have to get Billy Two-Feathers involved after all.

◆   ◆   ◆   ◆

An hour later, Mary was still sleeping. We had stayed up late taking advantage of our empty nest. I tend to get up at the same time no matter when I go to sleep, according to an internal clock I can't seem to turn off. If Mary stays up late, she sleeps in if she has a choice.

I called Buckley Clarke.

"Hello," a familiar female voice said.

"Gretchen?"

Dead air.

"Who's Gretchen?"

"My trusty assistant who thinks all men are rats," I said.

"Not anymore," Gretchen said in a sultry voice I had not heard before.

"Where's Buckley?"

"Asleep," she said. "He stayed up half the night working on this missing kids thing."

"Well, I hope it didn't get in the way of more important things," I said.

"Classified."

"Have him call me," I said.

An hour later, Buckley called back. Mary was still sleeping.

"Sorry I wasn't awake when you called," he said.

"Not a problem. I can see how you might have been extra tired."

"About that—"

I cut him off. "No need to explain. You're both adults I like very much, and your personal relationships are none of my business."

"Thanks," Buckley said. "At some point, I may want to talk more about it."

"Anytime," I said. "Now, tell me why you wanted me to call."

"I found two pairs of runaways who fit our profile," Buckley said. "A pair in Albuquerque and a pair in Denver. I called both police departments requesting information. They'll send me the files, and I'll bring them to your office to go over them."

"Good work," I said. "How long have they been missing?"

"The Albuquerque pair went missing three years ago and the Denver pair two years ago."

"Those trails are probably too cold to do us any good."

"Probably, but we have to take a look, don't we?"

"We do," I said. "Enjoy your weekend. I'll see you Monday."

"Sure thing," Buckley said.

◆   ◆   ◆   ◆

Ten minutes after I hung up, I heard sounds in the kitchen. I found Mary standing beside the kitchen island with her first cup of coffee, wearing her nightshirt and a pair of my pajama bottoms. She looked great.

"Nice bottoms," I said.

"My legs were cold."

"They fit pretty well," I said.

"That's because my ass is getting big."

"Your ass is perfect."

"Stop sweet-talking me," Mary said. "You got yours last night."

"Can't blame a guy for trying," I said, giving her a good-morning hug. "It snowed last night."

Mary looked out the kitchen window. "It sure did. I hadn't even noticed."

"Looks like it might snow all day."

She ignored the innuendo. "When did you get up?"

"Six o'clock," I said.

"What have you been doing?"

"On the phone, mostly," I said. "Both Buckley and T. Elbert asked me to call. I called T. Elbert first."

"What about?"

I told Mary about my conversation with T. Elbert.

"That's an interesting theory," Mary said. "But it seems like following that lead might be a waste of time. The trail is way cold."

"Probably," I said. "But you know how it goes. You start asking questions, and something useful turns up."

As we talked, I popped a Dunkin' Donuts K-Cup into our Keurig coffeemaker and brewed my second cup of the day.

"What did Buckley want?" Mary asked.

"Well," I said, pausing for effect, "when I called Buckley, he was asleep. Guess who answered?"

"Gretchen," Mary said.

"How'd you know?"

"Think about it."

"Girls' night out," I said, adding cream and sugar to my coffee.

Gretchen had recently joined Wanda and Mary for their weekly night out. Once a month, Mary took Lacy.

"Very good, Cowboy," Mary said.

"So how long has this been going on?"

"Not long," Mary said. "But they were circling each other for quite a while."

"You could have told me," I said.

"Gretchen didn't want me to."

"Why?"

"I'm not sure," Mary said. "Maybe she thought it was a conflict of interest. So don't mention their relationship unless she brings it up first."

"Don't worry, I won't."

"Now, why did Buckley want you to call?"

I told her.

"This case is starting to get complicated," Mary said.

"And then some," I said.

14

Sunday, the snow diminished to flurries, but the temperature was still in the twenties. Lacy and Biker showed up for a late breakfast and announced that the roads were fine.

"I hope you were careful out there," I said.

"You taught me how to drive in the snow, remember?" Lacy said.

"Uh-huh," I said. No point in arguing, since they had made it without incident.

I prepared challah-bread French toast, sprinkling one side with cinnamon and the other with nutmeg. I had fried a pound of bacon earlier and placed it on a warming rack in the toaster oven. I served the French toast with an apple compote and Vermont maple syrup. We sat around the kitchen island enjoying the fire, the food, and the conversation. I don't know if I'd ever been more content than sitting there in the relaxed atmosphere with two special young people and the woman I loved. *Youngblood, you're a hopeless romantic*, I thought.

Lacy snapped me out of it. "We have news," she said.

"Tell me."

Lacy looked at Biker as if to say, *Go ahead.*

"We asked around about who was the last person to see Clay and Julie leave the party the night of the accident," Biker said. "Anyway, it seems that Slinger Sloan and his girlfriend, Denise, were. Slinger and Clay are best friends. So I guess they're who you want to talk to."

Slinger Sloan was Mountain Center High's quarterback, and of course his girlfriend, Denise Ray, was the head cheerleader—funny how that worked. It made sense that Slinger would be Clay's best friend—a quarterback and a running back, both seniors.

"Ask if they'll come by the office one afternoon after school," I said. "I want to keep a low profile on this."

"Sure," Biker said. "They'll come. Slinger believes something funny was going on."

◆　　◆　　◆　　◆

Biker left the lake house in Lacy's Pathfinder in time to be home before dark. Snow was falling but not accumulating. Lacy made him promise to call when he got there. "Got to make sure my SUV is okay," she said as he walked out the front door.

"Sure you do," Biker said.

"And you," Lacy said, giving him a quick kiss.

I watched this scene and couldn't help thinking about the summer before her freshman year, when Lacy had walked into my office asking for help in finding her mother. It seemed like yesterday, and at the same time it seemed like a lifetime ago—the tricks of time and memory. From that day forward, my life had been a roller coaster. Lacy had grown into a young woman in front of our eyes. I had made the journey from confirmed bachelor with a lone dog to married man with a daughter and two dogs. I knew that was who I was meant to be. I couldn't have been happier. *Youngblood, the kinder, gentler private detective.* Well, maybe not.

"You okay?" Mary asked as Lacy went past us and up the stairs to her room.

"Never better," I said.

"You were gone there for a minute."

"Just thinking," I said.

"About Lacy?"

"You know me too well," I said, walking back into the kitchen.

"We won't have her much longer. She'll graduate and be off to college, and that will be that."

"Billy would say she has to find her own path," I said. "It's the natural order of things."

"That won't make it any easier," Mary said.

"No," I said. "It won't."

◆　　◆　　◆　　◆

As if reading our minds, Lacy brought up the subject of colleges that night at dinner. Mary had baked salmon in a miso sauce, accompanied by steamed broccoli with cheddar-cheese sprinkles and jasmine rice. I savored every bite.

"I've finished my research, and with the help of my guidance counselor I'm applying to three schools this week," Lacy said.

"Which schools?" I asked.

The answer totally surprised me. None of the schools was close to home.

"Arizona State, George Washington University, and the University of Pennsylvania," Lacy said,

Mary and I looked at each other.

"That's quite a diverse list," Mary said.

"It is, isn't it?" Lacy said.

"I'm sure those three schools have something in common," I said.

"You're right," Lacy said, enjoying the moment.

"So, are you going to tell us or keep it a secret?" Mary asked.

"I'm going to tell you," Lacy said. "They're all ranked in the top ten for law-enforcement degrees."

Mary and I again exchanged looks.

"You sure that's what you want to do?" I asked, although I was not surprised.

"My father is a private investigator, and my mother is a police detective," Lacy said. "I've seen what you two do and how you do it. I've seen you help people and catch bad guys. Law enforcement needs dedicated, honest people with integrity. I want to be part of that."

Wherever she goes, she should be on the debate team, I thought. I said nothing.

"Penn is an Ivy League school," Mary said. "It's hard to get into."

"I know that," Lacy said. "And as far as I can tell, it's the only Ivy League school with a law-enforcement degree. Don't worry, I'll get accepted."

"Do you have a first choice?" I asked.

"No," Lacy said. "Once I have my letters of acceptance, I'll visit each one and then make my decision."

I loved her confidence, but I knew college admission boards could be fickle. I hoped she wouldn't be disappointed.

"Is Biker applying to any of those schools?" I asked.

Mary snickered.

"All three," Lacy said.

Good grief!

15

Monday was cloudy and cold. I spent all morning running down information on missing kids and came up with only one new possibility, a pair who had gone missing four years earlier in Wyoming.

Gretchen arrived but had little to say—and absolutely nothing to say about Buckley.

"How was your weekend?" I asked.

"Good," she said.

I didn't press. I gave her assignments for the day, and she went silently to her desk, closing my door behind her.

About ten o'clock, I heard the faint sound of the outer office door opening and closing, followed by muted conversation. A couple of minutes later, my intercom buzzed.

"Special Agent Buckley Clarke from the Knoxville FBI office is here to see you," Gretchen said in her most professional tone.

"Show Special Agent Clarke in, please," I said.

Buckley, trying hard to look serious, managed to find his own way in and made himself comfortable in one of my oversized chairs. He opened his briefcase and handed me two files.

"Albuquerque and Denver," he said. "I should know more later today."

I read the files. Buckley waited quietly, working on his iPad. The two files were very much like the Michael Brand file. In each case, two boys had disappeared. Kidnapping was not suspected. One mother was highly concerned, the other not so much. One mother was a widow, the other divorced. One periodically checked for news, the other moved soon afterward without a forwarding address. *Too much coincidence*, I thought.

"Are you going to talk with the investigating officers?"

"Yes," Buckley said. "I'm expecting return calls anytime."

"Find out if these boys had any disciplinary problems or troubled backgrounds, things like that," I said. "And find out if they disappeared from summer camp. Find out everything you can about the mothers who took off. I want to develop a master file with as much information as possible for all the boys who fit our profile. Time of year they went missing, when they were last seen, where they went missing—you get the idea. Add anything else you can think of."

Buckley made notes. "If there are any juvie records, they'll be sealed," he said.

"I know. But it won't hurt to ask if any exist."

"Want me to interview any of them face to face?"

"That's up to you," I said. "I'd call them first. If you see a good reason, then do a face-to-face." I handed the files back to Buckley, along with a note on the missing pair I had found that morning. "Check out this pair and get back to me," I said.

"Sure thing." He put the files and the note in his briefcase and snapped it shut. He stood, walked toward my door, and turned. "Let's have dinner some night soon," he said. "I need advice from someone with experience."

"Sure," I said, not wanting to tell him that if he was seeking advice about women, I was the wrong person to ask. "Maybe one night this week. I'll let you know."

◆　　◆　　◆　　◆

Late that afternoon, after Gretchen left for the day, Lacy showed up. She was not alone.

"Dad," she said, "this is Denise Ray and Slinger Sloan. Guys, this is my dad, Donald Youngblood."

Lacy rarely addressed me as "Dad" unless she was teasing me or trying to make a point; most of the time, it was "Don." When she talked to or referred to Mary, it was always "Mom."

Slinger extended his hand. "It's an honor to meet you, sir," he said. His handshake was firm; he seemed excited.

Denise nodded and said nothing.

"You, too," I said. "I've seen you play. You-all had a great season."

"We did," he said. "But the championship doesn't seem very important right now."

We were still standing in the outer office.

"Let's go to my office," I said. "Lacy, grab one of those chairs from the conference table."

"I got it," said Slinger. He picked it up effortlessly and followed us in.

Once seated, I asked, "How is Clay?"

"Still in a coma," Slinger said. "His brain swelling is going down, and they're hoping he'll wake up in a few days. He's going to be really fucked up when he finds out Julie is dead."

"Slinger!" Denise said. "Watch your language."

"Sorry," Slinger said. "But it's the truth."

"How long had they been dating?"

"All senior year," Slinger said. "And he really liked her. They were friends a long time. I think it could have been long term."

Lacy remained silent.

"Does Clay have any other serious injuries?" I asked.

"Not that I know of," Slinger said.

I turned my gaze on Denise. "Did you see Clay and Julie leave the party?"

"Yes, sir," she said.

"How did they look?"

"Julie said she was really tired, like falling-asleep tired, and she wanted to go home. Clay said he was tired, too. We were supposed to ride with them, but we got a ride later with some other friends."

"Do you know if Julie was drinking anything alcoholic?"

"God, no," Denise said. "She would never." She started to cry. "We should have driven them. They'd still be okay."

"You couldn't have known what was going to happen," Lacy said. "It is not your fault."

I looked at Lacy. "Why don't you and Denise go get something to drink and wait for us in the outer office," I said.

Lacy understood immediately. "Sure. Let's go, Denise."

Denise seemed glad to leave.

Once we were alone, I asked, "Did Julie ever drink?"

"Never, that I knew of," Slinger said. "Honest to God."

"Clay?"

"No way," he said. "He was all about his body, staying in shape—no fast food, no smoking, no drinking. He could be a real pain-in-the-ass straight arrow."

"Is there anything you can add to Julie's account of when they left the party?" I asked.

"Nothing I can think of," Slinger said. "Clay said he was really tired, but he seemed okay to drive, and I knew he wasn't drinking."

"Any other thoughts?"

"There's got to be a reason for the accident other than that Clay fell asleep," he said.

"Maybe," I said. "I just can't think of what it might be."

"Maybe they got distracted by something that happened inside the car and Clay took his eyes off the road," Slinger said. "Maybe something was wrong with Julie."

"Maybe," I said. "Guess we'll have to wait until Clay wakes up to find out."

•   •   •   •

That night, the Mountain Center girls played at home against a team from Sullivan County. The final buzzer mercifully ended a 70–27 blowout, as Lacy and her teammates continued to roll. They had only two home games left before the district tournament. It was an exciting time of year.

16

Buckley called early the next morning—no caller ID, but I recognized his cell-phone number.

"What's new, Buckley?" I answered.

"Not much. The younger missing kids seemed to be a bit renegade, but apparently not enough to get in trouble with the law. They had some trouble at school—not handing in homework, grades lower than their ability, stuff like that. Both pairs were last seen at school, not at camp. But here's the thing. In both cases the older boys were excellent students and had been in school only about three months."

"Well, they had to transfer in from somewhere," I said.

"That was my thinking," Buckley said. "So I talked to the schools. Both of the older boys had supposedly been homeschooled."

"That could have been bullshit," I said.

"That's what I thought," Buckley said. "So I talked to their teachers, and both said the boys tested high for their grade level, which was consistent with homeschooling."

"What else?"

"The Wyoming pair is a little different," Buckley said.

"How so?"

"Both mothers are still around and inquiring weekly about their sons. Both are working mothers who know each other. The boys are average students—no trouble to speak of. They may be part of it, but this pair is different."

"Okay," I said. "Good work. Anything else?"

"I have another pair who might fit the profile. They're from Nevada. I'm looking into them."

"How long ago?"

"Last year," Buckley said.

"Good. The more recent, the better. Are there any fathers around in all of this?"

"None," Buckley said. "And I don't think that's a coincidence."

"Me either," I said.

"Anything new on your end?" Buckley asked.

"Now that you ask, there is."

I told him about my telephone conversation with T. Elbert. When I finished, Buckley was silent a moment or two.

"They'd make a nice little white supremacist startup group, wouldn't they?" Buckley said.

"Sure would. Why don't you check the FBI files and see if you come up with anything on that?"

"Why don't I?" Buckley said. "I'll call you after lunch."

◆   ◆   ◆   ◆

I still had plenty of morning left. I had managed to ingest only one cup of coffee, and my stomach was letting me know that was insufficient. It occurred to me that I hadn't seen much of Roy lately, so I called his private number.

"That you, Gumshoe?" he answered.

"That's Mr. Gumshoe to you," I said. "Want to meet me at the diner for breakfast? I'm buying."

"We important folk do have to eat," Roy said. "See you in fifteen."

Ten minutes later, I locked the outer office door and went down the back stairs to the alley. I turned left and headed toward the Mountain Center Diner, a two-block walk I had made many times. I slipped through the back door and was within a few feet of my table when Doris Black caught me.

"Ignoring my *Employees Only* sign again, I see," Doris scolded.

"Well, I am family of a part-time employee," I said. Lacy still worked at the diner from time to time, even during basketball season.

"Well, I guess that's good enough," she laughed. "What can I get you?"

"Coffee for now," I said. "I'm meeting Roy. He'll be here any minute."

On cue, Roy walked through the front door and headed toward my reserved table in the rear. He was wearing an expensive suit with an equally pricey shirt and tie.

"Make that two coffees," I said.

Doris bustled away as Roy sat down.

"Mr. *GQ*," I said.

Roy smiled. "Got to dress the part."

"You look very presidential."

"So what's the occasion?"

"None, really," I said. "I just haven't seen you in a while. You must be busy."

"Really busy," Roy said. "I love it, but sometimes I miss the good ole days when you were shooting people and getting beat up and Billy and I were right in the mix."

"Not that long ago," I said.

"Seems like a long time to me," Roy said.

Doris brought coffee, and we ordered. Roy had a government project starting, manufacturing parts for an unknown new weapon. Security would be tight. Dennis "Bruiser" Bracken—a college friend, former NFL lineman, and security chief at a top-end Las Vegas casino—had been hired by Joseph Fleet as head of security. Wanda Jones and Bruiser were dating—engaged, actually, but their wedding plans seemed rather vague. Roy talked to Fleet once a week. The last he heard, Fleet was in Italy—not alone, and for some reason I was pleased about that.

"Dennis will be in this weekend," Roy said. "The government project starts in one week."

Roy, Bruiser, Billy, and I had worked together on an earlier case, and Bruiser had become part of our inner circle.

As we ate, I told Roy what I was working on.

"I may want to go to Arizona," I said. "You're welcome to come along as hired muscle if you want."

"I wish I could," Roy said. "You'd better take Billy. If you go out there without him, he'll have a fit."

"I was planning to," I said.

"Let me know when, and I'll be sure the jet is available," Roy said. "After all, you *are* on the board of directors."

◆   ◆   ◆   ◆

Buckley Clarke didn't call me back that afternoon. Rather, he showed up a few minutes before four o'clock, just in time to see Gretchen.

My intercom spoke to me. "Buckley's here," Gretchen said.

"Send him in."

Buckley made himself comfortable. "I was in the area," he said.

"Sure you were."

"I'm waiting on a return call from Nevada," he said. "So I have nothing new to report there. I found a sparse file on the youth-camp disappearance. The tribal police did not request assistance from the FBI, and none of the parents contacted us. So the FBI did not get involved."

"That's weird."

"Not really," Buckley said. "An Indian reservation is like a foreign country. We cannot just barge in and hijack one of their cases. We have to be invited. We weren't."

My door opened. Gretchen stuck her head in, looked at me, and said, "I'm gone. See you tomorrow."

"Okay," I said.

She smiled at Buckley. "See *you* later." Her words were loaded with innuendo.

"Sure thing," Buckley said.

I thought he looked embarrassed. Gretchen closed the door, and seconds later I heard the outer office door close.

"What happens later?" I said, grinning ear to ear.

"Figure of speech," Buckley said.

"Okay, moving on," I said. "Do you know if the kids were ever found?"

"I don't," Buckley said. "There was no follow-up information in the file."

"Well, I guess I'd better go ask. Until then, keep this between us."

17

Two days later, Billy and I were in Fleet Industries jet number one, flown by Jim Doak. I had told Jim our final destination was Sells, Arizona, and after some research he had decided to fly into Tucson International Airport.

"There's a small airport in Sells," Jim told us when we boarded. Sells was in the heart of the largest Tohono O'Odham Indian Reservation. "But after taking a serious look at it, I decided on Tucson. The Sells airport is long enough and wide enough, but the tarmac doesn't look to be in good shape. I watched a pilot's video on YouTube. They've probably never had a small jet land there."

"How long a flight?" I asked.

Jim scratched his head. "Well, if I don't get lost and we don't run out of fuel, I'd say about three hours."

"Try not to do either," I said.

"I'll have Tucson send up smoke signals so the confused white man can find his way," Billy said to me.

"Good idea."

"You guys are hilarious," Jim said. "I didn't know Billy had a sense of humor."

"I was serious," Billy said, straight faced.

Jim smiled and retreated to the safety of the cockpit. He did not leave the door open. "You two buckle up so you don't fall out while I'm doing rollovers," he said over the intercom. It was his way of getting the last word.

"He likes us," Billy said.

"He does," I said.

◆　　◆　　◆　　◆

We had packed overnight bags just in case, but I thought it was unlikely we couldn't accomplish our mission in a day. I had briefed Billy on my reason for going to the Tohono O'Odham Nation, and he had made contact with its Safe Trails representative, a man named Thomas Wildfire. The Safe Trails Task Force was a joint operation of federal, state, local, and tribal law enforcement to reduce crime in Indian territory. Eighteen Safe Trails Task Forces were scattered across the United States from North Carolina to Washington State. Billy was a local representative for Swain County, working with the local Cherokee Indian police.

"Do you know what Tohono O'Odham means?" Billy asked.

"Is this a quiz? You're beginning to sound like Scott Glass."

"You need to be educated, Blood."

"Okay, so tell me."

"It means 'Desert People,'" Billy said. "Most of the tribe lives in the Sonoran Desert in southern Arizona and northern Mexico. There are four distinct Tohono O'Odham Reservations, one very large and the others relatively small. The one we're going to is the large one. The tribal police are headquartered in the town of Sells."

"Is it me, Chief, or are you talking more since you married a schoolteacher?"

"Maggie does encourage me to be verbal," Billy said.

"Okay, so how big is this large reservation?"

Billy smiled. "About the size of Connecticut."

"You're kidding," I said.

"I'm not," Billy said.

"How many people?"

"Hard to say," Billy said. "Twenty-five thousand max."

"That's a lot of land for so few people," I said.

"It is," Billy said. "But it's mostly desert."

"How big is Sells?"

"About three thousand people."

"You've done your homework." I must say I was impressed.

"I have."

"Should be an interesting visit," I said.

"Should be," Billy said.

It was.

◆　　◆　　◆　　◆

We landed. Jim Doak managed to find the private hangars—no small task, since he had never flown into Tucson before.

"Another airport to add to my list," Jim said as we exited the jet.

"How many is it now?" I asked.

"Thirty-four," Jim said. "You're responsible for at least four, maybe more."

I did not ask which ones. "Glad to help," I said.

We rented an SUV. I wanted a Lincoln Navigator, but Billy overruled me. "You don't want to go in there looking like a rich white guy," Billy said. We settled for a Jeep Liberty.

Billy had told me to dress down, so we wore boots, jeans, plain shirts that had some age on them, and our oldest leather jackets.

We drove out of the airport and found Highway 86 to Sells. Once we left Tucson, we traveled through a sparsely populated area where the traffic was almost nonexistent.

Less than two hours later, we were in the conference room of the Sells Tribal Police Department waiting for Thomas Wildfire. After fifteen minutes, I started to squirm. I did not wait well.

Billy sat motionless. "Patience," he said, sensing my agitation.

"Are we being tested?"

"Maybe," Billy said. "Maybe not."

Five minutes later, Thomas Wildfire walked in and shut the door behind him. I stood, and then Billy did the same. Thomas Wildfire was maybe five-ten, a dark-skinned, slender man with dark eyes. His silky black hair, showing strands of gray, was pulled back into a short ponytail. He looked up at Billy. It took him a few seconds to process it all.

"I'll bet nobody fucks with you in Swain County, North Carolina," he said. "You may be the biggest Indian I've ever seen."

"Billy Two-Feathers," Billy said, extending his hand.

"Thomas Wildfire."

"And I think the term is Native American," Billy said, grinning.

"Right," Wildfire said. "I should watch my language, me being one and all."

I could tell they had connected.

"Who is this?" Wildfire asked, looking at me.

"Meet Donald Youngblood," Billy said. "Best friend, first-class private investigator, and FBI consultant. I'm helping him with a case."

That's quite an introduction, coming from Billy, I thought. Those were things he would never say to me face to face. Wildfire and I shook hands.

"Okay," Wildfire said. "You guys have come a long way. Sit down and tell me what this is about."

Billy looked at me and nodded.

"About ten years ago, there was a camp for troubled youth somewhere on the Tohono O'Odham Reservation that disappeared without a trace," I said. "Do you remember that?"

"Sure," Wildfire said. "I was here at the time."

"What can you tell us about it?" Billy asked.

"Why are you asking about this thing ten years after it happened?" Wildfire asked.

Billy sat up straight and leaned forward. He chose his words carefully. I was impressed. "At the proper time, if we decide we can trust you, we might be able to share that information," Billy said. "For now, all I can tell you is that it's important. It could get political if we have to go through channels. I'm trying to avoid that for you."

It was a veiled threat, pure and simple. Wildfire and Billy stared at each other. Nobody said anything for what seemed like a long time. It was probably no more than ten seconds.

Wildfire stood. "I'll be back," he said.

He should have tried to sound more like Arnold Schwarzenegger in The Terminator, I thought.

Wildfire was gone for at least fifteen minutes, maybe twenty. He had left the conference-room door open, allowing us to take in the sounds of a working police station. Then he was back, shutting the door behind him and handing Billy a file.

"This is all I got," he said. "I'll give you some time to look at it. Come find me when you're finished."

It was a relatively thin file, but we took our time reading it. Billy started, and when he finished a sheet he slid it to me. It went like that until we were finished. A delivery man in charge of bringing supplies once a week had reported the empty camp about a month after the camp session began. The tribal police went down to have a look. Finding no signs of violence, they thought that maybe the camp was on some kind of camping excursion and would be back in a few days. One week went by, then two. The campers did not come back. A search by helicopter turned up nothing. The best trackers saw some evidence of tracks leading away from the camp heading south, but the trail, if it was there at all, was soon lost.

The file contained a copy of the lease agreement showing the lessor's name and Social Security number. I made notes. The police made three follow-up visits to the camp to see if anyone had returned. They had not.

As I read the file, I realized a lot of it didn't make sense. How could a whole camp disappear with so little media attention? Why weren't there parents up in arms about their missing kids? Why were there no records?

I finished the last sheet. "What do you think?" I asked Billy.

"I think there's more to this than is in the file," Billy said.

He got up and left the conference room. A few minutes later, he returned with Thomas Wildfire. Billy closed the conference-room door.

"What do you know that isn't in the file?" Billy asked.

"If I decide I can trust you," Wildfire said, "there might be a few things I can share that are not in the file."

Billy said nothing. He sat and stared out the window. Wildfire and I waited. It was Billy's play.

"I want to see the campsite," Billy said.

"That will take most of the afternoon," Wildfire said.

"Not a problem," Billy said.

"You buy me breakfast and I'll take you out there," Wildfire said.

Billy nodded. "I brought Blood along to buy breakfast," he said.

"Good thinking," Wildfire said.

Well, I was beginning to wonder why I'm here, I thought.

18

Thomas climbed into the front seat of our rental and directed us to the Desert Rain Café. It wasn't far.

"This place is outstanding for a town our size," Thomas said.

As it turned out, it would have been outstanding in New York City. The place was clean and well lit and had a casual café feel. We found a table in a corner.

"Good morning, Thomas," the waitress said, handing out menus.

"Good morning, Carmarisa," Thomas said.

"What would you like to drink?" Carmarisa asked.

"Coffee," I said.

"Coffee," Billy said.

"Make it three," Thomas said.

Carmarisa departed while we browsed the menu. She returned quickly with the coffee. "Ready to order?" she asked.

"I am," I said. I was long past ready. With the time change, it was past lunch eastern standard time, and I hadn't even had breakfast. "I'll have the three-egg omelet with spinach, cheese, and chorizo."

"That comes with a handmade whole-wheat tortilla," Carmarisa said.

"That will be fine."

She looked at Billy.

"Make that two," Billy said.

"Make that three," Thomas said.

"You guys are easy," Carmarisa said as she left to turn in our order.

I sat quietly until the food arrived, listening to Thomas and Billy exchange stories about the cases they had worked and the strange calls that had come in. Some of the stories were funny and some weird.

"We got a call one morning last year about a crazy man on Highway 19 trying to flag down vehicles," Billy said. "Of course, no one wanted to stop. The call said that all the man had on was his underwear. It was a cold morning, so I grabbed one of our jump suits and rushed to the scene. I got out of the car expecting who knows what, and all he says to me is, 'Thank God you're here. I'm freezing.' So I gave him the jump suit, and he put it on and got in my squad car. Turned out he was a professor at East Tennessee State University on a camping trip and a bear wrecked his tent and tried to have him for dinner. He managed to get out of his sleeping bag and wandered all night until he found the highway."

Thomas laughed. "No way."

"It's true," Billy said. "I took him to the hospital, and they checked him out. Except for some cuts and bruises, he was fine, so I took him to breakfast and then to buy some clothes and back to his SUV."

"What about his stuff at the campsite?" Thomas asked.

"He said he was done with camping, and whoever found it could have it," Billy said.

"That's a good story," Thomas said.

"It's the truth," Billy said.

Our table went quiet when the food arrived. It was exceptional. When we finished, I paid the bill and left a generous tip. We climbed into the rental, and Thomas directed us south out of Sells.

◆　　◆　　◆　　◆

After two hours of driving through some of the prettiest and most desolate country I'd ever seen, we arrived at the youth camp's location. It was midafternoon. We drove through a gate that had been left open. Fencing stretched for maybe a quarter-mile in all directions. The camp was in the middle of the fenced area. A cold February wind blew tumbleweeds past our rental as we stared at the deserted camp. It contained four flat-roofed buildings—one large rectangular building and three smaller structures of various sizes that were more or less square. They were scattered, not placed in any logical order. The buildings were a lot more than ten years old.

"This was something else before it was a youth camp," I said.

"It was originally an elite army training center for desert warfare," Thomas said. "It was built around 1990. Lots of security. Rumor was, they'd send twenty or so handpicked troops down for a six-week training session, then bring them back and send down another group."

"Middle of nowhere," I said. "Why did they pick this location?"

"Water," Thomas said. "About four hundred feet down. They drilled a well, put in a pump and piping. They had a really big generator."

"Did they ever come into Sells?"

"Never," Thomas said.

"When did they pull out?"

"Nineteen ninety-five. They had a five-year lease with the res and left when it was up."

I watched Billy while I talked to Thomas. He was walking from building to building, getting a feel for the place. Then he started walking south toward the distance fence.

"Where's he going?" Thomas asked.

"He's taking it all in," I said. "It's hard to explain, but Billy is just different."

"I've known a few in my tribe like that. They seem to know things without knowing how they know."

"That's Billy," I said.

Thomas nodded but said nothing. We were silent for a while, watching Billy in the distance.

"This place remained empty until the youth-camp people rented it," Thomas continued. "It's been empty since they disappeared."

"Did you know any of the camp staff?"

"I heard one or two were from my tribe, but I didn't know them," he said.

The wind picked up and bounced tumbleweeds over the top of our rental. I turned up the collar on my leather jacket.

"Let's go inside," Thomas said. "It's too cold out here."

◆　　◆　　◆　　◆

Half an hour later, Billy joined us. We were in the large building, which had probably been used as a barracks. Billy didn't speak, just walked around looking out various windows and opening doors to what I guessed were private quarters. He walked over to us and stood looking out the nearest window.

"Anything?" I asked.

"Nothing," Billy said. "I don't get a feeling that bad things happened here. When they were done with whatever they were doing, they just left. Headed north, I think."

Thomas said nothing.

"Is there any reason to stay here longer?" I asked Billy.

"None," he said. Then he looked at Thomas. "There's still a lot you're not telling us. Something that's not in the file. Something that only you know about."

Thomas acted as if he hadn't heard what Billy said. "Are we done here?" he asked.

"We're done," I said.

◆　　◆　　◆　　◆

We made most of the return trip in silence. The day had gone from partly sunny to mostly cloudy. The short winter days meant night would come soon.

"Where are you staying?" Thomas asked, breaking a long silence.

"We're driving back to Tucson and flying out tonight," I said.

"Long day," Thomas said.

"Very long," Billy said.

We arrived back in Sells at dusk. The thermometer on the dashboard told me the outdoor temperature was thirty-five degrees. Factor in the wind and it felt like twenty.

As we approached the police station, Thomas said, "You would honor my wife and me by spending the night with us."

"I appreciate the offer," I said. "But I think we'd better get back."

"We have two spare rooms, now that our offspring are both in college," he continued, ignoring the fact that I had declined his offer.

"We would be honored to accept," Billy said, surprising me.

It took me a minute before I understood. Billy saw the invitation as an opportunity to gain more information, or maybe to prove to Thomas Wildfire that we could be trusted.

"Like Billy said, we would be honored," I said. "But I insist that I take you and your wife out to dinner."

"Then it is agreed," Thomas said. "Follow me to my home. You'll meet my wife, and we'll show you to your quarters. I noticed you both packed overnight bags."

◆   ◆   ◆   ◆

We followed Thomas to his house. On the way, I called Jim Doak. "We're spending the night," I said.

"Sorry, but I can't wait for you," Jim said. "I've got to get back."

"Well, it's a tragedy, but I guess we'll have to fly commercial."

"A low-down dirty shame," Jim said.

◆   ◆   ◆   ◆*

That night after dinner at the Desert Rain Café, we sat at Thomas's kitchen table drinking coffee Edna Wildfire had made for us. Edna was a full-figured, medium-height, attractive woman with a pleasant personality who had spent most of the dinner talking about Thomas and her two children.

At one point, Thomas had said good-naturedly, "You talk too much, woman."

"I don't get out much," Edna replied, smiling. "Give a girl a break."

We had all laughed and let her continue to carry the conversation.

Edna went to bed early. We ate homemade mesquite oatmeal cookies, drank coffee, and talked about the disappearing youth camp.

Evidently, Thomas had decided he could trust us. "Everything I tell you has to be between us," he said.

I looked at Billy and shook my head ever so slightly.

"That might not be possible," Billy said.

"Well, at least you're honest about it," Thomas said. "So if you find you have to share, can it be from an unnamed source?"

Billy looked at me, and I gave a nod.

"We can live with that," Billy said.

Thomas looked at me.

"If Blood says he will not reveal your name, you can count on it," Billy said.

"Okay, I'll tell you everything I know," Thomas said. "The prevailing theory was that the camp packed up and went south across the border into Mexico. It would be easy to hide there. Border security at that time was not as tight as it has been the last few years. I bought the theory at first, but now I'm not so sure.

"Our chief told us not to waste any more time looking for those boys, since we didn't have any formal complaints about missing youths and no apparent laws had been broken. We thought they would turn up sooner or later, so we forgot about it. One day, I was sitting around with not much to do, and I thought about that camp and those missing kids. So I started nosing around. I reached out to some of our tribe in Mexico to find out if they had seen or heard of a group crossing the border. No one had. If they were in Mexico, I think someone would have heard or seen something. So I think Two-Feathers may be right. They might have gone north."

It was strange to hear Billy called by his last name, but it made sense that another Native American might do that.

My cell phone beeped and interrupted my train of thought. It was a text from Mary:

Girls win 80–37. Lacy had 28 points and sat out the fourth quarter. Safe travels. We'll be alone tomorrow night!

Billy looked at me.

"Eighty to thirty-seven," I said. "Lacy had twenty-eight."

Billy nodded.

"What?" Thomas said.

"Basketball," Billy said.

"Your son?"

"Blood's daughter. Number-two team in the state, and she's their best player."

"Nice," Thomas said.

"Please continue," Billy said.

Thomas took up where he had left off. "Anyway, I started asking around if anyone knew of any kids on the res who were all of a sudden no longer around. I came up with three. All the families had believable stories as to where these boys were, and I knew they were all lying. Then I visited one of the mothers when I knew she would be alone."

He paused to eat a bite of cookie and take a drink of coffee. His story had us on the edge of our seats, and he knew it and was enjoying the telling.

"What did you learn?" Billy asked, playing along.

"After a lot of promising and persuading, she told me her son was recruited to a special youth military movement," Thomas said. "The recruiter was a Native American, but not of our tribe. He told her if the family would sign their son up, the movement promised they would make a man out of him and the family would receive twenty thousand dollars. They had to sign a paper giving the movement legal guardianship."

"So they basically took a kid they didn't want and sold him to a domestic terrorist group," I said.

"In their eyes, it was a win-win situation," Thomas said. "Twenty thousand dollars is a lot of money on the res, and they got rid of a hard-to-handle kid, convincing themselves they were doing him a favor. Who knows, maybe they did."

Probably not, I thought, but said nothing.

"Did you confront the father?" Billy asked.

"No," Thomas said. "I promised the mother I wouldn't."

"Did you see the guardianship agreement?" I asked.

"No, the parents didn't get a copy."

"When did they get the money?" Billy asked.

"At the time the kid was picked up for camp," Thomas said. "He was picked up in a white van with 'USA Youth Camp' stenciled on the side panels."

"Cash?" I asked.

"Of course," Thomas chuckled. "My people are not stupid."

"Must be a well-funded group," Billy said. "They paid all the parents off so no one would come looking."

"Looks that way," Thomas said. "All the fathers had some extra money to support their other kids."

We were quiet as we drank coffee and ate cookies, immersed in our private thoughts.

"Is that delivery guy still around?" I asked. "The one who took supplies to the camp."

"As far as I know," Thomas said.

"I'd like to talk to him."

"I'll set it up," Thomas said. "Just let me know when."

"As soon as possible," I said.

Thomas nodded. He got up, went to get more coffee, and motioned the carafe toward us. I shook my head. Billy held out his cup.

"My researcher found a newspaper article about the missing kids online," I said. "Do you know anything about that?"

"Yes. It was done by our local weekly and was pure speculation."

"Is the person who wrote it still around?"

"No," Thomas said. "She moved a long time ago."

I paused to take a drink and eat some of my cookie. I looked at Billy to see if he had any more questions. He shook his head.

"Why did you keep quiet about all this?" I asked.

"I gave my word that if no law had been broken, I would keep quiet," Thomas said. "Nobody was interested anyway. Things on the res are different. That money did a lot of good. Each of those families sent kids to college."

It wasn't my place to argue morals or ethics with Thomas Wildfire, so I said nothing.

"Maybe I should have said something," Thomas said.

"Hindsight is always twenty-twenty," Billy said.

19

The next morning was cold and overcast. I again bought breakfast for the three of us at the Desert Rain Café.

Afterward, I said, "I want to go back to the campsite."

"Why?" Thomas asked.

"I had a thought during the night, and I want to check it out."

"Care to share?"

"Not yet," I said. "I know the way. You two don't have to come. But I would like to borrow some basic tools, and I need directions to a general store."

"You can take my toolbox," Thomas said. "And the only general store in Sells is just down the street."

"I'm going with you," Billy said.

"I've got to pass," Thomas said. "Come see me when you get back."

So I took Thomas Wildfire's toolbox, made a quick stop at the general store, filled the tank with gas, and headed back to the campsite.

◆   ◆   ◆   ◆

On the two-hour drive down, I told Billy what I was thinking.

"You always come up with something, Blood," Billy said. "That's a good idea."

Thomas had closed the gate the day before. Billy opened it, and we drove through. I parked in the center of the camp.

"I want to look around the barracks again," Billy said.

"I'll start checking the smaller buildings," I said. "What I'm really looking for is the head honcho's quarters."

The largest of the small buildings turned out to be the mess hall. It did not have what I was looking for. The second building seemed to be housing for two people. It had a main area with a room on either side, and each of those rooms had a bathroom. Bathrooms were what I was looking for. Each bathroom had a private shower. I took the shower drains apart and swabbed the inside with a toothbrush that I had duct-taped to a large screwdriver to get extra depth into the drain. I found hairs in both drains and bagged them separately.

I repeated that action in the smallest of the buildings, which proved to be quarters for one person, presumably the head man. I found hair in that shower drain also. When I was done, I had one final look around and then went back to the rental.

Billy was waiting. "Successful?" he asked.

"Yes," I said. "It's a long shot, but at least it's something to work with."

"I'm done," Billy said. "Let's get out of here."

We closed the gate behind us and drove back to Sells.

◆   ◆   ◆   ◆

Thomas Wildfire had the delivery man in the station-house conference room when we returned. I guessed he was around fifty, but with Native Americans it was sometimes hard to tell. They could be much older than they looked.

Thomas did the introductions. "Theodore Rainwater, meet Billy Two-Feathers and Donald Youngblood," he said.

We shook hands. Rainwater said nothing. He was probably concerned about being summoned to the police station.

Thomas motioned for all of us to sit down. "These two gentlemen are investigating a case that may have a connection to the missing youth camp," he said.

"I don't know anything about that," Rainwater said defensively.

"But you did deliver supplies there," Billy said.

"Yes."

"What kind of supplies?" Billy asked.

Billy was trying to get Rainwater to relax, so I said nothing.

Thomas Wildfire picked up on that. "Excuse me for a few minutes," he said. "I have to check on something."

We all watched him leave.

Billy turned his gaze back to Rainwater. "About supplies . . ."

"Food, mostly," Rainwater said. "All kinds of meat, fresh vegetables, potatoes, things like that. Flour, eggs, milk, bottled water, beer—all kinds of stuff. They sure ate well, I can tell you that."

"Who did you see when you made the deliveries?" I asked.

"The guy who ran the kitchen," Rainwater said. "I guess he was the cook."

"Anyone else?" Billy asked.

"A few kids sometimes. They would help me unload."

"Did you recognize any of the kids?" Billy continued.

"No," Rainwater said quickly.

"How many deliveries did you make in all?" Billy asked.

"Four, maybe five. It was a long time ago."

"Did you ever make deliveries when the army was down there?" I asked.

"No," Rainwater said. "I heard they brought in their own supplies."

"Did you ever see anything unusual?" Billy asked.

"Not that I can remember," Rainwater said.

Billy looked at me as if to say, *Anything else?* I shook my head.

"Thanks for your time," Billy said.

After Rainwater left, Billy said, "He was lying about not recognizing anyone."

"I know," I said. "Probably one of the three kids Thomas told us about. But I don't think that means anything. Maybe he knew about the money-for-kids deal. Who knows?"

"Or maybe he recognized one of the staff," Billy said. "Either way, it was a long time ago, and the trail is long cold."

◆　　◆　　◆　　◆

By the time we questioned Theodore Rainwater, it was too late to catch a commercial flight home without arriving after midnight. Thomas Wildfire insisted we again spend the night at his place, and I insisted I again buy dinner. We were still in the conference room.

"I need to get online," I said. "I assume you have wireless."

"We do," Wildfire said. "Look for 'Sells Guest.' You will not need a security code."

I checked email—nothing important. The Street was going nuts, edging over seventeen thousand. I was not surprised. Interest rates were nonexistent. CDs paid so little that they weren't worth the paperwork.

I checked out flights for our return trip. The times and connections were awful. So I called Roy and sounded as pitiful as I could, and he promised to send Jim Doak back for us. Jim would be in touch, Roy said.

An hour later, I got a text from Jim:

Pick you up at ten. Same spot I dropped you off.

That sure brightened my day.

◆　　◆　　◆　　◆

"I'm going to get in trouble for accepting food bribes for confidential information," Thomas kidded us at dinner. We were once again at the Desert Rain Café. *When you find a good thing, stick with it.*

"Tell them you're just taking advantage of a gullible paleface," Billy said.

"I can do that," Thomas said.

"Thank you very much for dinner, Don," Edna Wildfire said.

"You're welcome, Edna," I said. "I should make these two pay for their own meals."

Edna laughed. "You really should."

20

I sat on a barstool at the kitchen island at the lake house drinking a cold Amber Bock. I had been home only a few minutes. Mary was across from me drinking a glass of Blue Moon, smiling that smile I knew so well. We were alone.

Jim Doak had been at the Tucson airport waiting for us in the private hangar area. We were in the air by eleven and landed at Tri-Cities Airport by four in the afternoon, thanks to a substantial tailwind courtesy of a fast-moving jet stream.

I took a long drink and listened to the silence. With a teenager or two frequently in the house, silence was not the norm. The dogs lay quietly napping nearby, seemingly enjoying the silence as much as I did.

"Nice deal you've got going with Hannah's mom," I said.

"Suzanne," Mary said. "Hannah was here last night. The house wasn't nearly this quiet."

"I'll bet."

Mary finished her Blue Moon. "You must be really tired."

"Beat," I said.

"Maybe you should take a nap."

"Probably," I said.

Without another word, she took me by my hand and led me up the stairs to the master bedroom. She opened the door. The room was dark except for the glow of twenty or so candles, most of which were battery operated but looked real enough. Mary slid her jeans over her hips and let them fall to the floor and stepped out of them. I noticed she was not wearing panties. Then she pulled her T-shirt over her head and threw it aside. I observed she was not wearing a bra. *Observation is all.*

"Less tired now, Cowboy?" Mary asked.

"Way less," I said, gathering her into me.

◆　　◆　　◆　　◆

Much later, we dined—fettuccini Alfredo with Caesar salad and garlic bread. We shared an excellent bottle of South African Chardonnay. We set up our small table in front of the fireplace in the living room and had an intimate dinner.

"Tell me about your trip," Mary said.

I told all of it slowly. Mary was like T. Elbert; she liked the small details, right down to what was on the menu at the Desert Rain Café and what everyone had to eat. She seemed disappointed when I told her we all had the same omelet for breakfast.

"That's no fun."

I shrugged. "Not my fault. I ordered first."

As we ate and drank, I finished my tale, including the part about the tailwind that had allowed us to cut a half-hour off our trip.

"Was the trip worth it?" Mary asked.

"Yes," I said. "Meeting Thomas Wildfire and his wife was worth the trip. Seeing that part of the United States was worth the trip. Spending quality time with Billy was an added bonus. But I learned some things I didn't know before, and as T. Elbert says, 'Better to know than not to know." The other stuff, I'll have to wait and see. I'd like to take you there sometime."

"I'd like that."

I poured more wine. "Anything new in Mountain Center?"

"Oh, yeah," Mary said. "I almost forgot. Clay Carr woke up."

"When?"

"Yesterday morning. Big Bob sent me to interview him."

"And?"

"He doesn't remember a thing about the accident or the party, and he seemed hazy on the past few months," Mary said.

"Maybe he doesn't want to remember," I said. "Or maybe he remembers and for some reason doesn't want you to know it." It was simple enough to plead amnesia when you sustained a skull fracture. I knew from experience; I had done it myself once.

"I think the amnesia is real," Mary said. "It's consistent with his injury. They think he'll gradually get his memory back."

"Did he remember Julie?"

"He remembered who she was. He didn't remember that they had been dating. He was upset she was dead, but not upset like he had lost the love of his life."

We talked about trivial things as we sat there enjoying the fire and finishing the bottle of wine. Later, feeling buzzed, we made love again, on the couch in front of the fireplace.

21

Monday morning, I took the dogs to the office. They had not been in a while and seemed excited about it. I had a stack of call slips on my desk, many of which Gretchen had handled. The one that intrigued me was from Dr. Evan Smith: "Come by and see me. I'm working the early shift on Monday."

I didn't know when the early shift started, but my experience with doctors in general was that the later in the day you went to see them, the longer you waited. So I left the dogs, went down the back stairs, got in the Pathfinder, and headed for the Mountain Center Medical Center.

◆   ◆   ◆   ◆

Luckily for me, Evan Smith didn't have ER duty and I was at the hospital before his first appointment. I sat across from him in a not-so-comfortable chair in front of his desk.

"I have received the blood panels back on Clay Carr and Julie James," he said.

"You found something interesting, I take it."

"I did."

"One or both?"

"Both," Dr. Smith said.

"Bad?"

"Not good," he said.

"Tell me," I said.

"There were significant amounts of Zolpidem in their blood," Dr. Smith said. "It's otherwise known as Ambien, a sleep aid that's been linked to more and more sexual assault cases. But not in this case, since they both were drugged. I'd say Julie fell asleep first, since she had some alcohol in her system. Clay obviously fell asleep at the wheel. I made you a copy of both reports."

He handed them to me. I said nothing. My head was spinning. In essence, Julie James was murdered. The charge, if we ever found anyone to charge, would be manslaughter because the person who drugged them could not have predicted the accident that led to Julie's death.

"You okay?" Dr. Smith said.

"Not really. This means someone drugged them for some unknown reason and contributed to the death of Julie James and the injuries to Clay Carr. Now, I have to find out who and why. Can you tell me how many pills it might have taken?"

"No," he said. "They were probably mixed in a drink, and it's impossible to tell how much volume they drank. I'd guess four to six pills, if you put me on the spot."

I put the report in the inside pocket of my leather jacket and stood. "Thanks for doing this," I said. "And please keep this confidential."

"I would only reveal it at gunpoint," Evan Smith said.

"Well, let's hope it doesn't come to that," I said.

◆   ◆   ◆   ◆

"What a fuckin' can of worms this is," Big Bob said, getting more agitated by the second.

We were in his office. I had just delivered the news that Clay and Julie were drugged. He was pissed off, and I didn't blame him. I was pissed off.

"We're going to have to investigate everyone at that party, and we won't find out shit because no one is going to know anything, and if they did they wouldn't tell us," Big Bob roared.

I said nothing.

"I'll tell the D.A.," Big Bob said. "He might be considering a vehicular manslaughter charge for Clay Carr. If he is, I'll tell him to forget about it."

"Good idea."

Big Bob rapidly tapped a pen on a notepad on his desk. "You got any ideas?"

"I've got a few informants at the high school," I said. "I could get them to look into who might have had a grudge against Julie and Clay, thereby keeping MCPD out of it. We might get lucky. Right now, only you, me, and Dr. Smith know about this, and we can keep it that way. I'll probably tell Mary, but she'll keep it quiet."

"Informants, ha!" Big Bob said, his voice still raised. "Lacy and who else?"

"My informants are confidential," I said.

Big Bob laughed. He was running out of steam. "Well, tell your informants to be careful. We don't know what we're dealing with here."

In the end, he agreed. I would handle it until we had to go public, if and when that happened.

◆   ◆   ◆   ◆

When I got back to the office, I called Mary. I never called her while she was on the job unless it was important.

"What?" she answered, urgency in her voice.

"Is this Mary Youngblood—tall, blond, good looking?"

I could feel Mary relax. She knew I wouldn't be teasing her if there was a problem.

"Is this an obscene phone call?" She snapped.

"I wish. Stop by and see me when you have a minute. I need to share something I found out about the Clay Carr mess."

"You've found out something that surprises you?"

"I have," I said.

"On my way," Mary said. "By the way, Clay Carr slipped back into a coma."

That news did not thrill me. I had intended to interview Clay later that day.

◆   ◆   ◆   ◆

"Damn it," Mary said when I told her my news. "Some little bitch did this. I'd bet a million bucks on it."

Junior raised his head and looked at Mary, picking up on the anger in her voice. Jake snoozed on.

"You don't have a million bucks," I said, trying to lighten the moment.

"But you do," Mary said. "Besides, I know I'm right. It's exactly a thing one girl would do to embarrass another. Whoever did it was probably hoping Julie would pass out at the party and create a big scene."

"So why drug Clay?"

"Probably didn't mean to," Mary said. "I'll bet Clay and Julie were sharing a drink."

"That makes sense," I said. "So you're telling me a mean prank turned into manslaughter."

"Looks that way," Mary said. "Now what?"

"I have a few thoughts. For now, I'm staying away from high-school kids. We'll see what develops."

My thoughts did not include getting Lacy and Biker any further involved at the moment. I might, however, need them later.

◆   ◆   ◆   ◆

Robert Carr owned a local hardware store. I had known Robert pretty much all my life. His family went to our church. He was a few years older than I was and had married his high-school sweetheart. I sat in his office late that day, getting the obligatory small talk out of the way.

"I'm guessing this is not a social call," he said. "You don't need supplies for some project at the lake house, do you?"

I laughed. "Mary would say I need lots of supplies. But not today."

"This about Clay?"

"Yes," I said. "How's he doing?"

"Still in a coma," Robert said. "He's healing. The doctors say he should be awake, but he isn't."

"I heard he woke up."

"For a few hours. Long enough for me to call Big Bob and for Mary to talk with him. Then he was back under. We thought he was just tired, but he hasn't woken back up."

"I need to tell you something, and you have to keep it quiet," I said.

"I heard you were looking into the accident. You found something?"

"Clay and Julie were drugged," I said.

I told him the whole story.

"Somebody did this on purpose?"

"I don't think the person who did it meant for Clay to wreck and for Julie to be killed," I said. "I believe it was more like a prank gone bad."

"Do you know who?"

"I'm working on it," I said. "The less you say, the easier my investigation will be, but I thought you should know. I didn't want you to think Clay's carelessness caused Julie's death."

"I need to tell Julie's father," he said.

"I understand. Explain the circumstances and ask him not to talk about it. I think I can wrap this up soon."

"Thanks, Don," he said. "I appreciate your telling me this. It allows me to make a little sense out of this tragedy."

"If Clay wakes up," I said, "call me."

"I'll do it," he said.

◆   ◆   ◆   ◆

I was heading to the condo when I realized I had forgotten to do something. I went back to the office, prepared a UPS Next Day letter, and called for a pickup. Then I called David Steele.

"I have some hair samples I need DNA on," I said.

"Is this connected to the Midnight Riders case?"

"It is."

"Tell me about it," David Steele said.

So I shared everything I could think of about my trip to Arizona.

"How long have you known about this?"

"I just got back Saturday," I said. "I wanted to check it out before I bothered you with it."

"So you think this missing camp is connected to the Midnight Riders?"

"Maybe," I said. "I know the timing is right. If we can get a DNA hit and track somebody down and squeeze them, we might know for sure."

"Send me the samples," he said. "But it's going to take time, depending on how many you've got."

"I understand," I said. "You'll have the samples tomorrow."

22

The next morning, I was in the diner alone having my first mug of coffee and reading about the girls' win the night before. We had all been there to witness an 86–26 dismantling of a team from Greene County. Lacy had scored a career high thirty-one points.

My cell phone rang, interrupting my proud-parent alone time. I recognized the number.

"You're up early," I said, keeping my voice low, so as not to disturb the few early diners enjoying the peace and quiet. *Courtesy is all.*

"We may have caught a break," Buckley said. "I think."

"What does that mean?" I asked. "You think."

"Well, it fits the profile, but it's a little different," he said. "Missing kids, one a year older that the other, and the younger one rebellious. There's an Amber Alert out. Both mothers are still around, but the mother of the older one has been in the area less than a year."

"We need to interview the mother of the older kid right away," I said.

"I agree," Buckley said.

"What state?"

"California. San Diego."

"Get some of your guys to sit on the older kid's mother to make sure she doesn't take off. She probably won't, but better safe than sorry."

"Okay, I'll make that request," Buckley said. "When can you leave?"

"We'll have to fly commercial," I said. I wasn't about to ask Roy to have me flown to California on a Fleet jet right after returning from Arizona.

"I'll set it up for the earliest flight tomorrow morning," Buckley said.

"Okay. You said this one was different. How?"

"The missing kids are girls."

"Girls?"

"Girls," Buckley repeated.

"I've got to tell you, it doesn't feel right. But I guess they could recruit girls."

"I'll be in touch," Buckley said.

Girls?

◆　　◆　　◆　　◆

I busied myself with Wall Street for most of the morning, but my heart wasn't in it. The market had cleared seventeen thousand and seemed content on staying there. *Is eighteen thousand possible?* I wondered.

I got sidetracked thinking about the two cases I was working. As far as the Midnight Riders were concerned, our list was up to twenty pairs of missing kids who fit our profile, and only one pair was girls. *Something wrong there*, I thought. In every instance but one, the mother of the older missing kid had disappeared. That led me to believe the disappearing mothers and the older children were part of the plot. Maybe we had caught a break, but I didn't think so.

As far as the Clay Carr case, there was strong evidence the car wreck that had claimed the life of Julie James was not accidental. I had one solid thought on what my next step should be. I walked to the outer office and sat in front of Gretchen's desk.

"Visiting the little people, are we?" she said.

"Have to make the minions feel important."

"To what do I owe this honor?"

"I need some research," I said. "I need a list of every pharmacy in Mountain Center and the suburbs, complete with phone numbers, street addresses, and pharmacists; as much as you can find out."

"How soon?"

"Before you leave," I said.

"Starting now," Gretchen said, grabbing the phone book.

◆   ◆   ◆   ◆

Gretchen brought me the list around two o'clock.

"There are fifteen pharmacies in Mountain Center?" I said.

"Surprised me, too," Gretchen said. "I would have thought six or seven."

I looked at the list. We had three Walgreens, two CVSs, two in supermarkets, and one at Walmart. The rest were independents. This was going to be harder than I thought. I needed for all of them to cooperate, though I didn't have the authority to make it happen. *Well, I know how to change that,* I thought.

I picked up the phone and called Big Bob's private number.

"What now?"

"I need you to assign Mary to the Clay Carr investigation," I said.

"Why is that?"

I told him.

"Okay, Blood," he said. "That makes sense."

◆   ◆   ◆   ◆

Late that afternoon, Buckley called.

"What time are we leaving?" I asked.

"We're not," he said.

"Why not?"

"It's confusing, but the girls are alive and well," Buckley said. "Apparently, there was some abuse from the younger girl's mother's boyfriend, and the older girl persuaded the younger one to run away to relatives. The older girl went with her. The older girl supposedly left a note for her mother, which the mother didn't find until after the Amber Alert. An aunt and uncle of the younger girl now have temporary legal guardianship until the whole thing is sorted out. It's a mess, but not one we need to be involved in."

"That's good news for the girls, but it puts us back at square one. We need to find a fresh abduction and squeeze the mother involved."

"I hear you," Buckley said. "We've got alerts out to every Western state. I'll call the minute I hear something. Could be tomorrow, or it could be months."

◆   ◆   ◆   ◆

I was about to leave for the day when I heard the outer office door open and shut.

"In here," I said.

George James came in and introduced himself as Julie's father. I offered him a seat.

"Is it true what Robert Carr told me?" he asked. "Were Clay and Julie drugged?"

"Yes," I said.

"Robert said you were going to find out who did it."

"I am."

"I heard you were looking into it," he said. "One of Julie's friends told us the senior class hired you."

No secrets in a small town, I thought. I wondered how many people knew. That was not good; my prey could slip away.

"I thought they were just trying to protect Clay," he continued. "I didn't think you would find anything."

"That's what I thought," I said. "Then I did. I need for you not to talk about it. At this point, I want everybody believing it's just a whim of the senior class."

"You can count on me being quiet," George James said. "I want to catch this person more than anyone."

◆　　◆　　◆　　◆

We were at the kitchen bar in the condo having a drink—a Sam Adams Light for me and Bogle Chardonnay for Mary. Lacy was "studying" at Biker's.

Mary was excited. "I cannot believe we get to work together on a real case," she said.

"I need some real authority to put pressure on these pharmacists we're going to see. Some of them are going to play the confidentiality card. We need to convince them to do their civic duty."

"And you thought of me," Mary said. "How sweet."

"I did. You can be pretty convincing when you want to be."

"Can I convince you to come upstairs right now?" Mary asked.

I slid off my barstool. "See what I mean?" I said.

23

Like so many of my past cases, the Midnight Riders case was experiencing a lull. That almost always happened. Then, out of nowhere, a new lead would surface and I'd be off and running again. As strange as it seemed, we had to hope another pair of boys who fit our profile went missing. Then we might have a thread to hang on to. I feared that Buckley was right; it could be months. At this time of year, kids likely to disappear from school would probably already have disappeared. We might have to wait for summer school or summer camp. Meanwhile, I got to work a case with Mary—not a bad thing.

We had breakfast at the Mountain Center Diner, an event that left Doris dumbfounded. Mary rarely ate at the diner with me. We were rarely on the same schedule, and she liked to eat later than I did. We had just begun to drink our coffee when Roy came in. He smiled widely.

"Brought your bodyguard, I see," Roy said.

"Never know when I might need protection," I said.

"I wasn't talking to you," Roy said.

Mary laughed.

"You two want to be alone?"

"We're alone enough," Mary said. "Sit down."

"What's the occasion?" Roy asked.

"We're working a case together," Mary said.

"The local one?"

"Yes," Mary said. "Don's got the ideas, and I have the authority."

"Ideas and authority sound like a good team," Roy said. "Anything new on the case?"

Mary looked at me. I nodded. She told Roy about the Zolpidem.

"Had to be another girl," Roy said. "A wallflower, maybe. Definitely not a guy."

"That's the way I figure it," Mary said.

◆　　◆　　◆　　◆

We took Mary's unmarked car. Oddly enough, it was the first time I had ever been in it. The experience felt strange.

"You're awfully quiet," Mary said.

"I'm processing."

"What's the plan?"

"Let's hit the three Walgreens first," I said.

"Okay. We'll start with the one where I shop most. I know the pharmacist there. I'm afraid you're right. They're going to hide behind the confidentiality wall."

Mary drove to the North Mountain Center Walgreens and parked in back. She led me through the back door, marked *Employee Entrance*. It led to the waiting area. Luckily for us, no one was there. Mary went to the pickup counter, and a man appeared.

"Hi, Mary," the man said. He was wearing a nametag that said he was John Duncan, Pharmacist. "I don't think I have anything for you."

"I'm here officially," she said. "Is there someplace we can talk?"

"Sure, come on back."

He opened a side door and held it for Mary, and I followed. John Duncan was a little taller than me. He was also soft in the way that carrying extra weight can make you look. His was light complected, with blond hair casually kept, and I noticed he wore his pants too high. *This guy could have escaped from an F. Scott Fitzgerald novel*, I thought.

We followed him to his office. He went behind his desk and stood.

"Please sit," he said.

"John," Mary said, "this is my husband, Don."

"The private investigator," John Duncan said. "I'm pleased to meet you."

We shook hands.

"You, too," I said.

We sat.

"We're working a confidential case and need some information," Mary said. "We will share only what is absolutely necessary, and no one will know it came from you."

"What do you need?" John said.

Mary looked at me.

"Zolpidem," I said.

"Sleep med," John said. "Commonly known as Ambien. Zolpidem is the generic equivalent."

"We need a list of everyone who has had a prescription in the last year," I said.

He shook his head slowly. "Sorry," he said. "I'd like to help, but that information is confidential. There have been many lawsuits about pharmacists revealing patients' records to law enforcement without legal justification."

"We can get a subpoena," Mary said.

"That would be fine," John Duncan said. "Then I could share our information and feel safe about it."

"In the meantime, keep this conversation confidential," Mary said, standing. "Thanks for your time."

In the car, Mary said, "I was afraid of that. We're probably going to hear that from all of them."

"Maybe not," I said. "Let's try the independents. They might not be as rigid."

So that's what we did. We got basically the same result at the first two: *Come back with a subpoena, and we'll be glad to cooperate.*

24

Ridgetop Pharmacy was new to Mountain Center in the last two years. The owner promoted an old-fashioned motif featuring a grill, a soda fountain, counter stools, and a few tables and booths. All of that was in the front, which was busy and smelled good. The pharmacy, in the rear, was not busy at all. That's where we found the owner and pharmacist, Tomas Garcia, a short, stout, dark-haired man in his forties. Mary repeated the same spiel she had used all morning. Garcia looked nervous at first, then seemed to relax once he heard the name *Zolpidem*.

"Sure," he said. "I would be glad to cooperate. Come back around four and I'll have the list ready. Should not be too many names."

His English was good, but I detected a hint of an accent.

"*Keep this conversation confidential,*" I said in Spanish.

"*Most certainly,*" he responded.

"Show-off," Mary said as we walked toward the front of the store.

◆   ◆   ◆   ◆

We visited the other independent pharmacies without success, receiving much the same story about confidentiality. By that time, it was well past lunch, which neither of us needed, thanks to the Mountain Center Diner.

Driving away from the last pharmacy, Mary said, "I think it's time to talk to Big Bob."

"Didn't you think Tomas Garcia was a little too eager to cooperate?" I asked.

"Now that you mention it," Mary said. "He seemed eager and relieved."

"You might want to take a closer look at him," I said. "I'd bet a hundred bucks he's got something to hide."

◆   ◆   ◆   ◆

"Horseshit," Big Bob said when we told him we had hit the confidentiality wall. "They want a subpoena just to give you a list of Ambien prescriptions?"

Mary was in a chair in front of Big Bob's desk, and I was leaning against the doorframe.

"They do," Mary said. "All but one of the pharmacies we talked to mentioned *subpoena.*"

"Well, at least there's one in the bunch that has some balls."

"Maybe not," I said.

"You mind explaining that?" Big Bob said.

I sensed he was not going to like the answer. "The guy was spooked until we mentioned Zolpidem, like he was expecting us to mention something else. He couldn't cooperate fast enough. Mary and I agree that something is going on there."

Big Bob shook his head, folded his arms, came around to sit on the front edge of his desk, and said nothing. I knew him; he was thinking about our next step. Then he looked at Mary.

"Go see Judge Campbell for the subpoenas," Big Bob said. "I think she'll be sympathetic toward what we're trying to do here."

"Good idea," Mary said. "I'll take Don with me. She'll like that."

"And when you have time, look into this pharmacy guy," Big Bob said. "I can't ignore your husband's track record when it comes to finding trouble."

◆　　◆　　◆　　◆

We waited half an hour to see Judge Jerri Campbell, a spunky little blonde of maybe fifty years with a reputation as a man-eater and a body that went with the reputation. I followed Mary into the judge's chambers.

"Who's this hunk, Mary?" Judge Jerri asked. She had to know exactly who I was.

"Hands off, Your Honor," Mary said. "He's mine."

"Donald Youngblood, I presume," Judge Jerri said.

"Your Honor," I said.

"You lucky girl," she said to Mary, then switched to judge mode. "Sit," she said. "Tell me what this is about."

I let Mary do the talking. I just sat and tried to look like a hunk.

"So you think that by finding out who in Mountain Center is on Zolpidem, that will lead you to who caused this accident," Judge Jerri said.

"Yes, Your Honor," Mary said. "From that master list, we'll narrow it down to girls or parents of girls who attend Mountain Center High School."

"Okay, that makes sense. I'll grant the subpoenas, but I'll have some stipulations. First, when you narrow the list, you'll immediately discard the names not on it, and you won't mention them to anyone. I want your promise that you'll shred the master list once you have the secondary list."

"Yes, Your Honor," Mary said.

"Second, when you eliminate names on your secondary list, you'll drop those off on a daily basis and reprint the list and shred the old one. Understand?"

"Yes, Your Honor," Mary said again.

"I want only you and Don to know who is on those lists," Judge Jerri said. "Share with Big Bob only if you have to. By the way, my name will be on there."

"Mine, too," said Mary. "We'll eliminate you as a suspect."

"Thank you." Judge Jerri smiled. "I want to do individual subpoenas for each pharmacy. I'll have my clerk work on them today. You can pick them up in the morning."

"Thank you, Your Honor," Mary said as we stood to leave.

"You-all catch whoever is responsible for this, Mary," the judge said.

"You can count on it," Mary said.

◆   ◆   ◆   ◆

It was time to call it a day and go home. We swung by Ridgetop Pharmacy to pick up the list we were promised. The list was waiting, but the owner was not. Tomas Garcia had been right; it was not a long list.

As soon as we arrived at the condo, I took the dogs for a walk. After that, I changed into an old pair of jeans and a well-worn long-sleeved T-shirt and sneakers. Mary changed into cargo pants and one of my old button-down-collar shirts, which she tied in a knot at her waist. On her feet were short gray socks.

We opened a bottle of Cabernet, took that first glorious drink, and started to relax.

"You and the judge seem to have a pretty good relationship," I said.

"She's friends with Wanda," Mary said. "Wanda has brought her along for girls' night out a couple of times."

I started to ask how good of friends Wanda and the judge were but decided I really didn't want to know. I drank some wine instead.

"She would have jumped you right there in her chambers if you'd let her," Mary teased.

"No thanks," I said. "One blond bombshell is enough."

"This is really good wine. I'm starting to relax."

She was sending signals, and I was receiving loud and clear.

"When is Lacy going to be home?"

"Later."

"How much later?"

"Late enough," Mary said, coming off her barstool toward me.

25

The next morning, we again had breakfast at the Mountain Center Diner, which further perplexed Doris.

"My goodness," she said. "Two days in a row."

"We're working a case together," Mary said. "A Mountain Center Diner breakfast is a great way to start the day."

"Well, thank you, Mary." Doris blushed. "I should get you to do a commercial on TV."

"Anytime," Mary said.

◆   ◆   ◆   ◆

After breakfast, we went to the courthouse. Judge Campbell was in court, but the subpoenas were waiting for us.

The next stop we made was the North Mountain Center Walgreens.

"Hang on a second," John Duncan said when we handed him the subpoena. He disappeared into the back and returned seconds later with a letter-sized manila envelope. "I suspected you'd be back, so I went ahead and compiled the list. I hope it's helpful."

We thanked him and moved on. We covered two more Walgreens and two CVS pharmacies by lunch. Then Mary's police radio squawked: "Man brandishing a weapon at Walmart. All units respond."

Mary grabbed the mic. "This is Mary, on my way, ETA three minutes."

She flipped a switch, and a row of flashers in her back window came on as we raced toward Walmart. I knew she also had flashers in the grill of her car. She drove fast but in control. We heard other units responding over the radio and sirens in the distance. When we arrived, people were running from the store.

"Vests are in the trunk," Mary said, popping the release.

We put the bulletproof vests on as quickly as we could. I grabbed Mary's Taser from the trunk and slipped it in my jacket pocket.

"That's only good up to fifteen feet," Mary reminded me.

We ran to the entrance as two patrol cars pulled up. I had practiced with the Taser at home, shooting at an old chair in the den at the lake house.

"He's got a gun," said a man standing near the entrance doors in a Walmart vest.

"Where is he?" Mary said.

"Toward the back."

"Do you know him?" Mary asked.

"His name is Frank," the man said. "He got fired yesterday. I think he's looking for the store manager."

The uniforms arrived. I knew a couple of them.

"Stay here," Mary said to them. "We'll try to defuse the situation, and the fewer of us in there, the better. If you hear gunfire, come running. And get these people away from the entrance."

One of the uniforms handed Mary a walkie-talkie. "Keep in touch," he said.

She nodded, then looked at me. "Let's go."

None of the cops at the scene protested my involvement. Mountain Center was a small town. I was the Chief's infamous best friend; licensed to carry and not afraid to shoot. Beyond that I was married to the woman giving the orders. Besides, if anyone had to take a bullet they would just as soon it be me.

I followed Mary in. She motioned me to go right as she circled around to the left.

"Frank!" she yelled. "Where are you?"

I moved fast toward the far right of the store.

"Who are you?" a male voice yelled back.

"My name is Mary, Frank. You need to put the gun down and come talk to me."

"Not until I shoot that no-good son of a bitch Hollis," Frank yelled.

I was guessing Hollis was the store manager. I made it all the way to the right wall and headed left to the back of the store. From the sound of his voice, I guessed Frank was somewhere in the back center.

"You don't want to shoot anyone, Frank," Mary said. "That would not be good."

"Don't come any closer," Frank said, "or I'll shoot you."

"Do you have a wife, Frank?"

"The little whore left me!" Frank shouted.

Well, that didn't help, I thought.

I made it to the back of the store and turned left again, staying low against the wall. *Keep him talking, Mary*, I thought.

I didn't have to worry about that.

Frank screamed, "Hollis, you no-good chickenshit, where are you?"

Frank was close. Then I saw him maybe thirty feet away. I needed to get closer. He started to turn, and I ducked out of sight.

"Frank, put down the gun and come talk to me," Mary said again.

I looked up. Frank had turned in the direction of Mary's voice, briefly distracted. *It's now or never*, I thought. I opted for speed over stealth and went for Frank as fast as I could, Taser in hand. He heard me coming and turned as I was closing in. I saw his pistol come up. I fired the Taser as I dove to the right a second before I heard his gun go off.

Luck beats skill every time. The two tiny probes found Frank's chest, and he was instantly down in a heap, all his motor skills gone haywire.

"Don!" Mary screamed.

"I'm okay!" I called back as I got to my feet. "He's down."

◆   ◆   ◆   ◆

Two of the uniforms took Frank away. Among other things, he was having a bad hair day. His eyes were red and his skin pale. I was betting he was on something—probably not Ambien. Hollis, the store manager, came out of hiding and thanked us profusely.

Outside, more MCPD patrols cars had arrived. Mary waved a couple of uniforms over, one being Sean Wilson, Big Bob's younger brother.

"Everything okay?" Sean said.

"Nobody hurt," Mary said. "Don got to do the fun stuff."

"Yeah, like get shot at," I said.

Mary said to Sean, "See if you can get any eyewitness statements that might be helpful."

"Sure thing," Sean said. "Good work, you two."

At that point, Big Bob arrived. He got out of his SUV, put on his cowboy hat, and swaggered over.

"See what happens when you ride around with this guy?" Big Bob said, pointing at me.

I smiled.

"A thrill a minute," Mary said.

"Walk me through it," Big Bob said.

We did.

"Damn good work," he said.

Then the TV truck arrived. I looked at Mary. "Let's get out of here. Let Big Bob get some airtime."

"Sounds good to me," Mary said.

◆   ◆   ◆   ◆

"I was really proud of you today," I said to Mary. "You calmed and distracted Frank enough for me to take him down."

We had delivered the rest of the subpoenas and picked up dinner on the way back to the condo. We were in the kitchen having Chinese takeout with Lacy and Biker. The Walmart news was all over town. We had the TV muted, waiting for the six o'clock news so we could see what Big Bob said during his interview.

"Me, too, you," Mary said. "But you put yourself at risk. I wasn't too happy about that."

"You guys need to be careful," Lacy said. "I haven't had you for long, and I don't want to lose you." She paused. "But I'm really proud."

Biker said nothing.

"We're making it sound more exciting than it was," I said, looking at Mary.

"Don's right," Mary said. "I think the guy was just about ready to give up."

"Uh-huh," Lacy said, not buying it.

"You can't worry about us all the time," Mary said. "We're pretty good at what we do."

"I know," Lacy said. "I'm just saying, be careful."

Biker said nothing.

I looked at him. "Don't you have anything to say?"

He smiled. "Be careful."

The news came on, and Mary turned up the sound. The incident was the lead story. A picture of the Mountain Center Walmart flashed on the screen, then shrank behind news anchor Peggy Ann Romeo, who spoke directly into the camera: "There was some excitement today at the local Walmart as a disgruntled former employee roamed the store with a loaded firearm searching for the store manager, who had fired him the day before."

The screen changed to footage taken outside the store that included Mary and me talking to Big Bob. Then Big Bob was on screen with a young female reporter I didn't recognize.

"This is Traci Williams, and I'm here with Mountain Center police chief Big Bob Wilson. Chief, can you fill us in on what happened here today?"

Big Bob: "We had a male suspect with a loaded handgun inside the store apparently looking to shoot the store manager. Detective Mary Youngblood was first on the scene with her husband, Don Youngblood, who is a local private investigator. They were able to subdue the suspect without anyone getting hurt."

Traci Williams: "Were shots fired?"

Big Bob: "I don't know any more details at this time. That's all for now."

The camera followed Big Bob to the front of the store, where he spoke with his younger brother. Then it cut abruptly back to the studio, where Peggy Ann Romeo said, "We have subsequently learned that the suspect, Frank Watts, fired one shot as he was being subdued by Donald Youngblood with a Taser pistol. Mr. Youngblood was unharmed."

"School is really going to be fun tomorrow," Lacy said.

"I may go hide out at the lake house," I said.

"You will not," Mary said. "We have work to do."

26

Friday morning, I avoided the Mountain Center Diner and my office. Mary and I spent most of the day collecting lists of Mountain Center residents who had prescriptions for Zolpidem. There were well over a thousand names. A lot of people in Mountain Center were trying to get to sleep. Narrowing the list was going to take some time.

In the early afternoon, Mary and I sat in her unmarked car in a distant corner of the Walmart parking lot having a cup of Dunkin' Donuts coffee and a snack—two crullers for Mary, an apple fritter for me. Luckily for us, her radio was quiet.

"Two crullers."

"They're mostly air," Mary said. "You have more calories than I do."

"Calories are overrated," I said, taking a big bite of my apple fritter. *Justification is all.*

"We need to consolidate all these lists on one of our laptops," Mary said. "That's going to take awhile, and I don't have time. I have a couple of other cases going."

"I'll take care of it," I said. "I'll split the list with Gretchen."

"By *split* you mean giving her two-thirds of it," Mary said.

"Or three-quarters. Maybe all. I'll offer her some overtime."

"She cannot know what the list is or Judge Campbell will have my butt."

"She can't have it," I said. "It's all mine."

Mary laughed. "You better believe it."

"I'll black out any mention of prescriptions or pharmacies," I said. "Besides, Gretchen can keep her mouth shut. She's not curious like some people I know."

"Watch it, Cowboy," Mary said.

◆   ◆   ◆   ◆

Reluctantly, I was in the office by three o'clock.

"I saw you on the news last night," Gretchen said. "You just keep adding to that local-hero résumé."

"It sounded like more than it was," I said.

"I'll bet," Gretchen said.

I ducked into my office, where I found a list of detailed messages. Some had questions that I needed to answer; others were calls to return. Gretchen came in a few minutes later and sat in front of my desk, notebook in hand, awaiting comment. I answered all her questions and promised to return the calls.

Then I asked, "Want to make some overtime this weekend?"

"Doing what?"

"I have a list of names from different sources that I need compiled into a Word document," I said. "It'll take awhile."

"How many names?"

"Over a thousand."

"Is this about the case you and Mary are working?"

"Yes," I said. "And that's all I can tell you. I'll give you the list before you leave. After you finish, burn it to a CD and dump the Word doc."

"Understood," she said.

◆　　◆　　◆　　◆

One of the pink call slips was from Buckley. He had left his office number, not his cell-phone number. I dialed it.

"Agent Clarke," Buckley answered.

"You called?"

"I did," Buckley said. "I've developed quite a file on this Midnight Riders case. I'm seeing some tendencies. Would you like to take a look?"

"Sure," I said. "What do have in mind?"

"How about I come by Monday morning?"

"That will be fine. Are you going to be up here for the weekend?"

"Could be," Buckley said evasively.

"Gretchen could be pretty busy."

"Not *that* busy," Buckley said.

◆　　◆　　◆　　◆

Before leaving the office, I went online to take a quick look at the market and check email. The market was doing better than it had a right to—still over seventeen thousand and staying there. Sooner or later, it would come crashing down.

I answered a few emails from clients regarding stocks and then opened one from T. Elbert. It read: *Saw you on the news. I want to hear all!*

I wrote back and told him I would see him soon and tell him *the rest of the story.* I signed it, *Paul Harvey.*

27

Monday morning, I skipped the Mountain Center Diner, picked up coffee and bagels from a Dunkin' Donuts drive-through, and went to T. Elbert's. I had spent the weekend at the lake house getting caught up on a list of maintenance issues. I was glad it was Monday.

I had seen T. Elbert at Lacy's basketball games and even taken him to lunch, but I hadn't been on his front porch in some time. He was quick to remind me.

"Hey, stranger," he said. "It'll be three weeks tomorrow. That may be a record."

"One that I'll try to see stays on the books for a long time," I said.

"Don't worry about it. Records are made to be broken. I want to hear about this Walmart thing with you and Mary."

Of course, I had to tell it in great detail. T. Elbert listened, grunted, and shook his head a few times but said nothing.

"You took a big chance," he said. "You should have pulled your piece, taken dead aim, and told him to put down his weapon or get shot. Instead, you did it the hard way."

"I've killed too many people," I said. "Besides, I practiced with the Taser and felt I could take him down without shooting him."

"Worrying about the past can get you killed," T. Elbert said. "Remember that. It might be the single best piece of advice I ever give you."

"I'll try to remember," I said.

Thinking back, maybe I was reckless. If Frank Watts had turned a little quicker, I could have been shot—killed, even. Then Mary would have been a widow and Lacy would have been without a father. That thought shook me.

T. Elbert seemed to read my mind. "It's over," he said. "Learn from it."

"I will. And thanks for setting me straight."

◆   ◆   ◆   ◆

I was in the office by nine o'clock. Buckley was already sitting at the conference table, drinking coffee and working on his laptop. Gretchen had obviously given him a key.

"Did I give you a key?" I asked.

He smiled. "No."

"Breaking and entering would not look good on your FBI résumé."

"I didn't break anything," Buckley said. "I only entered. Gretchen said it was okay, that she ran things around here."

I laughed. "That's about right. Come on in."

We went into my office and got comfortable.

Buckley handed me a thick manila file folder. "I made you a copy of everything I have so far. I've seen enough that I see some patterns."

"Let's hear it."

"I ruled out a couple who looked like they fit the profile and then didn't," Buckley said. "What I have left are three distinct patterns. One, pairs of supposed runaway boys disappearing after school in mid-to-late October or early November. Two, pairs of boys disappearing after school in mid-February to early April. And three, pairs of boys disappearing during the night from summer camps in July or August."

"Tell me about group two," I said.

"In every instance, the older boy in the disappearing pair enrolled at midterm," Buckley said. "And the mother was gone within a month."

"Do you have any pictures of the older boys?"

"None so far," Buckley said. "The mothers told investigators they couldn't find any pictures and put on a good show about being upset over it."

"School pictures?"

"I'm working on it," he said. "So far, the few I've looked into were conveniently absent the day school pictures were taken. I'll bet that's the case in every instance."

"Keep after it," I said. "Check the camps. If a group picture was taken, it would be hard for a kid to avoid it. Talk to school administrators to find out if any casual pictures were taken for sporting events, school newspapers, glee clubs, like that."

"That's going to take some time."

"From your patterns of disappearances, it looks like we have some time," I said. "We need to alert law-enforcement agencies to let the FBI know about any runaway boys who fit our profile. If we can identify the next pair fast enough, we might be able to squeeze the mother of the older boy."

"I'm doing that," Buckley said. "It's a big job."

"Is there anything else?"

"Not now," he said. "How about dinner one night next week?"

"Monday," I said. "Seven o'clock. My treat."

◆   ◆   ◆   ◆

A half-hour later, Gretchen arrived, made herself a cup of coffee, entered my office, and got comfortable in the chair closest to the door.

"Buckley just left," I said.

"I hope you don't mind my giving him a key."

"What's he going to steal, our Keurig?"

"You've got a point," she said, taking a drink. "But if he steals the Keurig, I'll shoot him." She handed me a folder. "Here's your list. Some interesting names are on it."

"Forget you saw them," I said, "or a certain judge will be upset with Mary."

"They're forgotten," Gretchen said. "Any assignments for today?"

"No," I said. "Go back to what you were working on."

Gretchen returned to the outer office, and I started going down the list. There were indeed some interesting names. I needed to narrow the list. I started blacking out the names I knew had no possible connection to the case. When I'd gone as far as I could, I checked my online address book, found the number I was looking for, and made the call.

◆　　◆　　◆　　◆

We met at the Mountain Center Country Club for lunch. It had been awhile since I'd last seen him.

"I wasn't about to turn down lunch at the club," he said.

I had met Dick Traber when he was a middle-school principal soon after I first encountered Lacy. Now, he was the principal at Mountain Center High School. Over the years, I had gotten to know him. We often talked before or after Lacy's basketball games.

"Consider it my contribution to the Mountain Center school system," I said.

"On behalf of educators everywhere, I accept," Dick said.

"Why do I have the feeling this is not just a social invitation?"

"Because Mary and I need your help with an investigation we're conducting, and we didn't want to arouse suspicion by showing up in your office."

The waitress came, and we ordered.

"What investigation?" he said.

"Confidentially?"

"Sure."

"Some members of the senior class asked me to look into the Clay Carr accident."

He sat up straighter and leaned forward. "They don't think it was an accident?"

"More like they don't think it makes any sense," I said.

"And I take it that since I'm here, it's turning out to be more than an accident."

"Clay and Julie were both drugged. Whether or not the intent was for Clay to wreck and kill Julie, who can say?"

"My God," Dick Traber said. "Any idea who?"

"Mary thinks it was another girl in school."

"I could believe that," he said. "Girls are a lot more devious and calculating than boys."

"You should probably keep that thought to yourself," I said.

"It's no big secret among the staff," he said. "I'm always hearing stories. Obviously, Mary has similar feelings."

"She does."

Our food arrived—a Monte Cristo with fries for me and a chicken Caesar for Dick. We both drank sweet tea. The food and drink began to disappear.

"What kind of drug?" Dick asked between bites.

"Zolpidem," I said.

"What's that?"

"Commonly called Ambien."

"Somebody put them to sleep," he said.

"And then Clay ran off the road."

"What do you need from me?" Dick asked.

"Names and addresses of all the girls who attend Mountain Center High."

Dick thought for a moment. "I don't see why I can't do that," he said. "When do you need them?"

"The sooner, the better."

"I'll put it together and email it later today," he said. "But to be on the safe side, the list didn't come from me."

"Of course not," I said.

◆　　◆　　◆　　◆

That night was Senior Night for the girls basketball team. The three seniors being honored were introduced and walked to center court with their parents. I felt proud and sad at the same time—proud of Lacy, of course, and sad that this would be the last time I saw her play in her home gym. It had been a great four years. The team had not lost a home game in three.

The festivities ended, we took our seats, and the game started. Lacy was obviously fired up. The Lady Bears came out in a full-court press, and Lacy had two early steals and two easy layups. By the time the first quarter ended, the home team led 26–8 and Lacy had thirteen points. Lacy had a career-high thirty-three by the end of the third quarter. All the starters sat out the fourth quarter in a 90–38 win. The coach was obviously getting ready for the district tournament, which would begin two nights later.

I saw Dick Traber as I was leaving the gym. I waited until he was alone and went over to say hello.

"Thanks again for lunch," he said.

"My pleasure."

"I sent you an email earlier today."

"Really?" I said. "I don't think I got it."

"A pity," he said.

28

Tuesday morning, I again took Mary to breakfast at the Mountain Center Diner.

"Well," Doris said, "you're turning into a regular." She smiled, took our order, and hurried away.

"I don't think she likes my being here," Mary said.

"Why not?"

"She wants you all to herself."

"Doris?"

"You're her celebrity diner," Mary said. "She wants to hover and pamper you with food and service. I'm cramping her style."

"Doris?" I said again, having a hard time processing.

"Trust me," Mary said. "We woman know these things."

"Either that or you're paranoid."

Then again, maybe I was just being messed with.

◆　　◆　　◆　　◆

After breakfast, we went to my office with our lists and spread them out on the conference table. Gretchen was still an hour from arriving. Mary took the list of girls from Mountain Center High, and I worked from the master list Gretchen had put together. Both were in alphabetical order, which made things easier. We spent the morning going through the lists and crossing off names with a black marker so they would no longer be readable. I put a checkmark beside the names of parents on my list who had girls at the school. Some were fathers and some mothers. It would have been nice if the final list had two or three names. Instead, I was left with twenty-five.

"Now what?" Mary asked.

"I'll have to think about it."

"You do that," Mary said. "I have to get back to a B and E case I'm working on."

"By the way," I said as she got up to leave, "I had a thought about Tomas Garcia."

"I'm listening."

"Let me talk to Oscar about him. Oscar may know something."

"Good idea," Mary said. "I have plenty of other things to do. See you tonight."

"Not for dinner," I said. "I'm meeting Buckley at the club. I think he wants to talk about Gretchen."

Seconds later, Gretchen arrived as if on cue. Mary said hello, then goodbye.

"Looks like you've finished whatever you were doing," Gretchen said.

"We have," I said. "I need you to put together a new list, then shred the old one."

"Shouldn't take long," she said, looking at the edited list. "I'll get right on it."

◆　◆　◆　◆

Late that cold February day, after Gretchen left and the office was quiet, I sat and pondered my next moves in my two current cases.

First, the Clay Carr case. I had the final list. How was I going to investigate twenty-five high-school girls without raising a ruckus? The fact that I was investigating them meant they were suspects. I'd face outrage if I wasn't very, very careful. I wanted my investigation to remain confidential. There was one obvious question: who knew high-school girls better than anyone else? Answer: other high-school girls. I decided that at some point, I would get help from Lacy and Hannah.

I swiveled in my leather chair and faced the window. Night was descending on Mountain Center, and I was almost certain I could see snow flurries—wishful thinking.

The Midnight Riders case was now in awaiting-developments mode. My concern was that the Midnight Riders might get wind of being investigated and cease their recruitment plans. I was hoping we would soon get a break, a lead we could follow. If they shut down now, we'd find ourselves at a dead end.

As I pondered all of that, the night got darker. I could definitely see snow flurries in the streetlights.

◆　　◆　　◆　　◆

I sat at my favorite table at the Mountain Center Country Club, overlooking the eighteenth green, which was barely visible in the darkness. Buckley sat across from me. We ordered pints of draft beer.

"Nice," he said.

"It is," I said, looking at the menu. "Let's order when the drinks arrive. I'm hungry. Order anything you want. I'm required to spend so much per year on food, so don't be shy."

Our drinks arrived, and we ordered. Buckley wasn't shy. He got the most expensive steak on the menu. I opted for grilled salmon.

"Did you look over the file?" Buckley asked.

"Yes. You covered all the fine points during our meeting. But we're not having dinner to talk about the Midnight Riders."

Buckley drank some beer. "You were a bachelor for a long time," he said.

"I was."

"A lot of women, I'll bet."

"Enough," I said. "I don't know about 'a lot.'"

"You probably could have married some of them."

I knew where this was going, but I'd let him get there on his own. I drank some beer.

"Well, at least one," I said. "Probably more."

"Did you enjoy the playboy lifestyle?"

"I sure did at the time."

"And then you got married and adopted a daughter in the process," Buckley said.

"I did."

"Why?"

"I met Mary."

"Simple as that?"

"Relationships are never simple," I said.

"How did you know she was the one?"

"Everyone I trusted kept telling me," I said.

"You married her because your friends said you should?" Buckley said, looking confused.

"Of course not. I married her because I couldn't live without her. That and the fact that she proposed and gave me about ten seconds to decide. I took five."

"So how did you know she was the one?"

"Hard to explain," I said. "I just knew. I felt complete when I was with her and incomplete when I wasn't."

Buckley nodded and said nothing. He drank more beer and looked around. I drank more beer and waited quietly.

"I decided when I joined the FBI not to get married," Buckley said. "I thought it would be unfair to a wife to be married to an FBI agent."

"Probably best to let the potential wife decide that."

Buckley smiled. "I've come to that conclusion myself."

Our food arrived, and we dispensed with conversation for a while.

"Excellent steak," Buckley said.

"It is."

"I think I'm in love with Gretchen."

I had guessed that was coming, but it still caught me off guard. "You think?"

"Well, I'm new at being in love, but I'm almost certain. What you said about being complete and incomplete pretty much describes my situation."

I ate and said nothing.

"What should I do?"

"I'm probably one of the worst sources on the planet to give advice on affairs of the heart," I said.

"You're all I've got," Buckley said. "And you've been through it, so tell me something."

"Okay," I said. "If I were going to give you advice, I'd tell you to take it slow. If marriage is in your future, Gretchen will let you know eventually. Of course, I'm not going to give you any advice."

Buckley smiled. "Well, if you were, that sounds right on target."

29

I was in the office early Wednesday with the dogs. By the time I turned everything on and brewed a cup of coffee, the dogs were napping on their beds in my office. I settled in at my desk and booted up my laptop. I signed on, and a headline immediately caught my attention: "Colorado Supreme Court Destroyed by Bomb."

The article was short. A bomb had gone off around midnight. No one was injured. No one had claimed responsibility. Was it foreign or domestic terrorism? the article asked. I knew the bombers had to be the Midnight Riders.

I had just finished reading the article when the phone rang.

"Youngblood," I said.

"Did you see the news?"

"Just now," I said. "Looks like our homegrown terrorists are still active."

"You're right," David Steele said. "It was the Midnight Riders. This time, they left a two-word message scrawled below their symbol."

"Saying what?"

"It said," David Steele said with emphasis, "'Smoke this.'"

I couldn't help myself. I laughed. "A reference to legalized marijuana."

"Nothing gets by you, Youngblood," David Steele said.

"I have my moments. I'm surprised the press hasn't seen the Midnight Riders' symbol."

"We've been able to remove all of them without the press getting wind. As soon as we hear the words *bomb* or *courthouse* or *federal building*, we're all over it."

"Sooner or later, the press will have it."

"I'm catching a lot of heat on this from the director," he said. "How are you and Buckley doing? Any leads, anything I can share?"

I brought him up to date on the case.

"Did you talk with Sheila Buckworth?" I asked.

"Yes. I didn't get anything new. You told me all there was."

"Share as little as possible about this case," I said. "I don't trust anyone."

"I'll be vague. I'll say we have some leads we're tracking down, but nothing concrete."

"The ole federal two-step," I said.

David Steele laughed. "Yeah, but the director will see right through it. He won't be happy, but he'll understand."

"How about those hair samples I sent?"

"We've isolated two different males so far," he said. "No hits in any databases we've looked at."

"Another dead end," I said.

"Maybe. We still have more hair to look at. I've got to run. Keep in touch, Youngblood."

◆   ◆   ◆   ◆

That night, the Mountain Center girls team played its first game in the district tournament. It wasn't close. The starters sat out most of the second half in a 64–36 romp. The game was actually a semifinal, since the number-one-seeded Lady Bears had drawn a bye. Lacy played a solid game, scoring twenty points and playing inspired defense.

Later that night, I sat at the kitchen bar with my list of twenty-five girls from Mountain Center High who had a parent with a prescription for Zolpidem. Lacy and Hannah were across from me. We had just polished off a large pizza from Best Italian. I had two copies of the list.

"I have a list of girls from MCHS who I want you to look at independently," I said. "Don't ask me how I arrived at these names. See if anyone jumps out who might be obsessed with Clay or might not have liked Julie." I slid the lists across to them. "Take your time. Circle anyone who stands out."

They scanned the lists and at about the same time circled a name.

A few minutes later, Lacy said, "I'm finished."

"Me, too," Hannah said.

Lacy looked at Hannah. "The stalker?"

"Yep," Hannah said.

"Explain," I said.

"This girl, Ellie," Hannah said. "She was always around Clay, like she was following him. She couldn't take her eyes off him. We joked about it, called her 'the stalker.'"

The name both of them had circled was Elvira Moody. *Who names their kid Elvira?* I thought. No wonder she was called Ellie.

"You think Ellie had something to do with it?" Lacy asked.

"I don't know, but it's a place to start," I said. "And you two keep quiet about this. Don't even tell Biker or Al."

They nodded.

"Seriously," I said. "Not a word. If this gets out, it could all blow up."

Lacy looked hard at Hannah.

"Not a word," Hannah said. "I promise."

"One more thing," I said. "Was Ellie at the party?"

"I didn't see her," Lacy said.

"Me either," Hannah said.

"Whatever it's worth," Lacy said, "I don't think Ellie had anything to do with this. She would never do anything to hurt Clay."

"I agree," Hannah said.

"I value your opinions," I said. "But maybe you're being naïve."

"Or not," Lacy said.

◆   ◆   ◆   ◆

I woke in the middle of the night with an epiphany.

"Damn it," I said out loud, annoyed with myself. I should have thought of it sooner.

"What?" Mary said.

"Sorry. I didn't mean to wake you."

"It's okay," she said. "I was half awake anyway. What is it?"

"A moment of clarity on the Clay Carr case."

"Tell me."

I did.

"That's a damn good thought," Mary said.

"Except that I have to wait until morning to act on it."

"Well, I'm wide awake and you're wide awake," Mary said. "Any thoughts about that?"

"One or two," I said, reaching for her.

30

Early the next morning, I had breakfast at the diner. Doris seemed pleased that I was alone.

"You're early today," she said.

"Couldn't sleep."

"What can I get you?"

"Just coffee for now," I said. "I'll order later."

Doris poured coffee and scurried away. I waited to see if anyone would show up to eat with me. While I waited, I read the local sports page. The headline read, "How Far Can They Go?" The article was the story of the Lady Bears' undefeated season. *A bit premature*, I thought. Lacy Youngblood was mentioned more than once. I couldn't help feeling proud.

◆　　◆　　◆　　◆

When I reached the office, I texted Dick Traber:

Call me when you can.

I had slowly given in to texting. It was one way of avoiding small talk.

Five minute later, Dick called. "You need something," he said—a statement, not a question.

"A list of girls who are absent today, and how many days they've missed."

"I'll email you later," he said. "It's going to be a long list. The flu is going around. What are you thinking?"

"That if the guilty party got wind of my investigation, they might take off," I said.

"You mean run away?"

"Maybe," I said. "Or disappear with the help of a parent."

"I hope not," Dick said. "I'll be in touch."

◆　　◆　　◆　　◆

I had the list by early afternoon. Two names matched girls on my list of twenty-five. One of the names was Kathy Franks, the other Elvira Moody. I texted Lacy to call me when she could.

Ten minutes later, she did.

"I want to ask you about another name on the list," I said. "Kathy Franks. Would she have any connection to Clay Carr?"

"None that I know of," Lacy said. "Kathy has been going with the same guy for almost two years. I can't see her as one of your suspects."

"You're beginning to sound like a cop," I said. "Go back to school."

"What do you expect?" Lacy laughed. "I'm going to class now."

I called Mary.

"Elvira Moody has not been in school this week," I said.

"Interesting," Mary said. "Why is she out?"

"Flu, supposedly."

"I think it's time we had a talk with Elvira," Mary said. "I'll pick you up in half an hour."

◆　　◆　　◆　　◆

The Moodys lived outside town. But since the alleged drugging took place in Mountain Center, Mary was within her rights to pursue leads elsewhere. If jurisdiction became an issue, we could always get Jimmy Durham, the county sheriff, involved.

Ernest Moody owned Moody Farms, a local dairy that produced milk and ice cream. I didn't make the connection that Elvira Moody was his daughter until I took a closer look at the address.

Twenty minutes out of Mountain Center, we turned off the main road onto a secondary road. The day was pleasant for February—mid-fifties and windless, with a thin layer of clouds that diffused the sun but kept the day bright. Ten minutes after leaving the highway, we turned right under an arch that proclaimed we had arrived at Moody Farms. We drove past a number of buildings to the main house.

"Maybe I can get a sample of their mint chocolate chip ice cream," I said.

"I wouldn't count on it," Mary said.

An older man and two younger ones were working on a fence that surrounded the main house. We stopped in front of the gate that led to the house and got out. The three men followed the fence line around to where we waited. I leaned against the front fender of Mary's car. Mary took a few steps toward the men.

"Can I help you?" the older man asked.

"Are you Ernest Moody?" Mary asked.

"Ernie." He smiled. "The last person to call me Ernest was my mother, God rest her soul. These two handsome fellows are my sons."

"I'm Mary Youngblood." She showed her badge. "I'm a detective on the Mountain Center police force. We're investigating an incident at the high school and wanted to talk with Ellie."

"Ellie's got the flu," Ernie said. "What's this about?"

I watched Ernie and his sons closely. I didn't see any signs that they were uncomfortable with our being here. I was beginning to get the feeling this was a dead end.

"Did you hear about the accident in which Julie James was killed?" Mary asked.

"Sure," Ernie said. "Terrible thing."

"Do you know if Ellie was at the party that night?"

"No, she wasn't," Ernie said. "Ellie doesn't care much for basketball. Never goes to the games or the parties after. She loves football, though."

"Especially the running back," one of the sons cracked. The other one laughed. I was guessing they were both in their late twenties.

"She's kind of sweet on Clay Carr," Ernie said. "The accident really upset her."

"Would you mind if I say hello to her and ask how she's feeling?" Mary asked.

"Sure, come on in," Ernie said. "You two, get back to that fence."

Mary followed Ernest Moody into the house as the sons went back to their work. I remained leaning against the fender.

A few minutes later, Mary came out, said goodbye to Ernie, and got in the car. I nodded to Ernie and got in the passenger side.

"I didn't see or feel any red flags," Mary said as we drove away. "Ellie's not involved in this."

"You talked with her?"

"I did. A sweet, shy girl. Clay Carr is more of a hero to her than a love interest. According to Ellie, Clay is way out of her league. I think maybe we were influenced too much by what Lacy and Hannah said."

"You mean the stalker business?"

"Yes," Mary said. "Sometimes, teenage girls think they're being funny when they're really being cruel. I'm going to sit them down and give them a little lecture."

"Not a bad idea," I said.

We were quiet on our return trip to Mountain Center. As far as the Clay Carr case was concerned, I was back to a place I had been many times in previous investigations: square one.

31

Early Friday morning, I received a surprising phone call from the chief of detectives on the Provo, Utah, police force.

"Youngblood, I've got a live one for you," Jock Smithson said.

"Explain," I said.

"A pair of boys who fit your profile went missing in Ogden last Friday after school."

"Know any details?"

"Not much. But I do know the guy who caught the case. His name is Kent Watson."

"Okay," I said. "Do me a favor and call Kent and tell him the FBI will be in touch soon. Tell him to keep eyes on the older boy's mother."

"FBI?"

"Long story," I said. "Just do it, please."

"Right away," he said.

"Thanks for this, Jock. This may be the break we're looking for."

"My pleasure. But I want the whole story when you can tell it."

"You'll get it, I promise."

I hung up and called Scott Glass.

"I need you or one of your staff to go to Ogden as soon as possible."

"Explain," Scott said.

I did.

"Of course, she's not who she claims to be," I said. "Discreetly check out her ID. Don't let her know we're onto her."

"Leaving now," he said. "Are you coming?"

"As soon as I can," I said.

I called Roy.

"I need one of the jets tomorrow morning. I got a big break in the FBI case I'm working on."

"I'll tell Jim to be ready at eight," Roy said. "Good hunting."

Finally, I called Buckley.

"I think we have the break we've been looking for," I said.

I told him what I knew.

"I called SAC Scott Glass in Salt Lake City, and he's on his way up there. I'm going first thing tomorrow. Let me know if you want to come along."

"Let me check with my SAC. I've been working another case while we waited for a break in this one."

"I'll be at Tri-Cities Airport around eight o'clock tomorrow morning," I said.

"Okay," Buckley said. "I'll be in touch."

◆　　◆　　◆　　◆

That night, the whole gang was in the East Tennessee State University gym watching the girls district final between Mountain Center and a team from the Kingsport area. I was sitting between Billy and Roy. Mary, Maggie, and T. Elbert were directly in front of us. The first half had just ended. The Lady Bears led by twenty points. Lacy was having her usual solid game.

"I talked to Jim Doak," Roy said. "You're all set."

"Thanks," I said. "I appreciate it."

"How far do you think this team can go?" Roy asked.

"A long way," Billy said. "They're not that big, but they make life miserable for their opponents with their defense."

"I'm going to stretch my legs," Roy said. "Anybody want anything?"

Nobody did.

"I think we've caught a break in the Midnight Riders case," I said to Billy, lowering my voice.

"Tell me," he said.

I gave him the short version.

"How are you going to play it?" Billy asked.

"I don't know yet," I said. "But I'll know when I get there."

Roy returned with a Diet Coke and a large Butterfinger, one of my favorites growing up. I envied his metabolism.

"Nice snack," I said.

He smiled and took a large bite of the Butterfinger, making a show of enjoying it.

"By the way," I said, ignoring his taunt. "Have Oscar drop by and see me when he gets a chance. I need to talk with him about someone."

"Sure thing," Roy said, taking another bite.

32

By eight-thirty the following morning, I was cruising with Jim Doak at thirty-one thousand feet, heading west with the sun chasing us. Buckley had passed on coming along, citing a new case and the fact that David Steele thought Scott and I could handle things just fine.

Scott picked me up at the airport. Jim said he would hang around until tomorrow morning.

"What's the first order of business?" Scott asked.

"Let's go interview the mother of the older boy," I said. "I want to get a feel on how to play it, maybe shake her up a little."

"The name she's using is Marie Trout," Scott said. "All I can tell you now is that she doesn't hold a Utah driver's license. We checked on her employer and got her Social Security number, but it's bogus. She's had the job for two months. She's leasing a two-bedroom apartment for a year in a decent neighborhood. She has a few thousand dollars in her bank account and drives a two-year-old SUV she probably owns—no record of a car payment."

"You got that fast," I said.

"Thanks to John Banks," Scott said. John was an agent in Scott's office I had met while working the Three Devils case.

We left the airport and drove north on I-15 toward Ogden. Scott filled me in on what he knew so far. The boys had disappeared after school on Friday. They might or might not have gotten into a white van. A white van was seen in the area, but no one actually saw them get in.

"I talked to David Steele this morning," Scott said. "He says you're in charge of this case, so that means I'm taking orders from you."

"I don't want to be in charge," I said.

"Too bad. Orders from the associate deputy director."

◆　　◆　　◆　　◆

We knocked on Marie Trout's apartment door and waited for an answer. She cracked the door, and I heard the chain catch.

"Agent Glass, FBI," Scott said, showing his creds. "We would like to ask you a few routine questions about your son's disappearance. Can we come in for a few minutes?"

The door closed, and I heard the chain being removed. Then it opened, and we went in.

We sat in the living room. Marie Trout was a dark-haired, dark-eyed woman about five and a half feet tall. She looked muscular. She wore her hair short. She was attractive in a tomboy sort of way. She was calm while sizing us up. *Ex-military*, I thought.

"Why is the FBI interested in a runaway kid?" she asked.

"We just want to make sure it's not a kidnapping," Scott said. "Have you received a ransom note?"

"It's not a kidnapping," she said calmly. "My son has run away before. He's just trying to piss me off. I'm guessing he'll show up in school Monday morning."

"What about the other kid?" I asked. "Has your son run away before with another kid?"

"No," she said. "And there's no evidence my son is with the other kid. I doubt he is."

"So you didn't report your son as missing," I said.

"No," she said. "Someone told the police that the boys were together after school. The police came to question my son, and I told them I didn't know where he was. So they assumed the boys were together. I don't agree."

Marie Trout did not act like a mother with a missing kid. She acted like she knew exactly where he was.

"When will you start to get worried?" I asked.

"If he's not back by Monday morning, I'll call the police," she said. "I'll bet he's with a friend. I just don't know who his friends are. We haven't been in town long."

"Good enough," I said. "That's all for now. We'll touch base with you on Monday."

A look of concern passed briefly across her face, and then it was gone. I could tell Scott wanted to ask more questions, but I gave him a slight shake of my head to let him know not to. We thanked her for her time and left.

◆　　◆　　◆　　◆

"That whole thing was bullshit," Scott said. "Why did you end the interview?"

"Because I'll bet you a hundred bucks she takes off sometime in the next twenty-four hours," I said. "And I want her to. I want her to lead us to the Midnight Riders' home base."

Scott was quiet for maybe twenty seconds, then said, "No bet."

"We need to put a tracker on her car tonight."

"I'll need to get approval for that," Scott said.

"Go ahead and do it and then get approval," I said. "David Steele will approve it, and we don't want her taking off unless we can track her."

Scott drove and said nothing, but I could see the wheels turning. Then he made a call on his cell phone. "John," Scott said, "you're going to be working late tonight."

◆   ◆   ◆   ◆

By the time John Banks placed the tracker on Marie Trout's SUV, Scott had the approval from David Steele.

Later, Scott, John, and I sat in Scott's office polishing off a six-pack.

"You're sure she won't spot the tracker?" Scott said.

"Hell no," John said. "I'm not sure I could find it myself, and I put it there."

"All we can do now is wait," Scott said.

John Banks had software on his laptop that would allow him to track Marie Trout's SUV. Every ten seconds or so, he got a flash and a beep letting him know the tracker's location. So far, it hadn't moved.

"I'm going to take Don to his hotel and then go home and grab a few hours' sleep," Scott said to John. "I'll be back to relieve you."

"No hurry. Get a good night's sleep," John said. "I'm a night owl anyway."

Scott drove me to the Cottonwood Residence Inn.

"You might as well head home tomorrow," Scott said. "Nothing we can do now but wait for her to take off and see where she goes. I'll take you to the airport whenever you're ready."

"I'll call you in the morning," I said as I got out of his car.

I checked into a one-bedroom suite on the third floor and was sound asleep a half-hour later.

33

Early the next morning, before I could call him, Scott called me.

"Marie Trout's on the move," he said.

"What's her present location?"

"She's on I-80 East heading toward Cheyenne, Wyoming," Scott said. "She stopped for about forty-five minutes to have breakfast, and then she was on the move again. We have a car trailing her at a safe distance."

"Okay," I said. "Send someone to her apartment and see if you can get a usable print. I'd like to know who she is."

Scott laughed. "I've got a team on the way, Blood. This is not my first rodeo."

"Sorry, Professor," I said. "But you did say I was in charge."

"I did, didn't I? I think I'm regretting it already."

"I don't doubt it. I'll try to dial it down, but keep me posted. When she stops for the night, keep eyes on her. We don't want her switching cars or getting picked up by someone else and we don't know it."

"My guys already have instructions to do that," Scott said.

"Of course they do," I said. "Anyway, I'm heading home. I'm already at the airport. I took the shuttle from the Residence Inn. I'll be in the air in an hour. Call me when Marie stops for the night."

◆　◆　◆　◆

Jim Doak got the wheels up at nine o'clock. A little over three hours later, we landed at Tri-Cities Airport. I had parked the Pathfinder inside Fleet's private hangar.

Soon after leaving the airport, I stopped for gas. As I pulled out of the station, my phone rang. Caller ID told me it was Mary.

"Hello, Mrs. Youngblood."

"Where are you?"

"We landed a few minutes ago. I'm on my way home. Are you alone?"

"I am."

"Oh, goodie," I said.

Mary was waiting for me at the front door of the lake house wearing nothing but an XXL T-shirt. It was long enough to cover her gorgeous bottom, but just barely. Being totally distracted, I still have no idea what was on the shirt. Five minutes later, we were engaged in urgent sex.

An hour later, we sat in front of the fire having dinner and enjoying a bottle of King Estates Cabernet, an excellent wine for a cold February night.

"I really love these homecomings," I said.

"Me, too."

"Was I gone for just one night?"

"Uh-huh."

"Seems longer," I said.

"Uh-huh."

I knew that look. "What's for dessert?"

"Take a guess," Mary said.

34

Monday morning, we were out of bed at the same time. I used the downstairs bathroom and Mary the master bath as we got ready for work. We sat down for a cup of coffee together at the kitchen island.

"What are you working on today?" I said.

"As long as you're in town and in a holding pattern on the Midnight Riders thing, I thought *we* could work on the Clay Carr case," Mary said.

"I want to interview the girls on our list. If Kathy Franks is still out sick, I'll start with her, so as not to look like Ellie Moody was our prime suspect."

We talked it over and came up with a plan.

I called Dick Traber to explain what we wanted to do. Dick agreed. I found out that Kathy Franks was back in school, so we wouldn't have to interview her separately. We promised Dick to be at the high school at ten o'clock. He agreed to have things set up and ready to go.

"Follow me to the station. We'll go in my car," Mary said.

Mary's unmarked police cruiser was fully equipped with all the bells and whistles—computer, Kevlar vests, mace, shotgun. I had been in it a lot lately.

"I should probably take you to breakfast," I said.

"You definitely should take me to breakfast," Mary said. "But not to the Mountain Center Diner. We've been there too much lately. Let's try someplace else."

"How about Miss Piggy's?"

"Perfect," Mary said. "I love their biscuits and gravy."

You've got to love a woman who's not afraid to eat biscuits and gravy, I thought.

◆   ◆   ◆   ◆

On our way into Mountain Center, Scott called.

"Marie Trout spent the night at a Fairfield Inn in Aurora, Colorado, near Denver. She didn't make contact with anyone. We're monitoring her cell phone, and she didn't make any calls either."

"A little surprising," I said. "I thought she'd head north, near the Canadian border, maybe."

"Why did you think that?" Scott asked.

I told him about my trip with Billy to the Tohono O'Odham Indian Reservation and the abandoned campsite.

"Billy said they went north," I said. "Initially, I thought they probably went south to Mexico. But the more I thought about it, north made sense. Canada is a lot friendlier than Mexico."

"Maybe Billy was wrong," Scott said.

"You think so?"

"Not really," Scott said.

"Well, keep me posted," I said.

◆　　◆　　◆　　◆

After breakfast, we drove to the high school. Along the way, Mary said, "You know I'll never wear that in public."

"I don't want you to wear it in public."

Just for fun, I had just bought her an XXL T-shirt that said, "I pigged out at Miss Piggy's."

"Well, where then?" Mary asked innocently.

◆　　◆　　◆　　◆

Mary had decided we should question all the girls and then all the boys, so as not to arouse suspicion about our list. I thought that was a wise decision. Mary had some ideas on how to whittle down the list.

The girls were in the gym sitting in the bleachers and talking quietly among themselves. We would rather have had all three hundred girls at one time, but that would have been too many to handle. So we had decided on three groups. All the senior girls and some of the juniors were in the first group of maybe a hundred. They were more likely than the younger girls to have been to the after-game party. Once we questioned them, the word would be out and the element of surprise lost. That could not be helped.

Two tables were set up on the far side of the gym with a chair on each side. We walked in with Dick Traber.

"Ladies," Dick Traber said, "many of you know Mary Youngblood, who is a detective on the Mountain Center police force, and her husband, Don, who is a private investigator. They have asked the school's cooperation in investigating the car accident that killed Julie James. Please help them any way you can. Mary," Dick said, indicating the floor was hers.

"If you do not remember where you were on the night of the accident, raise your hand," Mary said.

No one did.

"Okay, then," Mary said. "Everyone remembers where you were. Raise your hand if you were at the after-game party that night."

About twenty hands went up.

"Those of you who raised your hands, please remain seated. The rest of you are dismissed," Mary said. "But please do not discuss what took place here until after school is out. To do so would be hindering our investigation, and you do not want to do that."

The girls who had not been at the party left quietly, sensing, I thought, that someone was in trouble. We dealt with the remaining girls one at a time, asking the same questions: *Did you see Clay or Julie? If yes, tell me what you saw. Did you see anything suspicious?* They sat across the tables from us with their backs to their classmates. They were shy and tentative. We dismissed the girls after we questioned them. When the last of them left, we compared notes.

"Anything?" Mary asked.

"Nothing," I said. Most hadn't seen Julie or Clay. Those who did had nothing to tell.

The rest of the day went much the same way. About eighty girls and more than a hundred boys had been at the party. None of them told us anything helpful.

We questioned three groups of girls, took a lunch break, and split a turkey and Swiss cheese sandwich, then questioned three groups of boys. One boy did say he thought he saw Clay Carr drinking out of a 7-Eleven cup.

By midafternoon, we sat in an empty gym about an hour before Lacy and the Lady Bears would have a short practice for tomorrow's regional tournament game.

"Think we wasted our time?"

"You never can tell," Mary said.

I was about to say something else when we heard one of the doors to the gym open and close. Walking toward us with a sense of purpose was Denise Ray, girlfriend of Slinger Sloan.

"I need to tell you something," Denise said to Mary.

"Can you tell both of us?" Mary asked.

"Sure," Denise said.

"Go ahead," Mary said.

"I don't want to sound like a rat, but I can't stand liars," Denise said.

"What do you mean?" Mary asked.

"One of the girls who left with the first group was at the party that night," Denise said. "In fact, I saw her with Julie James."

"Who?"

"Darlene Aaron."

Mary looked at me, and I shrugged.

"Okay," Mary said. "Thanks for telling us. We'll check it out. Don't mention this to anyone."

"I won't," Denise said. "I just thought you should know."

We watched Denise as she left the gym.

"How are you going to play it?" I asked.

"I'll come back tomorrow, get her out of class, and have a little talk with her," Mary said.

I did not envy Darlene Aaron.

◆ ◆ ◆ ◆

By the time I got to the office, Gretchen was gone for the day. The place was quiet, like the old days when I didn't have an assistant, when it was just Jake and me. I looked at the pink-slip messages Gretchen had left. There was one from Scott Glass. I dialed his cell phone.

"Where have you been, Blood?" Scott asked. "I tried to call."

"Sorry, Professor. I think my cell phone needs charging."

"Imagine that."

My frequently dead cell phone was high on the list of things that annoyed my friends.

"What's new?" I asked, ignoring the barb.

"Marie Trout is now on I-70 East heading for Kansas City," Scott said.

"Where the hell is she going, Blood?"

"I don't know. Maybe she spotted you-all and is leading you away from the Midnight Riders."

"Maybe," he said. "But I don't think so."

"Did you get any prints from her apartment?"

"No," Scott said. "It was wiped clean."

"Hair samples?"

"Not a one."

"Too bad," I said. "I was hoping we could learn her true identity."

"However . . . ," Scott said.

Scott was famous for playing little mind games, for making me work to extract information.

"Okay, Professor, enlighten me."

"We got a print off the door handle of her car in the middle of the night. We're running it now."

"Don't forget government and military databases," I said.

"Relax, Blood," Scott said. "We've got it covered."

◆　　◆　　◆　　◆

Just before five o'clock, Oscar Morales came through the outer door, walked into my office, and sat in the oversized chair directly in front of me.

"Hey, Boss," Oscar said.

I had met Oscar after helping Big Bob and the county sheriff's department take down a local meth lab. Oscar was on the wrong side of that but managed to skate when he cooperated with the authorities. He seemed like a decent guy caught up in a bad set of circumstances, so I helped him get a job with Fleet Industries. I had never been sorry, and neither had Joseph Fleet. Oscar was now Roy's right-hand man. From time to time, he did odd jobs for me. His nickname for me was Boss, and I let it go rather than make a big deal out of it.

"Are you familiar with Ridgetop Pharmacy?"

Oscar's smile disappeared. "*Si*," he said.

"Do you know Tomas Garcia?"

"*Si*," Oscar said, wary now.

"What kind of guy is he?"

"*Bueno hombre*," Oscar said. "He does a lot for the Spanish community. Why are you asking?"

I told him about our encounter with Tomas, and that I thought he had something to hide. Oscar was quiet. He stared out the window, deep in thought.

"He brings black-market prescription drugs in from Canada and sells them at a reasonable price," Oscar said. "If he didn't do that, a lot of my people wouldn't be able to afford them. Please don't jam him up, Boss. He is putting himself at risk to help people."

"It's not my call, Oscar, but I'll see what I can do."

"*Gracias*," Oscar said.

35

The next day, I had breakfast at the Mountain Center Diner. I ordered coffee and waited for a while to see if any of the gang would show up. Ten minutes later, I heard the phone ring. Doris answered.

"Yeah, he's here," I heard her say. "No, he hasn't. Okay."

Doris came over to my table and said, "Big Bob's on his way here. He said to wait on him to order."

Five minutes later, the big man showed up. As usual, the diner got quieter until he settled in.

"Thought I'd let you buy me breakfast," he said.

"Glad to."

Doris brought Big Bob a mug of coffee, and we ordered. I told him about my conversation with Tomas Garcia.

"Let me guess," he said. "You want us to forget about it."

"Seems like the right thing to do," I said.

"Well, I got bigger fish to fry," he said. "You talk to that wife of yours and tell her not to bring it up again."

"Will do."

Big Bob shook his head and tried to act annoyed. After a moment, he said, "What's going on with the Clay Carr thing? I've been missing Mary, so I figured I'd have breakfast with you and get the details."

"We spent most of the day interviewing teenage girls," I said.

"That must have been fun. Learn anything?"

"Not much. One girl supposedly lied about not being at the party. Other than that, nothing."

"I bet that won't turn out to be anything," Big Bob said. "She could have lied for any number of reasons. Maybe she wasn't supposed to be there."

"Maybe," I said. "Whatever the reason, Mary will get to the bottom of it."

"No doubt."

Our food arrived, and we concentrated on eating before our conversation turned to sports.

"Regional game tonight," Big Bob said. "Think it'll be a contest?"

"I doubt it," I said. "Our girls are really good."

"Especially Lacy."

"She can play," I said.

"Can you still beat her one on one?"

"Barely," I said. "My days of playing her one on one are almost over."

◆　　◆　　◆　　◆

The feta cheese omelet, home fries, and rye toast rode heavy as I headed down the alley to my office. It was after nine o'clock when I opened the door. I noticed the light flashing on Gretchen's telephone console. There was a message. I settled in at my desk and checked caller ID. The call had come in twenty minutes ago from *Private caller*, no number. I dialed my message service and picked up the message.

"I'm sure you'll be in soon," Scott said. "Call me."

I called. "I'm guessing you have more news, Professor."

"You guessed right, Blood," Scott said. "Marie Trout, who we will now refer to as Lisa Troutman, spent the night at another Fairfield Inn, this time in Independence, Missouri."

"So you're either psychic or you got a hit on the print," I said.

"You're the psychic," Scott said. "We got the hit in a military database."

"What branch?"

"Army," Scott said. "She served in Afghanistan. I'll send you the info I have."

"Do that," I said. "I'll try to add to it. I have a source at the Pentagon who might be willing to help. He thinks my life is a lot more exciting than his."

"He's probably right, Blood. It sure is more exciting than mine."

◆　　◆　　◆　　◆

Late that night, Mary and I were in bed reading. My book was a Raymond Chandler novel, *Farewell, My Lovely*. We had spent most of the evening watching the Lady Bears cruise to a twenty-point win in the quarterfinals of their regional tournament. Lacy played her usual solid game, scoring nineteen points and dishing our seven assists.

"I talked with Oscar about Tomas Garcia," I said.

"And?" Mary said, laying her open book on her chest.

I recounted the entire conversation with Oscar pretty much word for word. Mary was quiet. I knew she was conflicted.

"Any thoughts?" she asked.

"Well, let's say we were Spanish and Lacy needed a drug we couldn't afford . . ."

"Okay," Mary said. "I get it. I'll not mention Tomas Garcia again, but you need to talk with Big Bob. He'll listen to you more than he'll listen to me."

"I already have," I said. "Just don't bring Tomas Garcia up again."

"No problem," Mary said.

"Did you talk with Darlene Aaron?"

"Yes."

"Anything?"

"Not much," Mary said. "She wasn't supposed to be there, and on top of that she took a bottle from her father's wine cellar and shared it with four other girls."

"One being Julie James," I said.

"Correct," Mary said.

"So now we know where the alcohol in her system came from."

"We do," Mary said.

"Her father didn't miss the bottle?"

"She said his wine cellar has hundreds, with many duplicates."

"Sounds like someone we should get to know," I said.

36

Scott called early the next morning with yet another update.

"Lisa Troutman spent the night in Memphis."

"Where?"

"At a Springhill Suites," he said.

"That's three Marriott properties in a row," I said. "Have you checked to see what name she's using when she checks in? Those places usually require a credit card."

"I hate it when you think of things I should have thought of," Scott said. "I'll have John check that out right away."

"Every now and then, I have to think of something."

"She hasn't made contact with anyone and hasn't made any phone calls," Scott continued.

"Nothing we can do until she gets where she's going," I said. "If she's using a credit card, take a look at the charges over the last few years."

"I'll have John do that, too."

"John is going to be busy," I said.

"Better him than me," Scott said.

◆　　◆　　◆　　◆

After hanging up, I booted my office PC and checked email. I had one from T. Elbert asking what was new and saying he had news. I had a bunch of junk mail that somehow had avoided my spam folder, along with an email from Scott Glass with an attachment. I downloaded the attachment and opened it. The file name was *Lisa Troutman*.

I started reading. Lisa Troutman had been born in Orlando, Florida, in 1974. According to the file, her parents still lived there. She attended Cyprus Creek High School in Orlando. Less than a month after graduation, she enlisted in the army. She was an expert marksman with rifle and pistol and had spent time in Afghanistan. She held the rank of master sergeant. She was bilingual, Spanish being her second language. As I kept reading, I came across the most interesting part. Lisa Troutman was also an expert in explosives. She had left the army in 2004 with twelve years of service and an honorable discharge. No current address was listed. As far as I could tell, she had never been married.

How did a career military woman get hooked up with the Midnight Riders? I wondered. There had to be a connection somewhere. She probably knew someone who left the army before she did. I went to a phone-number file on my computer, found the one I was looking for, and dialed it. It rang twice.

"Culpepper," the voice said, sounding exactly like I remembered it. Lieutenant Colonel Bradley Culpepper worked at the Pentagon. I had met him while working on the Crane case. He had proven a valuable source for information regarding things military.

"Doesn't a big wheel like you have someone to answer his phone?" I said.

There was a moment of silence.

"Youngblood, is that you?"

"Yes, sir, it is."

"Well, how the hell are you?"

"I'm fine, lieutenant colonel," I said. "And yourself?"

"Well, it's colonel now. I have more responsibility and a bigger office, but it's the same old bullshit. Is this a social call, or are you working something interesting?"

"Something very interesting," I said. "And very classified."

"But you'll fill me in later," he said.

"If I'm allowed to," I said.

"Good enough. How can I help?" Bradley Culpepper said.

"Lisa Troutman," I said. "Born in 1974, enlisted in 1992, served in Afghanistan from 2002 until being honorably discharged in 2004." I told him what else I knew from the file.

"Lisa Troutman," he repeated. "Got it."

"I'll be grateful for anything you can find out about her that I don't already have," I said. "Any information might prove to be useful."

"Might take a day or two," he said.

"I appreciate it, colonel," I said. "And congratulations on that promotion."

◆　　◆　　◆　　◆

Later that morning, I called Buckley Clarke to catch him up on what was happening with the Midnight Riders case.

"So what's the plan?" Buckley asked.

"Wait until she lands somewhere and watch her," I said. "See if she makes contact with anyone."

"Surveillance," Buckley said.

"Right."

"I hate surveillance," Buckley said.

"Me, too."

Buckley said nothing. He knew what was coming.

"I'm putting you in charge," I said.

"Lucky me."

"I'll be in touch," I said.

"I'll be here," he said.

◆　　◆　　◆　　◆

That afternoon, Special Agent John Banks of the Salt Lake City FBI office called.

"You were right. She used her real name," he said. "What does that mean?"

"It means she's starting over," I said.

"How do you figure?"

"She's been using an alias," I said. "I think she's been with the Midnight Riders for some time now. The FBI shows up, and she decides to go to her backup plan, which is to go back home and start over. Tell me about the credit cards."

"How did you know?" John asked.

"Makes sense," I said. "Keep two or three cards active, make a few charges a month, set up a bill pay somewhere, pay on time, establish good credit, and you're all set when you're ready to run."

"You got it," John said. "One Visa card and one MasterCard. The charges were mostly gas and food. Both accounts were always paid on time out of a checking account in Orlando. Deposits into the checking account were sporadic."

"Tell Scott she's heading for Orlando," I said. "She might go all the way or make one more stop, but that's where she's going."

◆　　　◆　　　◆　　　◆

I called David Steele.

"The associate deputy director is in a meeting," his assistant said. She seemed annoyed that I had his private number.

"Tell him Donald Youngblood is on the line," I said firmly. "If he needs to call me back, fine."

"One moment, sir," she said—a definite attitude change.

"Youngblood," David Steele said. "Give me some good news."

I told him the latest.

"Sound like a good lead," he said. "Stay on it."

"We can't get in a hurry," I said. "We need to see if she makes contact with anyone."

"I agree. Let's watch her. Send Buckley down there to coordinate with the local office. If nothing happens in a week, you go down and put some heat on her."

"Will do," I said.

I called Buckley and gave him the good news. He was less than thrilled.

37

Nothing much happened for a couple of days. Buckley informed me that Lisa Troutman arrived in Orlando, spent two days with her parents, and signed a one-year lease on a furnished two-bedroom apartment. She moved in the day after signing.

I took some time to look at my investments and review my clients' investment lists with Gretchen. Gretchen did most of the boring research. I was interested in stocks that still had room for growth, yet paid a decent dividend, plus new technology stocks that might be worth a gamble.

I called Oscar and told him that Tomas Garcia had nothing to worry about.

"Thanks, Boss," Oscar said. "The Spanish community is in your debt."

Late that Friday afternoon, I was reading Gretchen's notes when the phone rang. Caller ID read, "Private caller." Gretchen had left for the day, so I had to answer my own phone; I was spoiled. I punched the talk button on my portable handset.

"Cherokee Investigations," I said.

"Hold for Colonel Culpepper," a male voice said.

I held for about a minute.

"Youngblood, you there?" Colonel Culpepper said.

"Yes, sir."

"I couldn't find out much more than you already had," he said. "I talked to her captain, and he vaguely remembered her. No black marks on her record. She did some special assignments in Afghanistan for a Colonel Jeffery G. Hayes that took her away from her regular duties for weeks at a time. No record of what those assignments were. That's about it."

"Is Colonel Hayes still around?"

"No," Culpepper said. "I had that same thought, so I checked. He put in thirty years, then took his pension."

"When did he opt out?"

"In 2003. Want me to gather some intel on him?"

"If it's not too much trouble," I said. "And while you're at it, check and see if his DNA is on file."

"It should be," he said. "He was a senior officer. I'll be in touch."

◆　　◆　　◆　　◆

I sat and thought. On the home front, the Clay Carr case was dead in the water. Clay was still in a coma. He shouldn't be, but he was. When he would wake up was anybody's guess. We would probably never know who had drugged Clay and Julie.

As for the Midnight Riders, there wasn't much to do until I talked to Lisa Troutman or she made contact with person or persons unknown. I was betting that would not happen. I had one thought: *Locate Colonel Hayes.*

I called Scott Glass.

"What's happening, Blood?"

"Not enough," I said. "I need to locate someone—Colonel Jeffery G. Hayes, U.S. Army, retired."

"Is he connected to Lisa Troutman?"

"Yes," I said. "She worked with him in Afghanistan."

"Okay, I'll see what I can find out."

"Something's going to break soon, Professor," I said. "I can feel it."

◆　　◆　　◆　　◆

The Mountain Center High gym was packed. The Lady Bears were hosting a regional semifinal game. The competition was better, but not nearly good enough. Lacy and her teammates took a twenty-point lead into the locker room at halftime. I stretched my legs by leaving the stands and walking down to where Dick Traber leaned against the wall just beyond one of the glass backboards. We shook hands.

"Best girls team we've ever had," he said. "How far do you think they can go?"

"To the states, for sure," I said. "After that, who knows?"

"How is your investigation going?" Dick asked.

"At this point, we've exhausted all our possibilities," I said. "If we find out who did this, we're going to have to get lucky."

"Well, good luck then," he said.

The teams came out for second-half warmups, and I made my way back to where Mary, Billy, Maggie, T. Elbert, and Roy were waiting. I sat between Billy and Mary.

"Sooner or later, they're going to get tested," Billy said. He paused briefly. "But not tonight."

They won by thirty-one points with the starters on the bench in the fourth quarter.

38

Saturday morning, I was up before dawn. Mary and I had spent the night alone and made up for lost time. I put on jeans, a long-sleeved T-shirt, and running shoes. I made coffee, booted up my laptop, and checked scores from the other girls tournament games. Thirty-two teams were left. Besides Mountain Center, two other girls teams were undefeated. If they all kept winning, the Lady Bears would eventually have to play both of them.

I checked the ski reports for Utah's two Cottonwood Canyons. There was lots of snow, and every trail at all four resorts was open. Maybe I should trade my private investigator's license for a Ski Utah season pass. *Wishful thinking.*

I checked email. Buckley informed me that nothing was happening in Orlando. No one had made contact with Lisa Troutman. She was now employed by a local Target.

While I was doing all that, the darkness outside changed to soft daylight, to the point where I could see the lake. I checked the outdoor temperature—forty five, mild by February standards.

I decided to visit the lake. I brewed a second cup of coffee in an insulated cup, removed a black fleece from the hall closet and put it on, unlocked the back door, and slipped outside. I smelled it immediately: faint cigarette smoke drifting on the breeze. Then an internal alarm went off. I ducked to go back inside and felt something whiz past my head. I heard a thud as it hit the side of my house, inches away. I had no doubt that it was a bullet. My cup went bouncing away as I plunged back inside the house, closing the door behind me.

I picked up the small pair of binoculars I kept on the kitchen bar and hurried to the front hall, where I had left my Ruger .38. I grabbed it and my cell phone, slipped out the front door, and ran up my driveway, moving fast. At the top, I stopped to catch my breath and calculated what to do next. I knew these woods like the back of my hand. Based on where the bullet had come from, I was pretty sure I knew where the shooter was. I was guessing that, having missed his target, he was on the move.

I stopped and called Mary.

"Don?" she answered, confused.

"Listen up," I said. "There's a shooter in the woods. He just took a shot at me. Stay off the back deck. I'm on the move. Call Jimmy Durham and tell him to get his butt out here with some backup. No sirens." I told Mary where I suspected the shooter was parked. "Take my Pathfinder and go there and wait. Be careful. Don't take chances. Shoot to kill if you have to."

"You bet I will," Mary said. "Watch your ass."

She was gone. I put my cell on vibrate and was on the move again. I plotted a course that I figured would intersect with the shooter's path.

I moved quickly, stopping every now and then to listen. I was hoping I wouldn't get ambushed, but I knew I had the advantage of knowing the terrain. To get to the spot I thought the shooter had fired from required at least a mile and a half of hiking. Unless he was moving really fast, I would be waiting.

Ten minutes later, I saw a black SUV. It was below me, off the road in a stand of trees. I hoped it belonged to the shooter. I knelt behind a large hemlock next to a small evergreen and waited. I listened for any signs of movement. The woods were quiet. And then they weren't.

I heard crunching sounds—someone coming my way, making steady progress. I removed the binoculars from my fleece and stared in the direction of the sounds. The woods were shrouded in darkness and shadows. In the distance, moving in and out among the trees, I saw the silhouette of a large man moving toward me. I peered with the binoculars through a small break in the evergreen. As he came closer, I slipped the binoculars back into the pocket of my fleece. He stopped to listen. I knew I was impossible to see; most of my body was hidden, and the right side of my face would be invisible in the shadows of the evergreen.

He kept coming, the rifle in his right hand dangling at his side. The rifle had a scope.

When he was within thirty feet, I stepped out with the Ruger raised, letting the shooter hear the sound of the hammer being cocked. He looked surprised. Then I saw a look of resignation.

"Halt!" I said loudly, thinking he might automatically respond to a military command.

He stopped in his tracks and said nothing.

"Place the rifle on the ground," I said. "Don't do anything stupid."

He switched hands with the rifle and knelt slowly, a barely perceptible smirk on his lips. At that moment, I knew this was not going to end well. As he placed the rifle in front of him to his left, I watched as his right hand went behind his back. I said nothing. I was done talking, and he was done listening. His hand came out fast with a pistol in it, and without hesitation I shot him in the head. I was a nanosecond late; the message from his brain to his trigger finger had been received, and he got a shot off. The bullet sailed wide to my left, hissing off into the woods, seeking a resting place in some unknown tree.

As I walked over to him to have a closer look, I heard car doors slam below me. I saw Mary get out of my Pathfinder and Jimmy Durham emerge from his cruiser. A county sheriff's squad car was pulling up behind Jimmy.

"Don!" Mary shouted.

"Up here!" I hollered.

I rolled the shooter over for a closer look. His head was a mess. He was probably six-three, two twenty, with close-cropped blond hair and blue eyes that seemed to look at me with total surprise. I opened his coat to see if he was wearing a Kevlar vest. He wasn't. I looked for ID; he had none.

I heard Mary and Jimmy Durham coming noisily through the woods and up the hill. As they did, I took out my cell phone and dialed David Steele's private number. He answered on the second ring.

"Talk to me, Youngblood," he said. "This has to be important or you wouldn't call on a Saturday."

"A sniper took a shot at me at the lake house about twenty minutes ago," I said. "I tried to take him prisoner, but he wasn't interested. He's dead. I'm at the scene. I'm almost certain this is the work of the Midnight Riders. I can't think of anyone else it might be. I thought you might want to send someone."

"Stay there and don't let anyone mess with the scene," he said. "Keep your cell phone on. We'll track your location."

Mary arrived ahead of Jimmy. She looked at the dead shooter, then at me.

"You okay?"

"Just dandy," I said. "I really wanted to talk to him, but he pulled on me, and I had no choice."

Jimmy arrived. Jimmy "Bull" Durham was a longtime friend and former high-school basketball adversary. We had collaborated on more than one case. He was usually calm and level headed. Today was no exception.

"You okay, Blood?" he drawled.

"Other than having just killed a guy, I'm fine, Bull," I said. "The FBI is on the way, so why don't you let this be their headache?"

"Works for me," Jimmy said. "We'll hang around until they get here."

◆　　◆　　◆　　◆

The FBI arrived in less than an hour. A gray Taurus parked behind the squad car, and two men in dark suits got out. One of the deputies pointed up the hill, and the two men made their way toward us. The lead man was older and, I suspected, senior. He glanced at the body and walked over to me.

"Youngblood?"

I nodded.

"Bannister," he said, extending his hand.

Introductions were made all around.

"We'll take it from here, sheriff," Bannister said. "No paperwork on this one, okay? This never happened."

Jimmy nodded and looked at me. "Let's have breakfast sometime soon, Blood," he said. It was his way of saying he wanted to know what was going on.

"I'll call you, Bull," I said.

Jimmy went back down the hill toward the road.

"You can go," Bannister said, turning to Mary.

"She stays," I said. "This is my wife, Mary. She's also a police detective, and a damn good one."

He thought about that, then nodded, turned, and walked to the body. He studied the scene for a few seconds.

"That's an M24 sniper rifle," he said. "Military issue."

I said nothing.

"Walk me through it," Bannister said.

I did. He listened without interruption. Below us, I heard the sheriff's cars driving away.

"A head shot is pretty risky," he said.

"I thought he might be wearing a vest," I said. "I was going to get only one shot."

"Damn good shooting," he said.

I made no comment.

"I've got some more guys on the way," he said. "They'll clean this up. You don't have to hang around unless you want to."

I had seen the work of a government cleanup crew on one of my previous cases. I had no doubt that, when they were gone, there would be no trace of what had happened.

"I'm starved," I said to Mary. "Let's get some breakfast."

That's cold, Youngblood, I thought. *You just killed a guy, and all you can think about is your stomach?*

Mary nodded.

We crunched down toward the road, leaving the two agents alone in the woods.

◆   ◆   ◆   ◆

We sat at my favorite table overlooking the eighteenth green at the Mountain Center Country Club. The golf course would not open for at least another month. The scruffy grass on the green looked as tired as I felt.

The country club had Saturday and Sunday morning buffets that were well stocked with a wide variety of delicious breakfast fare. Our waitress brought coffee. Mary and I had said little since leaving the scene of my latest killing. I was trying to sort out my feelings. Part of me was glad the shooter had pulled on me. He had tried to assassinate me from a distance, and I was more than a little shaken. I had killed him with angry intent, but he had given me no choice. I was amped and agitated. I needed to calm down.

"Not your fault," Mary said. "I would have killed him myself if you hadn't. He tried to kill you. That makes me mad as hell." She seemed as strung out as I was.

I smiled at her and said, "I love you."

"I love you, too." She smiled widely and placed her hand on mine. We stared at each other. "And thanks for that nice compliment to the FBI geek."

"Just telling the truth, ma'am."

I relaxed a little. The tension was starting to drain.

We took a long time eating. We went to the buffet, got a few samples, returned to our table, and ate slowly. We repeated the process a couple of times. Our waitress was prompt with hot coffee. I was surprised the food and coffee tasted so good. Maybe my nearly being killed had heightened my senses.

As we walked to the parking lot, Mary said, "You've got to find these bastards before they make another run at you."

"You got that right," I said.

◆   ◆   ◆   ◆

That night, we made love—a hungry, urgent coupling. When we had given all we had, Mary lay naked in my arms.

"I could have lost you today," she said. "That scares the hell out of me."

"I know," I said.

"Maybe it's time we both retired."

"Maybe it is," I said. "But I've got to put an end to this Midnight Riders thing first."

"I know," Mary said, snuggling closer. Within minutes, she was asleep.

For me, sleep would not come easily. I lay wide awake, thinking I could be dead. It frightened me. I'd be a fool not to be frightened. The sixty-four-thousand-dollar question was, if this was the work of the Midnight Riders, how did they know I was working the case, and why did they target me?

I went downstairs to the kitchen and poured myself a large glass of milk. I took it up the short flight of stairs, turned left, went down the hall, and made a right into a small room where I had set up an office I rarely used. I removed a legal pad and a number-two pencil from the top right drawer of the roll-top desk. At the top of the pad, I wrote, "Possible Leaks." I began making a list, taking into consideration all the people who knew about the Midnight Riders or the missing children connected to the case. Somebody had tipped somebody. I ruled out the obvious. My list looked like this:

Someone in the Provo PD
Someone in the FBI
Someone at the Pentagon
Lisa Troutman
Someone on the Tohono O'Odham IR

I studied the list and drank my milk. I crossed out the Provo PD. That was too big a stretch. Less of a stretch was a mole in the FBI or at the Pentagon. I thought the Pentagon was more of a possibility than the FBI. The last two were also possibilities, but it had been a month since I was on the Tohono O'Odham Reservation. The timing didn't fit. However, the timing for Lisa Troutman fit perfectly. It might have taken her a day or more to get the word back to the Midnight Riders and then some time to get the shooter to Mountain Center and scout his position. The shooter also had to find out that I was at the lake house on weekends. The hole in that theory was that Lisa Troutman didn't know my name. Scott had never introduced me. That led me back to the Pentagon. Assuming the Midnight Riders were ex-military, they very well could have a source at the Pentagon. When Colonel Culpepper went snooping, he could have raised a red flag. I didn't want to jam up the colonel, so I'd have to find a way around that if I was going to find the leak.

"What are you doing?" Mary asked, startling me as she came sleepily into my pseudo office. Disappointed and thankful at the same time,

I noticed she was no longer nude. She was wearing the Miss Piggy's nightshirt.

"Unless someone from my distant past has a grudge to settle, the Midnight Riders are responsible for this attempt on my life. I'm just trying to figure out how they found out about me."

Mary looked over my shoulder at the list. "Lisa Troutman," she said. "The timing's right."

"My thinking exactly," I said as I swiveled my chair to face her. "There's only one problem with that."

"What?"

"Scott never introduced me when we went to question her. As far as I know, she has no idea who I am."

Mary said nothing for a moment. "You need to get down to Orlando and squeeze Lisa Troutman and find out what the hell is going on. And the sooner, the better."

"I'll go tomorrow," I said.

I finished my milk, cut off my desk light, and spun my chair back to face Mary. She put her hands on my shoulders, bent forward, and kissed me on the lips. I couldn't help myself; I cupped my hands around her breasts and fondled her.

She smiled. "Come back to bed."

"Love to," I said.

39

The following morning, Jim Doak flew me to Orlando. It was time to have another chat with Lisa Troutman. While I was in the air, I called David Steele.

"What kind of authority do I have to cut a deal with Lisa Troutman?" I asked.

"Whatever it takes, unless she set one of the bombs," he said. "I'm willing to let her skate if she wasn't directly involved. She has to convince you of that, and she has to have some good information."

"Okay," I said. "Any promises I make, you have to back."

"Not to worry," he said. "I trust your judgment."

I then called Bradley Culpepper on his private home number.

"Donald Youngblood, colonel," I said. "Sorry to bother you at home on a Sunday. The case I'm working on is really heating up. I wondered if you found out anything more on Colonel Hayes."

"I did some digging Friday afternoon," he said. "The guy's a ghost. I couldn't find a damn thing more on him. It's like someone got into our system and erased his file."

"Well, thanks for trying," I said. "If you do find out anything more, you have my number."

"Take care, Youngblood," he said. "And call me when this is over."

◆　　◆　　◆　　◆

We landed in Orlando, and I rented a Navigator. I set up Hilda, my annoying GPS. As I was leaving the airport, I called Buckley.

"Where is she?"

"She just went into a Cracker Barrel on Semoran Boulevard at Butler National Drive," Buckley said.

I programmed the address into Hilda and followed her instructions to the letter, since I had no idea where I was going. I was there in five minutes. I walked through the front door to the seating station.

"One?" the hostess asked.

"I'm looking for someone," I said. I described Lisa Troutman.

"She's all the way over in the third section in the front corner," the hostess said.

I walked through sections one and two, then spotted Lisa at a table for two by the window. She was drinking coffee and working on her laptop. Her back was to me. Unless she looked over her left shoulder, she couldn't see me approaching her. I walked past her, pulled out a chair, and sat down opposite her.

"Hi, Lisa," I said. *Youngblood, the friendly PI.*

Her face was a mixture of surprise and confusion. She was trying to remember where she had seen me. Then she did.

"FBI," she said.

"Kind of."

"How did you find me?"

"Doesn't matter," I said.

"Matters to me," she said.

"Tracking device on your SUV," I said. "We got a print off the door handle. We ran it through a military database, found out who you are."

She nodded.

The waitress came by. "Coffee?" she asked me.

"Sure."

"Are you-all ready to order?"

"Later," I said.

She turned without another word and walked away.

"Could I see some ID?" Lisa Troutman asked.

I showed her my FBI consultant's ID.

"Donald Youngblood," she said.

I nodded. If she recognized my name, she didn't show it.

"Consultant?" she asked.

"In charge of this case," I said.

"What case?"

"The FBI calls it the Midnight Riders case," I said.

She went a little pale but said nothing.

"I know you were part of them," I continued. "I want to know as much as you can tell me about the Midnight Riders."

"Never heard of them," she said.

The waitress came back with my coffee and refilled Lisa's mug.

"Lisa," I said, the concerned big brother, "you need to talk to me. If you don't, the FBI will turn you over to Homeland Security, and they'll lock you up for twenty years."

She went a little paler. Homeland Security evoked fear like the Gestapo. Their authority was wide and undefined, and they took full advantage of it.

"And if I tell you everything I know?"

"As long as you don't lie to me, and as long as it's worth something, you can continue with your new life. But let's get one thing clear. If you try to warn them we're coming, I'll see that you're locked up for life."

She smiled and made a soft noise, as if chuckling to herself. "You don't understand," she said. "I don't care if you take them down. I hope you do. There are some good people who are caught in a sadistic trap. The leader is totally off the rails. If you go in at night and catch them off guard, you can minimize the damage."

Spoken like a true soldier, I thought.

"So why didn't you come to us, rather than run?"

"Because I wasn't sure I could cut a deal," she said.

"Okay," I said. "I'll buy that."

We stared at each other a few moments. Lisa looked tense. She took a drink of coffee.

"How will you know if I'm lying?"

"I'll know," I said. "We know more than you think we do."

"For instance?"

"For instance, we know about a youth camp that mysteriously vanished about ten years ago," I said.

"A youth camp?" She looked genuinely surprised.

I nodded.

"Then you know more than I do," she said.

"Probably not."

She said nothing. I needed to nudge her a little, so I took a chance.

"I know about Colonel Hayes," I said.

She started to say something, then let out a deep breath and looked out the window. I had played one of my trump cards. She was silent for a while, and I let her be that way.

"Are you going to record me?"

"Have to," I said.

She nodded. "Here?"

"No. FBI headquarters in Orlando."

She nodded again. "When?"

"After breakfast," I said. "I'm buying."

She smiled and seemed to relax, like a person who had made a decision and was relieved.

"Why not?" she said. "A girl's got to eat."

40

The Orlando FBI office was actually in Maitland, a northern suburb. The building was a modern concrete and glass structure four floors tall. I sat at a desk in a vacant office kept for visitors. Lisa Troutman sat across from me. A tape recorder was between us on a nearly empty desk. I pushed the button and nodded at Lisa.

"The first thing I have to tell you is that Jeffery sent out a sniper to kill someone giving us a problem," Lisa said.

"How do you know that?"

"I have to check in from time to time," she said. "I'm close friends with the woman I check in with. Our resident sniper went missing the day before you showed up with Agent Glass."

"You sure it was the day before?"

"Positive," she said. "I phoned her right after you two left, and she said he had left the camp the day before."

I made a mental note. If she was telling the truth, then Lisa wasn't the source who had given my name to the Midnight Riders. I would have to give that some more thought.

"Did you ever hear my name mentioned?" I asked.

"No, why?"

"Your resident sniper came for me."

"And you're still alive?" She looked incredulous.

"And he's dead," I said. "I had to kill him."

"Then you're either very good or very lucky," she said.

"Very lucky, for sure."

"And probably very good, I'm guessing."

"Good enough," I said, though I wasn't feeling as confident as I was acting.

She said nothing.

"Tell me more," I said. "So far, I think you're telling me the truth."

She nodded and continued. She had joined the military with the intention of making it a career but had slowly become disenchanted. She met Colonel Hayes in Afghanistan, and they became lovers. Hayes, she said, was ultraconservative and was fanatically concerned that our country was "going to hell in a handbasket." He vowed to send a wakeup call. He formed the Midnight Riders before she finished her final tour. He was well funded, but she didn't know by whom.

She had joined "the Riders," as she called them, more to be with Hayes than to be a "patriot" with a cause. She described Hayes as good looking, charismatic, and secretive. Hayes built his private army by brainwashing troubled kids to join the cause.

"He wanted them young and needy," she said. "In a year, they thought he was God. He fed them and clothed them and made them feel important. They'd do anything for him."

"So you used older boys to pick out the most likely candidates," I said.

"Yes, and then started planting seeds," she said. "When the younger boy was ready to take off, we'd leave. If an older boy brought back a candidate, he was promoted."

"What was the success rate?"

"I'm not sure," she said. "Not 100 percent. Every now and then, Jeffery would mention a failed mission, but not often."

"How many times did you personally do this?"

"This was only my second time in ten years," she said. "Jeffery wanted to avoid anyone being identified twice as a mother. We hit different states and focused on schools in districts with low-income families. Those kids are more likely to want to start a new life."

"What about their education?"

"Homeschooled at our camp," she said. "They were motivated and did well. They were always far ahead of their public-school classmates. The camp is run like a military school."

"Where is the camp?"

"I don't know," she said. "Anytime anyone goes in or out, they're blindfolded and flown by helicopter or private jet. There was a helicopter pad and a private airfield for small jets. Everything came in after dark. The helicopters delivering supplies came from small airports, I guess. The jets would fly in from major airports. Sometimes, they would fly all the way to camp. Other times, they would land at small airports and fly in by helicopter. When we flew, none of us ever knew where we were, and we didn't care. Not knowing was for our own protection. All I can tell you is that the camp is remote—probably in a northern state because it's cold in the winter. It might even be in Canada."

"How often did jets and helicopters come in?" I asked.

"Jets, not very often," she said. "Mostly with new arrivals. Helicopters came in once or twice a week with supplies."

"Was there a road?"

"Not much of one," Lisa said. "Good enough for a Humvee and not much else."

"Describe the camp," I said.

"It was a long, flat building, three floors," she said. "But two of the floors were underground, so it looked like a one-story building. The roof was camouflaged, so it was impossible to see from the air. There was a small, enclosed observation deck on the roof that allowed a 360-degree view. The top floor, the one above ground, was called 'the first floor.' The next floor down was 'the basement,' and the bottom floor was 'the lower basement.'"

"How big?"

"Big," she said. "Maybe two football fields long and another football field wide."

"Football fields?"

She shrugged. "I'm a fan."

I smiled. It was hard not to like a woman who was a football fan.

"Did you have access to all the floors?"

"No," she said. "The lower basement was off limits. Most of us thought it was for weapons storage."

"So there must have been elevators," I said.

"Yes, a few regular elevators and one really big elevator accessed from the outside."

"Did you ever see it in use?"

"No," she said.

"Were lookouts posted on the observation deck?" I asked.

"Twenty-four/seven."

"How was it accessed?"

"Stairs or elevator," she said.

"Any outside cameras?"

"Not that I know of."

"When helicopters came in with supplies, where did they land?" I asked.

"On the roof near the observation deck. They would unload and take the supplies down to the mess hall using the elevator. Then the helicopter would fly to a nearby hangar to be stored until the next trip. The hangar was big enough for a small jet and the helicopter. There was also a Humvee in the hangar. The hangar, like the main building, was well camouflaged."

"Did the copter radio in before its arrival to deliver supplies?"

"No," Lisa said. "Orders were to maintain radio silence unless there was an emergency."

"Was anyone notified once the copter was down?"

"No. Whoever was on duty just unloaded the supplies and took them to the mess hall."

"How many were involved in the unloading?"

"The pilot, the lookout, and one other adult assigned to make the trip to pick up the supplies."

"What time did the supply helicopter usually arrive?"

"Sometime after midnight," she said. "I know because I had to pull lookout duty from time to time. Every adult did."

"Did anyone ever see anything to report?"

"I never did," she said. "I heard we had to run off some hunters once."

"How many people would be awake after midnight?"

"Hard to tell. We had to be in quarters by ten o'clock, and we weren't supposed to leave until six the next morning. The top two floors had guards who patrolled, although I'm not sure why."

"Internal cameras?"

"No," she said.

I was quiet, trying to picture taking the place down and wondering what other questions I needed to ask.

"I'll need you to sketch a layout of the top floor and basement as best you can remember," I said.

She nodded. "I can do that."

"How many people were in the camp?"

"I don't know. We were responsible for our own meals. We had a schedule to follow and not much free time. All of us were never together at the same time. We were compartmentalized, so as not to know too much."

"What about the children?"

"Each child was assigned an adult," Lisa Troutman said. "Sort of a substitute parent. They stayed together until the child was sixteen. Then they were considered adults."

"Any girls?"

"No," she said.

"Did you ever meet a kid named Michael Brand?"

"I don't know," she said. "New arrivals were given numbers. Then, when they earned it, the kids received new names—one-word names, sometimes an animal name, sometimes something else."

"What name was given to the kid killed in Texas?" I asked.

"Oh, that was Falcon," she said. "Nice kid, not cut out for the Riders."

"What did they call you?"

She smiled. "Trout."

The door opened, and Buckley came in with bottles of water and set them on the desk. I stopped the tape recorder.

"Thought you might be thirsty," he said.

"Thank you," Lisa said, immediately opening a bottle and taking a drink. She downed about half of it.

I opened my bottle and took a couple of swallows. "Thank you, Agent Clarke," I said.

"You are welcome, sir," Buckley said.

He nodded and exited the room. I waited until Lisa screwed the top back on her bottle, then started the recorder again.

"Did you ever get to go outside?"

"Yes," she said. "Everyone had a two-hour window for recreation. Not the same two hours—it was staggered so we weren't all recreating at the same time. We had an indoor basketball court and a racquetball court. We had a couple of ping-pong tables and three pool tables. We had a large gym. Strength and conditioning sessions were mandatory. There were miles of hiking trails through beautiful country."

"Snow in the winter?"

"Lots of snow," she said.

"So what's the point? Why go to all this trouble to blow up a few buildings?"

"I used to ask the same question," she said. "Jeffery said it was something big. He would never tell me what, but he said it was big and it would happen soon."

"Any idea what?"

"None."

"Where did Colonel Hayes get the money to fund this operation?"

"I don't know," she said. "He wouldn't talk about it. He only said money was not a problem."

I was getting tired of asking questions. It was time to let Buckley have a crack at her. I was curious about one thing, though.

"If you and Hayes were lovers, you must have cared for him," I said.

"I did, once," she said, eyes lowered, staring at the table.

"So why give him up now?"

She looked at me with a mean little smile. "Someone else is in his bed now," she said.

Hell hath no fury like a woman scorned, I thought.

◆　　◆　　◆　　◆

Early that evening, I had dinner with Buckley. We got a corner booth in a Bonefish Grill near the airport. We ordered draft beer and the Bang Bang Shrimp appetizer—crispy shrimp in a spicy cream sauce. We were halfway through our first beers when the shrimp arrived.

"Before we discuss the case," I said, "I need to ask you not to mention the shooting to Gretchen."

Buckley smiled. "I never discuss cases outside the office with anyone not involved, even other agents."

I nodded. "Find out anything else worth knowing after I left?"

"Maybe," Buckley said. "Time will tell. Lisa identified some of the players from a list we compiled of probable members of the Midnight

Riders. One was the guy you killed yesterday. He was a sniper in Afghanistan, last name Adams. Those guys are good. You were lucky."

"Maybe," I said. "Or maybe it was supposed to be a warning. Killing me would have only brought more heat."

"How close did he come?"

"Close enough," I said. "I really wanted to interrogate him, but he was not about to be taken alive. I don't think he expected to be confronted."

We were doing major damage to the shrimp, which were just spicy enough to make the beer go faster. We ordered another round of beer.

"Something else is going on here that I can't quite put my finger on," I said.

"Which is?"

"I'm not sure. The unanswered question is, who would fund this operation? Who profits from chaos? Blowing up a single government building here and there is like guerrilla warfare. Who does that sound like?"

"An extremist group?"

"Exactly," I said. "I'm not buying this Midnight Riders manifesto. I think that's a cover for something else."

"You think they're funded from overseas," Buckley said.

"Makes sense. Either Colonel Hayes is doing the bidding of an extremist group or he's using them to promote his own agenda."

"This is getting complicated," Buckley said.

"It sure is."

"So what's next?"

"We need to find that camp and shut it down," I said.

"That's not going to be easy, based on what Lisa Troutman told you. The camp sounds pretty well hidden."

"We need to put some feelers out about private helicopters in Minnesota, North Dakota, Montana, and Idaho, for starters. Have the local offices start snooping around at private airfields for helicopters that go out at night."

"That's a needle in a haystack," Buckley said.

I was left to mull that thought when the waitress showed up to take our order. I ordered the Chilean sea bass and Buckley the fried shrimp.

I had another thought. "How about we check land purchases since 2000 for large tracts in the middle of nowhere?"

"That idea," Buckley said, "I like."

◆   ◆   ◆   ◆

That night at the lake house, I sat at the kitchen island with Mary enjoying a bottle of full-bodied burgundy from France. I was beat, and it showed. But I was also wired and needed to come down.

"Long day," Mary said.

"Very."

"Tell me about it."

I told her in great detail. She listened silently, peering at me over the top of her wineglass. As always, her wine was disappearing faster than mine.

"You believe her?" Mary asked.

"I think so. She volunteered the sniper information. She didn't have to do that."

"What do you think the big thing is that's going down?"

"I have no idea," I said. "But it scares me. If it involves a small army, people are probably going to die. We need to find that campsite soon and neutralize it."

41

Monday morning, I was in the office early when I got the call.

"Clay's awake," Robert Carr said.

"That's great news."

"Praise God," Robert said. "Our prayers were answered."

"Do me a favor," I said.

"Anything."

"Keep this quiet. For a couple of days, don't tell anyone who doesn't need to know, especially the press."

"Okay."

"I'm on my way," I said.

I hung up and called Mary.

◆　　◆　　◆　　◆

I was all too familiar with the Mountain Center Medical Center. It was a little over five years old, and I had spent two overnights there and had been to the emergency room twice, once for Mary.

Mary met me at the main entrance, and we went to the information desk.

"Is Clay Carr still on the third floor?" Mary asked.

"Visiting hours start at ten o'clock," the receptionist said. She was an older woman and appeared to be all business.

Mary flashed her badge. "I need to know now, please," Mary said.

"Certainly." The receptionist pecked her keyboard. "Room 312," she said.

◆　　◆　　◆　　◆

Clay's parents were with him. We stopped in the hall, and I made eye contact with Robert Carr. He walked out of the room to meet us.

"Clay seems pretty groggy," Robert said. "He doesn't remember the accident. He doesn't remember the first time he woke up. He doesn't know about Julie or being drugged. The doctor thinks you should wait a day before you talk with him. He should be more clear headed tomorrow."

I looked at Mary.

"We've waited this long," she said. "I don't think another day will make any difference."

"We appreciate it," Robert Carr said.

We left. Mary went back to work, and I went for breakfast.

◆　　◆　　◆　　◆

I settled in at my reserved table in the back and called Big Bob.

"I'm at the diner," I said. "Join me for breakfast."

"I'm too busy," the big man growled.

"I don't give a damn how busy you are," I snapped. "Give me a half-hour."

"You okay?"

"Yes and no," I said.

"I'm on my way," he said.

Ten minutes later, Big Bob slipped in the back door. He sat down quietly, tossing his cowboy hat on an empty chair.

"Clay Carr woke up," I said.

"That's good news," he said. "But you could have told me over the phone."

At that point, Doris interrupted us with mugs of hot coffee and took our orders. Then she hustled away, leaving us alone.

"What else?"

"I killed someone Saturday morning," I said.

"What?" His face showed disbelief.

I nodded and said nothing.

"Why didn't I hear about it before now?"

"The FBI put a lid on it," I said.

"Tell me about it."

As I told him, I could see his agitation. When I finished, he let it out in a controlled but animated anger.

"You need to quit this shit, Blood," Big Bob said. "You've got all the money you could ever need, a gorgeous wife, and a lot of good years ahead of you. Send Lacy off to college and take Mary and travel and have some fun."

Leave it to Big Bob to put things in perspective.

"I'm thinking about it," I said.

"Well, think harder."

Our food arrived, and we ate in silence. *I've killed four people since I've become a private investigator,* I thought. *I really should get out of this business.*

Big Bob seemed to read my mind, as good friends do from time to time. "Don't worry about it," he said, softening. "You're on the front line facing some really bad guys. They all had it coming. Better them than you."

"Well, at least we can agree on that," I said.

◆　　◆　　◆　　◆

When I got back to the office, Gretchen was on the phone at her desk.

"One moment, please," she said. "He just walked in." She punched the hold button. "Associate deputy director of the FBI on line one," she said, as smugly professional as she could possibly be.

"I'll bet you've waited a week to say that," I said.

Gretchen smiled. "Two, actually."

I walked into my office, shut the door, took a seat at my desk, and picked up my phone.

"Dave," I said.

"One moment, please," a female voice said.

"Youngblood?" David Steele said after a moment. The old drill instructor just couldn't get away from last names.

"I'm here," I said.

"How are you?"

"Thinking more and more about the future," I said.

"I know what you mean. That was a close call. We could have lost you."

"The more I think about it, the more I think it was a warning," I said. "The showdown in the woods wasn't supposed to happen. He planned on getting away clean."

"Too bad you killed him."

"He didn't give me any other choice," I said.

"He thought you'd hesitate and he could take you out. Too bad for him he hadn't read your file."

"I don't think that would have made a difference," I said. "He wasn't about to be taken alive."

"What's next?"

"I've got Buckley working on a few things we learned from the Lisa Troutman interview," I said. "I can feel us getting closer. I think their camp is somewhere near the Canadian border."

"The sooner we find it, the better," David Steele said. "And watch your six."

"I will," I said. "And Dave, see if any of those hairs I found in the desert is a DNA match to Adams."

◆   ◆   ◆   ◆

That night, Mary and I met Billy and Maggie in Morristown for the girls basketball regional championship game. The Lady Bears were playing a local team. For a while, it looked like it might be a game. Mountain Center led by five points at the end of the first quarter, then stretched it to fourteen by halftime. The Lady Bears ran away with it in the second half, leading 58–33 by the end of the third quarter. The starters sat in the fourth quarter, and the backups ran wild. The final score was 85–40.

After the game, we had a late dinner at the Millstone at 74 Main Bistro, an upscale local restaurant recommended by Jessica Crane, a former client. I had called Mrs. Crane that afternoon for a recommendation and to see how she was doing after the death of her husband. She seemed okay.

We had a corner booth. Most of the dinner crowd was long gone, and the place was quiet. We engaged in small talk as we ordered and ate at a leisurely pace.

Then Mary said casually to Billy, "Don had some excitement Saturday."

Billy looked at me. I said nothing. He looked back at Mary.

"An ex-army sniper tried to kill him," Mary said. I could tell she was still upset.

"That's terrible," Maggie said.

"And failed," I said.

"Tell me all of it," Billy said.

Mary told it from her perspective. Billy listened without showing any emotion, as if he were hearing a weather report. But I knew he was seething inside. When Mary finished, Billy looked at me.

"I want to hear your version."

So I told him all of it from my perspective.

"My God," Maggie said, looking at Mary.

Mary said nothing.

"When you take these guys down," Billy said, "I want to be in on it."

"I second that idea," Mary said.

"I'll see what I can do," I said to Billy. "I'd be more than happy having you watch my back."

42

When I arrived at the office the next morning, I had a voice mail from Robert Carr that Clay was ready to talk. Clay knew about Julie, Robert Carr said, and his memory was quickly improving. I called Mary and told her.

"Go by yourself," she said. "You're a local hero among our high-school boys. You can probably pull more out of him than I could. Call me later and fill me in."

◆　　◆　　◆　　◆

Clay Carr's mother greeted me politely when I arrived, then turned to address Clay. "Clay, this is Mr. Youngblood. He wants to ask you a few questions, okay?"

"Sure," Clay said.

"I'm going to the cafeteria to get some breakfast," she said on her way out.

I was alone with Clay. I sat in a chair beside his bed.

"You're Lacy's father, right?" Clay asked. "The private investigator."

"I am."

"She's a really good basketball player," he said.

"She is pretty good," I said.

"I like watching her play. She's always under control. She never gets excited."

"Kind of like you on the football field," I said.

"Yeah," Clay smiled. "I guess so."

I waited to see if he would continue. He didn't.

"How do you feel?" I asked. No need to charge right in.

"Not bad. The doctor said everything is healing fine."

"How did you sleep last night?"

187

"I didn't sleep much," he said. "I was afraid that if I went to sleep I wouldn't wake up."

"I can imagine," I said. "When are they going to release you?"

"Day after tomorrow, as long as everything looks good."

"Have you been up?"

"I walked around a little early this morning, but I was pretty dizzy," he said.

I was running out of small talk. "Do you remember the night of the accident?" I asked.

"Not one thing," he said. "Isn't that weird?"

"Maybe not," I said. "I'm not a doctor, so I can't say. What's the last thing you remember?"

"I'm not sure. I remember Julie. I remember my last football game. I remember some basketball games I went to. I remember lots of bits and pieces, but I don't know how they fit or what time frame they fit in."

I said nothing.

"My parents told me you were investigating the accident," he continued. "Have you learned anything?"

"I know it wasn't your fault," I said.

"How do you know that?"

"You were drugged with Zolpidem, a sleep medication commonly known as Ambien."

"What?" Clay Carr sat up straighter in bed. "How?"

"I guess someone slipped it into whatever you were drinking," I said. "Did you and Julie usually share drinks?"

"All the time," Clay said. "Diet Coke. It was our thing."

"Both of you had the drug in your system. Julie more than you."

"That makes sense." Clay smiled. "Julie was always hogging our drinks. It was a joke between us. God, I can't believe she's gone." He swallowed hard and fought back tears.

"Not your fault," I said slowly.

He nodded, and I saw his face change.

"Well, whoever's fault it is, I hope you frag his ass," he said angrily.

"Whoever is was, and it was probably a she and not a he, probably didn't mean for anyone to get hurt," I said. "And I'm sure they didn't mean to get Julie killed. They couldn't have known that would happen. It was probably a prank that went wrong."

"It doesn't matter," Clay said. "Julie's dead, and I want whoever did it found and made to pay."

"Tell me about Julie," I said, hoping to calm him.

"She was my best female friend. We knew each other since grade school. She was cute and sweet. She didn't have a mean bone in her body. We dated off and on all through high school as friends. This year, we decided to go steady, but we didn't make a big announcement or anything. I was comfortable around her. I think we were headed for a long-term relationship. Now, that's gone."

I could have said, *I know how you feel*. I could have said, *there will be other girls*. I could have said, *you're young and you'll get over it*. I could have said, *you have your whole life ahead of you*. But at that point, I didn't think anything I said would make a difference. So I said nothing.

Clay was fighting back tears. A few escaped, and he wiped them away. "Sorry," he said.

"Don't be. I lost my parents when I was in college, and I cried plenty."

He nodded, took a deep breath, and was quiet. I wanted to leave, but I didn't want him to think I was bailing on him. I waited. Clay's mother came back.

"Did I give you-all enough time?" she asked.

"You did." I stood and looked at Clay. "Call me if you think of anything I should know," I said. "Your father has my number."

◆   ◆   ◆   ◆

When I got back to the office, I called Mary on her cell phone and filled her in on my conversation with Clay Carr. "He's pissed," I said.

"I don't blame him," Mary said. "We need to get him closure on this."

"We'll need a break. Whoever is responsible isn't going to come forward and confess."

"Probably not," Mary said. "Any thoughts?"

"One," I said.

"Let's hear it."

"Why don't we give the whole story to the *Mountain Center Press* and the local TV station? We can invite them to my office at the same time, give them the story, and answer questions. We can ask that anyone who knows anything helpful get in contact with us. It might shake something loose, and we've got nothing to lose."

"Not a bad idea," Mary said. "I like it. Some people might feel more inclined to talk to a private investigator than to the police."

"Especially women," I said.

"Careful, Cowboy."

43

The next morning, I was sitting on T. Elbert's front porch with Roy and T. Elbert drinking coffee and eating a toasted poppy seed bagel with cream cheese. Roy had visited a Dunkin' Donuts drive-through on his way to T. Elbert's. I had called Roy and told him to meet me there. I then called T. Elbert and told him we were coming. I made it sound as if there were no agenda. In truth, I wanted to tell them about the Saturday shooting.

The morning was cold, but T. Elbert's overhead heaters kept the porch at a reasonable temperature. We ate and drank and talked about nothing in particular. Then I dropped the bomb.

"Somebody tried to kill me Saturday," I said casually.

Nobody said anything. Roy looked at T. Elbert. T. Elbert looked at Roy. Then they both looked at me. They waited.

"Sniper," I said. "In the woods. Just missed me. Fifteen minutes later, I killed him."

They exchanged glances.

Then T. Elbert said the predictable: "Details, Donald. I want to hear the details."

Roy said nothing.

I told them all of it.

When I finished, Roy said, "Why didn't we hear about this on the news?"

"I'm guessing the FBI came and cleaned up the mess," T. Elbert said.

Roy looked at me. I nodded.

"Who else knows besides Mary, Jimmy Durham, and the feds?" T. Elbert asked.

"Other than those at the scene, you two, Big Bob, Billy, and Maggie," I said.

"Sarah Agnes?" Roy asked.

"Not yet," I said. "But I'll tell her eventually."

"How do you feel about it?" Roy asked.

"It was him or me," I said. "How am I supposed to feel?"

"Lucky to be alive," T. Elbert said.

I drank more coffee and said nothing.

◆　　◆　　◆　　◆

That afternoon, Peggy Ann Romeo and Gail Fields, a reporter I didn't know from the *Mountain Center Press*, sat across from me in my office. Mary sat beside my desk on one of the conference-table chairs, looking professional in a charcoal-gray pantsuit and light gray turtleneck. Peggy Ann was with the local television station and had exchanged favors with Mary from time to time. Her cameraman waited in the outer office.

When everyone was settled, Mary looked at me and nodded.

"Do you-all remember the Clay Carr accident?" I asked, knowing full well they did.

The body language of the two reporters changed immediately. They were on high alert. Both nodded.

"As you probably know, Clay has been in a coma. You may not know that yesterday he woke up." I had their full attention, as if I had just reported an Elvis sighting. "We invited you here today to give you the rest of the story. I have one condition that the TV station needs to agree to," I said, looking at Peggy Ann.

Peggy Ann smiled. "In the interest of fairness, you want us to wait until the eleven o'clock news."

I smiled back at her. Women were always reading my mind.

"Exactly," I said. "Are you okay with that?"

"Sure," Peggy Ann said.

"We appreciate it," Gail Fields said.

"I'd like to film this," Peggy Ann said.

"Not yet," I said. "First I tell you the story, and then we'll decide what to film."

"Can I record it?" Peggy Ann asked.

"As long as you don't use the recording on the air," I said.

Peggy Ann smiled again. "What are you afraid of?"

"Edited recordings have a way of changing the context," I said. "And if you quote us, it has to be word for word."

"Agreed," Peggy Ann said.

I looked at Gail.

"Agreed," she said.

I looked at Mary. "You start," I said.

Mary began with the night of the accident and finished with the initial conclusion that for some unknown reason Clay Carr had run off the road.

"Your turn," she said.

I picked up the story at the point where Lacy had asked me to investigate on behalf of the senior class. I continued with my visit to Proffit's Garage, the blood work results that proved both Clay and Julie were drugged, and my meeting with Big Bob Wilson to share what I had learned. I left out some things on purpose, such as the alcohol in Julie's system and Evan Smith's name. Mary and I had agreed there was no need to go there.

I looked at Mary and nodded.

"At that point, Chief Wilson thought it would be a good idea if Don and I worked together on the case," Mary said. She continued with our questioning of students who were at the party that night but was vague that we actually thought one of them did it. She didn't mention the drugstore subpoenas, which would point directly at the students.

She looked at me.

I picked it up again at the point when I interviewed Clay Carr, telling how he was very upset but didn't remember anything about the night of the accident. I concluded that we were at a dead end and would like anyone who knew anything to contact either Mary or me.

"I want both of you to emphasize that Clay Carr is completely innocent of any wrongdoing," I said. "The accident was not his fault."

They nodded simultaneously.

"Any questions?" I asked, knowing there would be. They were, after all, reporters.

"Do you think a high-school student drugged their drink?" Gail Fields asked.

"It is certainly a possibility," Mary said. "But so far, we have no evidence of that."

"So you're hoping that by going public with the story someone might know something helpful," Peggy Ann said.

"It's a long shot," I said. "But it's all we have."

"And we know about you and your long shots," Mary said, smiling at me.

◆　　◆　　◆　　◆

After Mary, Gail Fields, and Peggy Ann Romeo left, I called Robert Carr.

"You and your family should be sure to watch the eleven o'clock news tonight," I said. "There will be a story about Clay's being cleared of any wrongdoing in the death of Julie James. The story will also be in the *Mountain Center Press* tomorrow morning."

"That's great, Don," Robert said. "I cannot thank you enough."

◆   ◆   ◆   ◆

We stayed up for the news. We were propped up in bed watching the new sixty-inch TV on the opposite wall. There was a teaser at ten o'clock during a commercial break: "Star tailback wakes from coma."

Clay Carr was the lead story. Peggy Ann Romeo appeared on the screen with a picture of Clay in his football uniform as a backdrop. She stared earnestly at the camera and said, "On Monday morning, all-state Mountain Center running back Clay Carr came out of a coma he had been in since a car crash that killed his teenage girlfriend, Julie James. The crash, thought to be an accident, has since been investigated by private investigator Donald Youngblood. The senior class hired Youngblood soon after the accident to investigate, and after Youngblood discovered that both teenagers were drugged, the Mountain Center Police Department joined the investigation and classified the death of Julie James as manslaughter. The search continues for the person or persons responsible. Youngblood is working with his wife, Mountain Center police detective Mary Youngblood, in the ongoing investigation. The Youngbloods ask that you call either of them at the numbers listed below if you have any information regarding this case."

My office number and Mary's extension at the MCPD appeared at the bottom of the screen.

Peggy Ann continued, "Clay Carr has been absolved of any wrongdoing in the accident. Carr, who has a football scholarship to the University of Tennessee, is expected to make a full recovery. We will bring you more on this ongoing investigation as information is made available to us."

I turned off the TV as Peggy Ann Romeo switched to another story.

"We didn't get any face time," Mary said.

"Thank God."

"Speak for yourself, Cowboy."

"I don't want all those horny guys out in TV land to see what a babe I'm married to," I said.

"You're such a sweet-talker," Mary said, moving closer.

44

The next morning, my butt was dragging. One thing had led to another after the news, and by the time I drifted off to sleep it was past one in the morning. I was at my desk drinking coffee, my first cup, and thinking I'd like to take a nap. I dared the phone to ring, so it did.

"We might have something," Buckley said.

"I'm listening."

"There's a big parcel of land in North Dakota that sold in 2003. The owner is listed as Greenbelt Trust. They appear to be a holding company, with very little information available. The sale was handled by a fleet of lawyers and is considered highly confidential."

"On the surface, it sounds like a conservation group," I said. "But those guys like to get press by buying up large pieces of land that won't be subjected to the horrors of industry. So I'll bet you a steak dinner that when you peel back all the layers, you're going to find oil-company involvement."

"No bet," Buckley said. "I was thinking the same thing. There have been a lot of recent oil discoveries in the Dakotas. We did satellite imagining and didn't see any buildings. But those images are being analyzed by our experts, since Lisa Troutman said the building was well camouflaged. If we turn up anything, I'll let you know."

"How close is it to the Canadian border?" I asked.

"Not that close," Buckley said.

"So you think it's probably nothing," I said. "So why did you call?"

"Because Associate Deputy Director Steele wants you to be apprised of every little detail," Buckley said.

"Lucky me," I said.

◆   ◆   ◆   ◆

Things were quiet in midafternoon. I was surfing the market, looking for potential bargains. In my opinion, there were none. Solid stocks that paid a decent dividend were the way to go, and my clients and I owned enough of those, so I didn't do any buying.

I was trying to figure out what the next big thing would be when I heard the outer office door open and shut and someone ask Gretchen if he could see Mr. Youngblood.

Gretchen came through my open door and shut it behind her. "A kid out there claims he might have some information for you about Clay Carr. He said he read in the *Mountain Center Press* this morning that you're looking for information."

"Kid?"

"Early twenties," Gretchen said. "College boy, probably."

"Okay," I said. "Send him in."

Gretchen opened my door and said, "Put your jacket on the coatrack and come on in."

A few seconds later, a young man entered. He was a little shorter than I was and weighed at least twenty pounds less. He was clean cut and good looking, with dark hair and quick eyes. I noticed he wore an East Tennessee State University class ring, signifying he was an upperclassman.

He took a fast look around as he extended his hand. "Lonnie Lawson," he said.

"Don Youngblood," I said, shaking his hand. "Sit down, please."

I nodded at Gretchen, and she went back to her desk, shutting the door behind her. I looked at Lonnie and waited.

"I read the article in the *Mountain Center Press* this morning," he said.

"You have something for me?"

"Yes, sir. It's probably not much, but I figure every little piece of information could be helpful."

"You're right about that," I said. "What can you tell me?"

"I work at the 7-Eleven out on the highway," Lonnie said. "The one near the high school."

The minute the kid said 7-Eleven I knew that I had missed a clue. The devil is in the details T. Elbert had said. During my questioning of the Mountain Center High School boys one of them had said he saw Clay drinking out of a 7-Eleven cup.

"I know the one," I said. I knew what was coming.

"Anyway, the night of the accident, Clay Carr bought a large Diet Coke around eight o'clock," Lonnie said.

"How do you know it was Clay Carr?"

"I played high-school football and I'm kind of a football junkie, so I had been to some of the Mountain Center games," Lonnie said. "I've also seen his picture in the paper."

I waited for more. Lonnie said nothing.

"Anything else?"

"No, sir, not really," he said.

I could have said, *Thanks, see you later,* but I did what any self-respecting private detective would do—I started asking questions. You never know when someone knows something they don't even know they know.

"Was Clay alone?"

"Yes, sir."

"You didn't see his girlfriend?"

"No, sir," Lonnie said. "I guess she was waiting in the car."

I made a note on my pad. *Professionalism is all.*

"Were you busy that night?"

"Yes, sir," he said. "Friday nights are always busy after a ball game."

"Did Clay say anything?"

"I said, 'Congratulations on winning the state championship,' and he said, 'Thanks.' That was all."

I nodded and fiddled with my pen. "Does the 7-Eleven have a security camera?"

"Yes, sir," Lonnie said. "We're monitored by Safeway Security. We even have a hot button."

"Hot button?"

"Yes, sir. On the floor. If there's trouble, you step on the hot button and a signal goes to Safeway, and they call the police."

"Ever used it?"

Lonnie smiled. "Not yet."

"Do you know how long Safeway keeps security footage?"

"No, sir, I don't."

I had nothing else. "Okay, Lonnie," I said, standing. "Thanks for coming in."

We shook hands. He turned and opened my office door and disappeared into the outer office, closing my door behind him. For the next few minutes, I heard muted voices. Finally, the outer office door shut. A minute later, Gretchen was back in my office.

"Cute kid," she said. "Pre-law at ETSU, working his way through school."

"Thinking of robbing the cradle?"

"No way," Gretchen said. "I'm happy with my FBI guy."

"How's that going?"

"It's going."

I smiled back at her and said nothing.

"When I asked Lonnie why he didn't just call you rather that come in, you know what he said?"

"No clue," I said, although I had a pretty good idea.

"He said he wanted to meet the famous Donald Youngblood."

"Imagine that," I said.

"Don't let it go to your head," Gretchen said on her way back to her desk.

I sat and wondered how I had missed the 7-Eleven connection. Maybe I was being too hard on myself but it was a cold reminder to always pay attention to every little detail.

◆   ◆   ◆   ◆

Mary and I sat at the kitchen bar after dinner finishing our drinks. Biker and Lacy were down in the den watching a *Hunger Games* movie on Blu-ray. I had about half a pint glass left of my new discovery, Blue Point Toasted Lager, a Long Island brew. Mary was finishing a glass of Hands, a very good South African Chardonnay. She was listening to my account of my conversation with Lonnie Lawson that afternoon.

"Sounds like nothing," Mary said, finishing her glass.

"Maybe not."

"So?" Mary poured the rest of the bottle into her glass.

"So I'd still like to see the security footage from that night," I said.

"Why?"

"Better to see it than not to see it. I'm just trying to cover all the bases."

"So take a look," Mary said.

"Safeway Security might not be too forthcoming with the security footage for a private detective," I said.

"Not even for the famous Donald Youngblood?"

I shrugged. Mary smiled.

"You want my help?" she asked.

"I do."

45

Safeway Security had a third-floor office in a recently built professional building in North Mountain Center. The next morning, Mary and I walked into its office promptly at nine o'clock. We had just come from breakfast at Miss Piggy's. Mary had reluctantly declined the biscuits and gravy in favor of eggs Benedict. I threw caution to the wind and ordered scrambled eggs with hot sausage patties and for good measure tossed in a side order of biscuits and gravy. "You rat!" was Mary's response to my order. She tried not to look envious. But I was a gentleman and shared half a gravy-laden biscuit. Chivalry is not dead in the South.

"May I help you?" an attractive brunette at the front desk asked. I guessed she was about Mary's age.

"You may," Mary said pleasantly, flashing her shield. "We need to see whoever is in charge."

"May I ask what this is about?"

"You may not," Mary said less pleasantly.

"Very well," the brunette said icily. "May I have your name?"

"Mary Youngblood. Mountain Center police detective."

The brunette got up and disappeared through a door behind her, shutting it as she went.

"That was friendly," I said.

Mary stared hard at me and said nothing.

"Maybe we should guard the back door," I said. "They might make a run for it."

"Remember, you asked for my help, funny man," Mary said.

"Good point."

We waited in silence. A minute passed, then another. Finally, the door opened, and the brunette came back with a pleasant-looking blond man following. Probably mid-forties and maybe a few inches shorter than me, he was slightly overweight and soft looking, like he spent too much time behind a desk.

"Detective Mary Youngblood," the brunette said formally, "this is Warren Morris, the owner."

Mary and Warren shook hands. Then Mary introduced me, and Warren and I shook hands.

"Is there a problem?" Warren asked.

"No problem," Mary said. "We need your help with something. Can we talk in your office?"

"Sure," Warren said. "Follow me."

We followed Warren Morris past a row of cubicles occupied by young employees pecking away on laptop computers to the back of the building and straight into his office.

"Please have a seat," he said. "How can I help you?"

Mary looked at me and nodded.

"You monitor the 7-Eleven convenience store near the high school," I said.

"Yes, we do," Warren said. "And we monitor quite a few other businesses in Mountain Center and the county."

"How long do you keep security footage for the 7-Eleven?" I asked.

Warren tapped a few keys on the open laptop in front of him. He hit *Enter* and then appeared to do some scrolling.

"Three months," he said. "That's our minimum. We might have some footage older than that, depending on how fast we dump the files. The system we have in place downloads every twenty-four hours into a master file."

"Then you have the footage we want to see," I said. "Six weeks ago today, let's say from seven to nine in the evening."

Warren looked at Mary.

"It's part of a police investigation," Mary said. "I could get a subpoena, but I can't see any reason you wouldn't want to help us."

"None at all," Warren said, scribbling a note on a Safeway Security notepad. "We're always happy to cooperate with the police department. I'll have my wife take care of this today and attach the file to an email. She's the real techie in the family. Where do you want me to send it?"

I handed Warren Morris my card. He took a long look.

"I've heard about you," he said. "It's nice to finally meet."

I could have said, *Aw, shucks,* but instead I ignored the compliment and said, "It was nice meeting you, too."

As Warren escorted us back toward the front door, I asked, "Is the woman at the front desk your wife?"

"Yes, she is," he said proudly. "Twenty years this June."

I thought I saw Mary flinch.

We walked past the brunette at the desk. She was busy on her laptop and ignored us as we exited.

Halfway to the Pathfinder, Mary stopped.

"How did you know that woman was his wife?"

I started to say, *I'm a private investigator, and we know things,* but I figured that might get me slapped. Instead, I said, "She seemed a bit too protective, and she was about the right age, and I noticed a glance between them that could have been you and me."

"How did I miss that?"

"I think you were busy sizing up Warren."

◆   ◆   ◆   ◆

That night, Johnson City's Freedom Hall hosted a round-of-sixteen game in the Tennessee girls state basketball tournament. The Mountain Center Lady Bears were playing a team from Knoxville. I thought the Lady Bears would win easily, and so did Billy. We were wrong. Billy and Maggie were the only members of our inner circle to make the game. Roy was traveling, and T. Elbert was under the weather with flu-like symptoms.

The Lady Bears led 16–14 at the end of the first quarter and 30–26 at the half. Everyone's game seemed off, even Lacy's. They missed easy shots, missed free throws, and made turnovers. Early in the fourth quarter, the team from Knoxville tied the game at 50. But they could not get the lead, and the Lady Bears eventually pulled away and won 68–60. It was hard to watch. I fidgeted and yelled and talked to myself the entire game. Billy sat stoically, as if he were watching the sun come up.

"Damn lucky to win that one," I said to Billy after it was over.

"Finding a way to win when you're not playing your best is the mark of a good team," Billy said. "They will learn from this one."

"One can hope," I said, still annoyed. But I knew he was right.

"You worry too much, Blood," Billy said.

◆   ◆   ◆   ◆

Later than night, Mary and I shared a bottle of Bogle Phantom Red, a terrific full-bodied red from California, while we waited on Lacy to get home. She eventually came in, poured herself a Diet Coke, and sat with us.

"God, we stunk tonight," she said. "Myself included."

"That's okay," I said. "You're going to have a bad game every now and then. It's tournament time, and you won. Survive and advance."

Youngblood, the voice of reason. Billy would have been proud.

"You need to tell that to the coach," Lacy said. "She called an eight o'clock practice tomorrow morning. She was really pissed."

"Well, then," Mary said, "you better get to bed and get some rest."

"Good idea," Lacy said. "I'm beat. Good night, you two."

She took another gulp of Diet Coke, then slowly made her way up the stairs to her bedroom. Ten minutes later, the light showing underneath her door went dark.

Mary and I talked softly about nothing in particular and finished the red. Soon after we were in bed and sound asleep.

46

Early Monday morning, I found an email from Safeway Security with an attachment—a video of the footage I had requested. I downloaded the attachment and transferred it to a DVD. Then I deleted the email. I decided to watch the DVD later.

I was hungry, and the Mountain Center Diner was calling my name. It had been a week, and I was surprised Doris hadn't sent out a search party looking for me.

I locked the office, went down the back stairs, and turned left into the alley. It was still early, it was winter, and it was cold. The sun had yet to make an appearance. The streetlights were still on. A few illuminated the alley, but there were lots of shadows where bad guys could hide. I felt safer knowing I was armed. *You're paranoid, Youngblood*, I thought.

I reached the back door of the diner without incident and had a last-second thought that it could be locked. It wasn't. I walked through the storage room and out another door that was close to my table. Much to my surprise, my table was occupied.

"How was your trip?" I asked as I sat down.

"Uneventful," Roy said.

"Best kind."

I noticed Roy already had coffee.

"Well, hello, stranger," Doris said, setting a mug of hot coffee in front of me. "I haven't seen you in a while."

"It's only been a week," I said.

"Well, it seems longer," Doris said. "What can I get you-all?"

Doris took our orders and hurried away. I could see to the street from my back table. It didn't look like daylight was making much progress.

"Looks like it could snow," I said.

"I heard it might," Roy said.

I added cream and sugar to my coffee and took a drink.

"I saw the game score," Roy said. "Must have been pretty exciting."

"Not for me," I said. "I like blowouts."

"What's their schedule?"

"They leave later today for the state quarterfinals at Middle Tennessee State. They play tomorrow afternoon at four. If they win, they stay and play again on Thursday in the semifinals. The finals are on Friday."

"If they make the finals, I'll be there," Roy said. "I'll bring T. Elbert if he's able."

"I talked to him over the weekend. He said it was just a bad cold. He didn't sound good. I need to go by there."

Our food arrived, and we attacked it immediately. Occasionally, we exchanged small talk, but we were comfortable in our virtual silence. When we finished, Roy left a ten-dollar bill.

"What's the soup of the day?" I asked Doris as I was leaving.

"Chicken noodle," Doris said.

"Perfect. Save me a large container. T. Elbert's not feeling so great, and your chicken noodle soup should really perk him up."

Doris smiled at the compliment. "I'll send it over later," she said.

◆   ◆   ◆   ◆

That afternoon, I viewed the 7-Eleven security footage. I watched people come and go for an hour before I saw Clay Carr. Most of the customers looked like high-school kids. They bought sodas, candy, popcorn, and various kinds of chips—the junk-food generation. Clay appeared with a large drink, set it on the counter, and moved out of the frame. Someone stopped to pay for something, then someone else moved across the frame, and then Clay was back with a bag of chips. Given what Slinger had said about how particular Clay was with what he ate, I was betting the chips were for Julie. He paid, picked up his drink, and left. I watched for another half-hour and saw nothing of interest. *So much for that idea*, I thought.

◆   ◆   ◆   ◆

That night, Mary and I were in our usual spots at the kitchen bar after dinner discussing our day and finishing off a bottle of French Bordeaux. The condo was quiet. Lacy and the team were settled in for the night two hundred miles away, having just finished practice for their Elite Eight state tournament game. I knew that because we had just hung up with her after a short conversation. She was excited and in no mood for a long talk.

"I saw the footage from Safeway Security today."

"Anything there?" Mary asked.

"Nothing."

"I didn't think there would be," she said, drinking more wine.

"Worth a try."

"How's T. Elbert?"

"He has a bad cold," I said. "On my way home, I took him some chicken noodle soup from the diner. He was pleased but wouldn't let me in the house. Said he didn't want me to catch his cold. I told him if he wasn't better by Thursday, Roy was taking him to the doctor."

"What did he say to that?"

"He said, 'Like hell he will.'"

Mary laughed. "Well, he's not too sick to be ornery."

"True enough," I said.

47

The rest of the week would be filled with basketball.

We left Mountain Center on Tuesday at ten o'clock and took the shortest route to I-40 West. The day was clear and cold, perfect for driving. Since we were in no big hurry, I drove.

I had booked two top-floor two-bedroom suites and one one-bedroom suite at a newly opened Residence Inn close to Middle Tennessee State University.

Our two-bedroom suite was booked for four nights. Billy and Maggie would join us that day in time for the quarterfinal game.

The other two-bedroom suite was for Roy and T. Elbert. I was betting on T. Elbert's recovery, based on an earlier email that said he was feeling much better.

The one-bedroom suite was for Elizabeth Durbinfield, Lacy's maybe-or-maybe-not grandmother. Lacy had never known her father. Recent events had revealed the possibility that he was Elizabeth's son, John Cross Durbinfield, a renegade rich kid who had died violently in West Virginia. Only I knew the truth, revealed to me by a DNA test Wanda Jones had secretly run. The results, which I had not shared with anyone, were locked in my safe-deposit box in the bank below my office. Neither Lacy nor Elizabeth wanted a DNA test, each convinced they were grandmother and granddaughter, and each not wanting anything to change that. They had grown close since they first met. The plan was for Lacy to fly back to Long Island with Elizabeth, since spring break started the following week.

We checked in early. Fifteen minutes later, Billy and Maggie arrived. We went to lunch at nearby B. McNeel's Southern Kitchen, down-home Southern-style cooking at its best. After lunch, we drove to the MTSU campus, found parking, and made our way to the arena. We were early, and Lacy's game was the first of two, so we were able to get good seats. While Mary and Maggie talked a mile a minute, Billy and I sat in silence and watched the two teams warm up. Our focus was on the team from Memphis, whose girls were bigger than the Lady Bears. Time would tell whether they were quicker or not.

"What do you think?" I asked Billy.

"I think we win," Billy said.

I felt better. Billy was rarely wrong.

The game began slowly, each team feeling the other out. Then Lacy hit a pair of three-point shots, and the Lady Bears grabbed a six-point lead at the end of the first quarter. The Memphis team was big but not quick. The Lady Bears led 29–17 at the half and 47–25 by the end of the third quarter, and I began to relax. The subs put an exclamation point on a 64–35 blowout. Lacy led all scorers with twenty points.

We saw her briefly after the game.

"You played great," I said.

"Did you think we would win, Chief?" Lacy asked Billy.

"I never had any doubts, Little Princess," Billy said.

Little Princess was a nickname Billy had given Lacy soon after they met. He was the only person who called her that, and she called him Chief. They had a special connection that had started because neither knew who their father was.

"Good game," Mary said, hugging Lacy.

That was echoed by Maggie, who gave another hug.

"I'll call you guys later," Lacy said. "We're going to watch the next game, and then we're having a team dinner."

She disappeared into the locker room.

"We play the winner of the next game," I said to Billy. "Want to stay and watch?"

"Sure," Billy said.

"Give me the car keys," Mary said. "Maggie and I will do some exploring. Call us when you're ready, and we'll pick you up."

◆　　◆　　◆　　◆

Game two was an undefeated team from Clarksville against a three-loss team from Knoxville. Recent polls ranked the Clarksville team number three in the state, right behind the Mountain Center Lady Bears. We watched as the Clarksville team systemically and methodically built a ten-point halftime lead.

"They play like Mountain Center," Billy said.

"They do," I said.

The second half was more of the same. The final score was 64–48.

"What do you think?" I asked Billy.

"The Lady Bears are going to have their hands full," Billy said.

I was afraid to ask if he thought they would win.

48

We didn't see Lacy on Wednesday. The team had a light morning practice and then saw some of the sights around Nashville. She called Mary a couple of times, excited about her day. That afternoon, the team went back to the arena to watch the other four teams play in the Elite Eight. One was a local team from Nashville, undefeated and ranked number one in the state.

Mary and Maggie slept late. Billy and I quietly left the suite early and went down to the dining room and had coffee. I left Mary and Maggie a note to come join us when they got up. Billy and I sat at an out-of-the-way table and talked quietly about what was going on in our lives. He said the biggest problems his department faced were DUIs, petty thefts, and meth labs.

"We'll never win the meth battle," Billy said, sounding depressed. "All we can do is slow it down."

"Well, that's something," I said. "Maybe you'll save a few lives."

"I certainly hope so," Billy said.

I told Billy the latest on my two cases. He listened like he always did, patiently and silently. When I finished, he was quiet. I waited. He was processing.

"Sounds like the Midnight Riders thing is coming to a head," he said. "I still want to be in on that."

I nodded.

"The Clay Carr thing is harder," he said. "You don't have much to go on. But my money is on you, Blood. You'll find something. I can feel it."

"I hope you're right," I said.

"Right about what?" a voice behind me said. It belonged to the lovely Mary Youngblood. Mary and Maggie had "thrown something on" and come down to have coffee with us. They both looked gorgeous.

"Billy thinks I'll eventually get a lead in the Clay Carr case," I said.

"I don't doubt that for a second," Mary said.

◆   ◆   ◆   ◆

Later than morning, we went to the Loveless Café for breakfast. It was a bit of a drive from where we were staying, but I had been there before and knew it was worth it. The Loveless has been a Nashville institution for over sixty years, serving so many country-music legends and other celebrities that it needed a wall of fame just to remember them all. Their world famous biscuits, made from a recipe that remains a secret, were a major attraction. We ordered way too much food and ate it all.

Mary wanted the four of us to do something "touristy." After much deliberation, we decided on the Country Music Hall of Fame and Museum in downtown Nashville. As country music evolved into what it is today, I had become a bigger fan. We spent the afternoon looking at and listening to everything the museum had to offer.

That night, Mary and Maggie turned in early. I set up my laptop on our kitchen table to check email, and Billy went downstairs with his cell phone to see what was happening in Swain County. I had an email from Buckley saying the North Dakota land purchase was exactly what we thought: a speculation purchase by an oil company. He was still searching, but it was taking time. An email from T. Elbert said he was feeling "much, much better," and that he and Roy would see me tomorrow. I spent another ten minutes looking at the market and then shut down.

Fifteen minutes later, I slipped in beside Mary. The day had been fun. It had been awhile since we'd done something so different. I fell asleep wondering why.

49

The following day, Mary and Maggie went shopping. Later, they would meet Mary's son, Jimmy, for lunch. Billy and I had a light breakfast at the hotel and then found a full-service gym and spent an hour and a half working out.

Around noon, I went to pick up Elizabeth Durbinfield at the Smyrna/ Rutherford County Airport, a large general aviation airport that catered to private and corporate aircraft. The runway would handle a Boeing 747, so it had no problem with the small Durbinfield jet as it landed ten minutes after I arrived. I met a smiling Elizabeth as she descended the stairway.

"It is good to see you again, Donald," she said, extending her hand.

"I think we're way beyond handshakes," I said as I gave her a hug.

"You're quite right. What was I thinking?"

We walked to where I had parked. A few minutes later, Elizabeth's pilot wheeled her luggage toward us and loaded it in the back of my Pathfinder. Elizabeth introduced him to me as Chester Jessup.

"Pick me up at noon on Saturday," Elizabeth instructed.

"Yes, ma'am," Chester said. He turned and walked back to the jet.

"I thought I'd take you back to our hotel and get you settled in, and then we can have lunch," I said. "And then I have some friends you need to meet."

"Lunch sounds perfect," Elizabeth said. "And I look forward to meeting your friends."

◆　　◆　　◆　　◆

The Mountain Center Lady Bears were playing the first semifinal game that evening against the Clarksville team Billy and I had watched on Tuesday. Both teams were undefeated, and the gym was packed and loud. Our little group had good seats, thanks to T. Elbert's wheelchair, which demanded a premium location. Roy and T. Elbert had arrived that afternoon in T. Elbert's Hummer, the Black Beauty.

Minutes before tipoff, I again asked Billy, "What do you think?"

"I think it's going to be a battle," Billy said.

I waited for more. Billy said nothing. I was nervous.

Elizabeth, who was sitting on the other side of me, overheard. "They're playing a very good team, I take it," she said.

"Undefeated," I said.

"The bigger the challenge, the greater the reward," she said.

The game started slowly. Both teams played good defense and missed tough shots. The first quarter ended with the Lady Bears down 13–12. They were still down by a point at halftime, then scratched their way to a 38–36 lead at the end of the third quarter. The game was exciting, and the crowd was into it. With thirty seconds left, the Lady Bears led 53–51, but the Clarksville team had the ball. They called a timeout to set a play.

"You okay?" Mary asked, leaning across Elizabeth.

"Sure," I said.

"Liar," Mary said. Then to Elizabeth, she said, "He gets really nervous watching Lacy's games."

With fifteen seconds left, Clarksville's best player drove the lane, heading for the tying bucket. Lacy got there just in time and drew a charging call. Mountain Center was awarded possession. The Lady Bears' point guard inbounded the ball to Lacy, and she was immediately fouled. Lacy went to the other end to shoot a one-and-one. She made the first, and the other team's coach used her final timeout.

"It's over, Blood," Billy said. "You can relax now."

"I'll relax when the clock reads zero and we're ahead," I said.

Billy smiled and shook his head as if to say, *Ye of little faith.*

Lacy went back to the line and calmly made the second free throw to up the lead to 55–51. The Lady Bears went to a full-court press, and the team from Clarksville threw the ball away, fulfilling Billy's prophecy.

◆　　◆　　◆　　◆

Billy and I stayed to watch the second game. Lacy and the rest of her team did not. By halftime, I understood why. Their coach didn't want them to see what they were up against. The number-one team, Nashville's Riverside Academy, started slowly against a big Memphis team, leading by four points at the end of the first quarter. By halftime, Riverside had the game under control, leading by sixteen. The final score was 85–62. I didn't ask Billy what he thought. I already knew.

50

The gym was packed for the championship game. It should have been. The number-one and number-two teams in the state were playing. They were both undefeated and had been ranked at the top for the last half of the season. In the world of sports, it didn't get any better.

Riverside came out hot and raced to a ten-point lead. Mountain Center's coach called a timeout to settle her team down. It worked. The Lady Bears clawed their way back to within two points at the end of the first quarter. Lacy had eight of her team's sixteen points. A scoring burst at the end of the half gave Riverside a 43–36 halftime lead. I was proud that our girls were that close.

"They're doing the best they can," Billy said. Those were the first words he had spoken since the opening tip.

"I know," I said.

"That team has at least three major-college recruits."

"For sure," I said.

We sat as we had the night before, hoping for every piece of luck we could muster. Beside me, Elizabeth was silent but totally invested in the game.

Apparently, nobody told the Lady Bears they were seriously overmatched. They came out on fire in the second half. By the end of the third quarter, the score was 58–54, Riverside still leading. I couldn't have been more proud. The game stayed close until the final minute and a half, when the Lady Bears had to start fouling to get the ball back and conserve the clock. Like the number-one team they were, Riverside hit their free throws to seal the victory, 78–69. Lacy had played every minute and had one of her best games of the year, considering the competition.

After the game, we stayed for the presentation ceremony. The Mountain Center Lady Bears received the runner-up trophy, and Lacy was announced as a member of the ten-player all-tournament team.

"Congratulations," I said on the floor after the game, giving Lacy a hug. "That was a great effort."

"Thanks," she said. "They were just too good. I'm proud that we hung with them."

"We're proud of you," Mary said, her eyes wet as she hugged Lacy.

Lacy hugged Elizabeth. "I'm so glad you're here." She looked at Roy and T. Elbert. "Thanks for coming," she said. "It means a lot."

They nodded and said nothing. I think they both blushed.

She looked over my shoulder at Billy. "Not a bad way to go out, huh, Chief?" Lacy said.

"Not bad at all, Little Princess," Billy said.

51

The next morning, Lacy, Elizabeth, Mary, and I saw T. Elbert and Roy off to Mountain Center. Then we said goodbye to Maggie and Billy.

"Keep in touch," Billy said, which meant, *Don't take down the Midnight Riders unless I'm in on it.*

"For sure," I reiterated.

◆   ◆   ◆   ◆

When we got to the airport, Elizabeth's jet was waiting, gleaming in the cold sunlight, stairs down. The wind and mid-thirties temperature had forced all of us to button and zip our coats and jackets to the top. We stood at the bottom of the stairs to say goodbye. Introductions had been made.

"Chester, why don't you take Lacy and Mary and show them around the jet," Elizabeth said. "I'll be on board soon."

"Right this way, ladies," Chester said, climbing the stairs.

Lacy hugged me goodbye. "Love you," she said.

"Love you, too," I said. "Have fun."

"I know I will," she said. She was up the stairs and out of sight in seconds, Mary following.

Elizabeth and I were alone.

"I had a good time," she said. "I'm so glad I got to come. I liked your friends, especially Billy. I can tell he cares a great deal for you."

"He can be a mother hen."

"Good for him. You need to be around for a long time."

"That's my goal," I said.

"And thank you for allowing Lacy to come visit," Elizabeth said. "That means more to me than you'll ever know."

"I know you'll look out for her, and I know it will be a great experience for her."

Elizabeth hugged me. "Until we meet again," she said.

"Until then," I said.

◆　◆　◆　◆

Mary and I stood in the reception area and watched the little jet taxi to its takeoff position.

"God, I'm going to miss her," Mary said.

"She'll be back before you know it," I said. "What are you going to do when she goes off to college?"

"I don't want to think about that," Mary said.

We could hear the jet's engines rev. Then it started moving down the runway faster and faster and gently lifted off the tarmac. Within seconds, the jet was a black dot in the crystal-blue sky.

"Let's go home," Mary said.

52

L acy called shortly after we arrived at the lake house on Saturday night. She had a hard time squeezing all her words into her excitement, overwhelmed by the wealth and ostentatiousness she was seeing. I hoped she wouldn't be seduced by it all. She had taken pictures with her iPhone and sent them to Mary. The Durbinfield estate was beyond impressive, both inside and out.

After the call, we went straight to bed and straight to sleep, too exhausted to do anything else.

Sunday, we lounged. The trip had taken a lot of physical and emotional energy, and we needed to recharge. Lacy called again, calmer, to replay her day.

Early Monday morning, I sat at my desk in my Mountain Center office lost in memories of the weekend when my outer office door opened. I heard him walk in and pour himself a cup of coffee. He came into my office, tossed his hat in the far chair, and took his usual place in the near chair in front of my desk. He took a drink.

"Best coffee in town," Big Bob said.

"You mean the best free coffee in town."

"That, too," he said. "Tell me about your trip."

I hit the highlights, thinking I was glad T. Elbert had been there to see it all so I didn't have to tell him about it with all the details thrown in. Big Bob was happy with the highlights.

"One hell of a season," Big Bob said. "You should be proud of your girl."

"I am."

"Anything new on Clay Carr?"

I told him about the security footage. As I talked, I had the nagging feeling I had missed something. I had looked at it twice. I was convinced nothing was there, but still . . .

"I sure would like to get to the bottom of this," Big Bob said. "Whoever was responsible for the death of Julie James shouldn't skate."

I nodded and said nothing. There was nothing to say. Big Bob drank more coffee. Then he got up, put on his cowboy hat, said "Later," and left.

◆   ◆   ◆   ◆

I had a stack of pink slips regarding phone calls that had come in while I was in Murfreesboro watching basketball. Most were from financial clients wanting advice. Three calls were not finance related. One was from Sister Sarah Agnes Woods, a nun on a mission in the backwoods of Connecticut. "She wants to get caught up," the message said. The second call was from Raul Rivera, a college friend and rich international playboy living in Miami. Raul and I had stayed in touch and he had actually helped me on an earlier case involving Joseph Fleet's daughter, Sarah Ann. The message read: "Things in paradise are very good. Call when you can." The final message was from Sheila Buckworth: "Please call soon."

I made notes for Gretchen on most of the call slips and put them on her desk. I called Raul's cell phone, no answer. I left a message that everything was fine on my end and to call back when he could. That might be another month. I put Sister Sarah's pink slip aside. I would call her when I had time for a lengthy conversation.

I called Sheila Buckworth.

"It's been awhile," she said. "I thought maybe you had forgotten about me."

"Yes, it's been too long. I apologize for that. No, I have not forgotten you."

"Have you made any progress on what happened to my son?"

"Yes," I said. "Quite a lot, but nothing I can share just yet."

"When?"

"Soon, I think. Maybe a couple of weeks. When the whole thing is over, we'll sit down and I'll tell you all of it. It's a whole lot bigger than the loss of your son."

"Nothing is bigger than the loss of my son," she said sharply.

"Sorry," I said. "Poor choice of words. I just meant there's a lot more to your son's death than you could imagine."

"I thought there might be," she said. "But it doesn't make it any easier."

"I know," I said. "If it's any consolation, you might have saved hundreds of lives by coming to me. I'll explain when I can."

"Thank you," Sheila Buckworth said. "If I've waited this long, I can wait a few more weeks."

◆　　◆　　◆　　◆

Early that afternoon, I got the call I wanted.

"I think we found the Midnight Riders," Buckley said.

"When?"

"Sunday."

"Why didn't you call me?"

"We wanted to be sure."

"Where?"

"Northeast Montana, a large piece of land northwest of Glasgow quietly acquired from different sources over a period of five years. At its closest point, it's about fifteen miles from the Saskatchewan border. There's no oil in the area, so it wasn't about that. We took a look and saw the building Lisa Troutman described. She was right about its being well camouflaged."

"Saw it how?" I asked.

"That's classified."

Silence. He was waiting.

"Surveillance drone," I said.

Buckley laughed. "Associate Director Steele said it wouldn't take you long to figure that out. But it wasn't just any run-of-the-mill drone."

"A drone disguised as a bird."

"How'd you know that?" Buckley said.

"I read about them," I said. "I'm always looking for new technology or medical breakthroughs that make sense to invest in."

"Okay," Buckley said. "Tell me what kind of bird."

"You sound like Scott Glass. He loves guessing games. It had to be something large, like an eagle or vulture or hawk. I can only guess which."

"Red-tailed hawk," Buckley said. "Not yet available on Amazon."

"But soon," I said.

Buckley laughed again. "It wouldn't surprise me."

"How big is the building?"

"Over six hundred feet long and two hundred feet wide."

"So Lisa Troutman was pretty close," I said.

"She was."

"Any signs of life?"

"None," Buckley said.

"Do you think they've pulled out?"

"Probably not," Buckley said. "We staked out some private airports in the area, and late last night a rather large helicopter came in to one of them, picked up what looked like supplies, and then took off."

"You sure it was the Midnight Riders?"

"Pretty sure. It took off in the general direction of where we think they are. Anyway, our guy did some asking around and found out they pick up supplies twice a week, Mondays and Fridays, always after dark. They've been doing it for years, so no one gives it a second thought. Their cover story is it's a secret government maximum-security prison and anyone caught trespassing will be shot on sight."

"That would sure cut down on the curiosity factor," I said. "Where's this airport?"

"About thirty miles west of Glasgow."

"That's good work, Buckley."

"Thanks," he said. "What's our next step?"

"I need for you to get with your local Montana agents and find the floor plan. There's got to be one somewhere."

"Okay," Buckley said. "I'll get right on it."

"We need it fast. We shouldn't go in there without it."

"Anything else?"

"Let me think a minute," I said.

Buckley waited silently.

"Get down to Orlando this afternoon. Sit with Lisa Troutman and someone who has some architectural experience and help her sketch out a floor plan, just in case we can't find the real one. Call me when you're finished."

"What else?" Buckley asked. He was pumped. I could feel his excitement.

"That's all for now," I said. "I need to talk with David Steele. I'll be in touch."

◆   ◆   ◆   ◆

I called David Steele on his personal line and got his voice mail: "This is Steele. Leave me a message."

"This is Youngblood," I said. "Call me."

A few minutes later, the phone rang. Gretchen was still in, so I waited for her to answer. That was her rule. If she was in, she answered the phone. If she was on another line and the phone rang more than three times, I was allowed to answer. I didn't argue. It was fine with me. The phone rang twice. I waited—nothing. *Must not be David Steele*, I thought. A couple of minutes later, Gretchen's voice came over the intercom: "Mary on line one."

I picked up. "What's happening, doll?" I said in my best Bogie.

Mary laughed. "I'm cooking for you tonight, big boy," she said, playing along.

"Cooking what?" I asked, dropping the Bogie imitation.

"Country-fried steak. We've eaten out so much, I felt we needed some comfort food—mashed potatoes with gravy, green beans, biscuits."

"All of a sudden, I'm hungry," I said.

"Control yourself. No need to be home early. Dinner won't be ready until around seven. I don't want you hurrying me."

◆   ◆   ◆   ◆

I sat at my desk long after Gretchen left, staring out the window as darkness descended on Mountain Center. The bank clock across the street let me know it was thirty degrees. I tried to convince myself that I could see snow flurries in the streetlights, but it was wishful thinking. I had wanted to take Lacy out west to ski during her break, but then the invitation came from Elizabeth, and we had let Lacy decide what she wanted to do.

"I can't say no," Lacy had told us one night at dinner. "It wouldn't be right."

"I understand," I said.

"It's the right choice," Mary agreed.

I was feeling a little sorry for myself when the phone rang.

"Youngblood," I answered.

"You're in late," David Steele said.

"Mary's cooking tonight. She didn't want me pacing the kitchen with my tongue hanging out."

"What's on the menu?"

I told him.

"That sounds good. *Bon appétit*," David Steele said.

"*Merci.*"

"Did Buckley fill you in?"

"He did."

"We need to move fast on this. You and Buckley put together a SWAT team and take that place down."

"We're going to need quite a few of your people," I said.

"I know, but this is top priority."

"What kind of authority do I have?"

"You're in charge of this operation and report directly to me," he said. "You have the authority of the office of the associate deputy director of the FBI."

"You're putting a lot of faith in a lowly consultant." *Youngblood, the humble private eye.*

"Cut the crap," David Steele said. "You're the best guy for the job. You're smart, cool under pressure, and not afraid to shoot first and answer questions later. Besides, I trust you, and I don't trust many people. Get back to me soon with a plan."

"How about I get with Wolf and we put a team together? Let Wolf report directly to me," I said. "I'll work with him, and we'll come up with a plan."

"Perfect," David Steele said. "Wolf's damn good. He'll be pleased to be in on this. Unless you hear from me, he'll be in your office sometime tomorrow."

53

Early the next morning, I sat at my desk with a cup of Dunkin' Donuts coffee and texted Billy on his cell phone to call me at the office. I reluctantly had to admit that texting had its benefits. One was that it cut down on lengthy phone calls—not that lengthy phone calls were a big problem with Billy.

Thirty seconds later, my office phone rang.

"Why text rather than call, Blood? You knew I would be up."

"I didn't want to disturb Maggie," I said.

"Very considerate," Billy said, teasing.

"I'm meeting an FBI SWAT team leader today to plan the takedown of the Midnight Riders. Want to be here?" Wolf had called my cell phone and left a message that he would see me that afternoon.

"When?"

"Around three."

"I'll be there," Billy said.

◆　　◆　　◆　　◆

Later that morning, Buckley called.

"We can't find anything on the building—no records anywhere. I have a pretty good floor plan I was able to piece together from details given to me by Lisa Troutman and filling in the blanks with one of our agents who has an architectural degree. It's not like having the original, but it's better than nothing."

"It will have to do," I said. "We have an afternoon meeting around three-thirty. Can you be here?"

"I'll be there," Buckley said.

I hung up, took a relaxing deep breath, and thought for a few minutes. How did a building appear out of nowhere? Only one answer made sense. It was already there. So, if it was already there, it made sense that Colonel Hayes knew about it, and that he and his financiers had started purchasing the property and the surrounding land. Hayes had known about the training camp in Arizona. I would lay odds he knew about the Montana building, too. I'd lay even better odds that it used to be military. There had to be a floor plan somewhere.

I made a phone call. The man himself answered.

"Culpepper."

"Colonel, it's Don Youngblood. I need more of your help. It's a matter of national security involving the FBI."

"Tell me what you need," he said, resigned to the fact that he had to help whether he wanted to or not.

"There's a building in a remote part of northeastern Montana. It's about the size of two football fields, three stories, two of them underground. I think it's military, and I think it's old. I think the government sold it shortly after 2000. I need you to locate the floor plan and tell me anything else you can find out. This is urgent. Five minutes ago wouldn't be too soon."

"You will, of course, tell me all about this when it's over," Colonel Bradley Culpepper said.

"Yes, sir," I said. "In great detail."

"I'll be back to you as soon as I can, Youngblood."

◆ ◆ ◆ ◆

Bradley Culpepper called back at two that afternoon.

"You pretty much had it figured out, Youngblood," he said. "It was a military installation for cold-weather training and storing surplus weaponry. Uncle Sam sold it in 2001."

"Why did they shut it down?"

"I'm guessing we stored nukes there. We don't like to keep them in one place too long. It was probably too expensive to keep as a training center, and the war game changed. The weapons and training of twenty years ago are obsolete today. I'm sending you a file attached to an email. It's a complete floor plan, very detailed. You'll have to print it and then piece it together floor by floor. It shouldn't be too difficult."

"Sounds like a job for my office manager," I said. "Thanks for the quick response, colonel."

"I hope it helps."

"Not only does it help, it's probably going to save lives."

"I appreciate your telling me that, Youngblood. Now, go do what you've got to do and trash that email as soon as you download the file."

"Yes, sir, colonel," I said.

◆ ◆ ◆ ◆

Fifteen minutes later, I had the file. I downloaded it, printed it, placed it in a secure file, and permanently deleted the email with the attachment. It took twenty-four pages to print the file.

I took them to Gretchen. "I need you to tape these together," I said. "When you're finished, you'll have three long sheets. I think you'll be able to figure it out. It's a floor plan—three floors, eight sheets per floor. Use the conference table. When you're finished, turn them face down and leave them there."

Gretchen quickly shuffled through the sheets. "Shouldn't take too long. Is this top priority?"

"It is."

She nodded. "I'll let you know when I'm finished."

"Also, I'm expecting Billy, an FBI agent named Wolf, and your main squeeze in a half-hour or so."

I didn't wait for a response. I turned and went back to my desk, preoccupied with the events of the next few days.

◆　　◆　　◆　　◆

Billy arrived first, as I had planned. As always, he was relaxed, like he was dropping by for a cup of coffee, not laying plans to take down a domestic terrorist group.

"This could be dangerous," I said.

"Could be," Billy said.

"Yes, but you're a husband and father now. You really don't need to get involved in this." I knew I was wasting my time, but I felt compelled to make this little speech, probably more for me than for Billy.

Billy smiled. "You also are a husband and father."

"Well, Lacy is almost grown, and Mary is a cop and understands this is what I do."

"And watching your back is what I do," Billy said. "Besides, in case you haven't noticed, we're hard to kill. We'll be fine, Blood."

End of discussion. For some reason, it gave me a sense of well-being.

We waited in silence, but not for long. My intercom buzzed.

"Wolf is here," Gretchen said.

"Send him in."

Wolf was a big man—six-three, maybe—and he looked rock solid. Like Billy, Wolf was someone you would want on your side. He had the look that he could take care of himself. I had met Wolf while working the CJK case. He had headed a SWAT team assigned to take down a farmhouse where we thought the killer might be.

Wolf sat in the chair nearer the window. Introductions were made. Billy and Wolf sized each other up and seemed to approve.

"I saw where you finally got James Hyde at that farmhouse we checked out," Wolf said. "I read the report. Lucky thing you decided to secure the woods the day we were there."

"Luck counts," I said.

"Big time," Wolf said.

"I'm expecting Agent Buckley Clarke," I said. "He's been involved in this since the beginning. While we're waiting, do you have any questions?"

"How soon do we go?" Wolf asked.

"Friday night, unless I find a good reason not to."

As soon as I said it, the intercom buzzed.

"Agent Clarke is here," Gretchen announced.

I resisted a smart remark. "We're coming out," I said.

◆　　　◆　　　◆　　　◆

We spread the floor plans on the conference table. Gretchen had been meticulous in piecing them together. I complimented her on her work, then suggested she use my office while we looked at the plans. She took the hint.

The plans were extremely detailed. We compared them to the ones Buckley had brought with him to see if there were any glaring differences.

"You-all did pretty well," I said to Buckley.

"I just watched," Buckley said. "They couldn't do the bottom floor because Lisa had never been down there, but it looks like everything else is pretty close."

"What's this?" Billy asked, pointing to the plan for the lower basement.

"Looks like an escape tunnel," Wolf said. "About two hundred yards long."

"I wonder how many people know about that tunnel," I said.

"Not many, I'll bet," Wolf said.

The room went quiet as we studied the plans.

Wolf broke the silence. "These are exactly what we need. How do you want to play this?"

I recapped my conversation with Lisa Troutman.

"So the plan is, we commandeer the supply helicopter, fly in at midnight, take out the guard, go quietly room to room taking prisoners, and secure the building," I said.

Wolf smiled. "Sounds simple enough. I'll get with my team leaders and work on the details and get back with you late tomorrow. Their helicopter and a couple of ours ought to hold enough of our people to do the job. I'll call if I have more questions."

I looked at Buckley. "Have one of the Orlando agents pick up Lisa Troutman and have her in the office there by three o'clock tomorrow afternoon."

"Will do," Buckley said.

I looked at Billy. "Anything?"

"Let's hope it turns out to be as easy as it sounds," Billy said.

"I heard that," Wolf said.

54

Wolf and I met late the next afternoon in my office. Billy was back in Cherokee and Buckley in Knoxville.

"I met with the team leaders at Tri-Cities Airport for lunch," Wolf said.

"How many?"

"Six, including me. Eight-person teams. We think that'll be enough. There will be at least one woman on each team."

"Smart," I said.

"We'll go in quiet and systematically, clear them room to room, and take them to the mess hall. If anyone resists, we'll Taser them. If anyone breaks free, we'll shoot them."

I must have grimaced.

"I don't think it will come to that," Wolf said.

"I hope not."

"We'll commandeer their helicopter at the airport and fly it back using our own pilot. Once we land on their pad, we could have a problem."

"The sentry," I said.

"Right," Wolf said. "I hope I don't have to kill him."

"Or her."

Wolf frowned. "I'd hate to have to kill a woman."

"Thinking that way might get you killed," I said.

Wolf shrugged. "Might."

I picked up my phone and dialed Buckley's cell.

"Do you have Lisa?"

"She's here," Buckley said.

"Put her on."

I pushed the speaker button on my phone so Wolf could hear.

"Yes?" Lisa said.

"When the supply copter comes in, what does the sentry on duty do?" I asked.

"He's supposed to go out and help the pilot unload," she said.

"How well lit is the area?"

"It's not," she said. "The sentry turns on a couple of outside floods while they unload, but it's just barely enough light to see. Then he turns them off when they're finished."

"Does the sentry wear body armor?" I asked.

"Not that I've seen," Lisa said. "I didn't wear body armor when I did sentry duty. They're really not expecting trouble."

I looked at Wolf as if to say, *Anything else?* He shook his head.

"Okay, thanks," I said. "That's all."

I disconnected.

"So we put a man in the pilot's uniform, make sure the sentry doesn't get a good look at him, and take the sentry down with a tranquilizer pistol when he comes out," I said.

"Should work," Wolf said. "As soon as we immobilize the guard, we'll get the rest of my team off and get their copter out of there, then bring in the other teams in two more copters. If all goes well, we should secure the place in ninety minutes, give or take. Once that's done, another team of agents will come in and go over the place to see if we can get any intel on the group and what their targets might be."

"Sounds easy," I said.

"Might be if we do it right," Wolf said.

"Well, then, let's do it right."

Wolf nodded and stood. "I'll see you tomorrow night," he said.

◆   ◆   ◆   ◆

"I don't like it," Mary said. "Too many things could go wrong."

"Or not," I said.

We were having after-dinner drinks at the kitchen bar, and I was trying to minimize the danger of the mission. Mary wasn't buying it.

"Don't be a smart ass. You know what I mean."

"Stop worrying," I said. "The SWAT team will do the heavy lifting."

"I know you," Mary said. "You have an agenda no one knows about."

I smiled.

"You're going to kill Colonel Hayes for what he did to all those kids, aren't you?"

"I'd like to kill the bastard," I said. "But he's too valuable alive. And he'll have information he'll deal for a lighter sentence. I've given this a lot of thought, and I'm convinced that if he gets wind of what's going down he'll end up in one of two places. I'll be in one place, and Billy will be at the other. One of us is going to bring him down, and I sure hope it's me."

"Wrong," Mary said. "You and Billy will stay together. Promise me."
After a long pause I said, "I promise."

55

We were in the air at thirty thousand feet on the same FBI jet where David Steele had introduced me to the Midnight Riders case. We were flying to Glasgow, Montana, to meet Wolf and his team.

David Steele wanted in on the action. He and Billy sat across from me, a small table between us. We were having a lunch of premade club sandwiches, potato chips, and Diet Coke. The sandwiches were surprisingly good. My hunger probably made them taste better than they were.

"This is your and Wolf's show," David Steele said. "I'll just be observing from the background."

"And then taking the credit if all goes well," I said.

"Of course," David Steele said.

"Works for me," I said.

Billy said nothing.

"Tell me the plan," David Steele said.

I told him.

"You armed?"

"Glock Nine in my backpack," I said.

"Billy?" David Steele asked.

"Same," Billy said. "And a couple of knives."

Billy didn't like guns but had begun carrying one ever since he became a deputy sheriff. I didn't even know if he could shoot. But something told me he was good, as with everything he did.

"Did you ever consider that Lisa Troutman might have second thoughts and try to warn them?" David Steele asked.

"I did," I said.

"And?"

"I had Buckley fly down to Orlando last night. He'll be with Lisa until this is over."

"I'll bet he was thrilled about that."

"Actually, his response was, 'Fine with me. I don't like cold weather.' I told him that once the building was secure, he could fly up and be in charge of the geek unit. He's done a lot of work on this case, and I'd like him to get some recognition."

"You sure have a lot of authority for a consultant," David Steele said.

"I'm friends with the associate deputy director."

Billy said nothing. He was pretending to be asleep. Or maybe he was asleep. I never knew with Billy.

◆   ◆   ◆   ◆

We flew to Glasgow International Airport in Montana, a small regional airport with two mile-long runways serving the greater Glasgow area. How it got the *International* in its name was a mystery to me, since it was served by only one regional carrier.

"Buckle up tight, gentlemen," our pilot said over the intercom. "This one could be a little rough."

That was the understatement of the year. Our landing was an adventure. I felt like I was on the old wooden roller coaster at Dollywood, a ride I had once shared with Lacy and did not wish to repeat. We were tossed to and fro as we saw the ground getting closer. Then the bottom briefly fell out. If not for the seat belts, we would have been scraping ourselves off the ceiling.

"Shit," David Steele said. He looked pale.

I gripped my armrest tightly and said nothing. I looked at Billy, who appeared as calm as if he were on a back-porch swing enjoying the afternoon, a faint smile on his face. I took solace in the knowledge that the pilot wanted the jet safely on the ground as much as we did. I felt the wind push us to the right, felt the jet drop, felt the thrust of the engines, felt the smack of wheels on tarmac, felt the engines reverse, and felt myself exhale as we coasted to our private hangar.

"Well, that was fun," David Steele said. He removed a microphone from the side of his seat. "Good job, Todd."

"Thanks, boss," the pilot said.

◆   ◆   ◆   ◆

When we deboarded, a white Chevy Suburban was waiting for us. Wolf was leaning against the front fender, arms folded across his chest, calmly waiting as we made the long walk toward him. David Steele carried an oversized briefcase. Billy carried a small gym bag. I carried my backpack with my computer and the bare necessities for a one-night stay.

"We have reservations at the Cottonwood Inn," David Steele said. "Everyone needs to rest. It's going to be a long night."

Wolf pushed away from the Suburban and stood tall as we approached.

"Are we set with the rooms?" David Steele asked.

"All set," Wolf said. "My team is resting. We'll meet for dinner at eight and leave the Cottonwood Inn at nine. We'll drive to the Hinsdale Airport and be completely set up when the Midnight Riders' copter arrives. The other teams will be in the area awaiting instructions."

"Good," David Steele said. "Let's get to the inn."

◆   ◆   ◆   ◆

I wanted to lie down and rest but couldn't. I was too pumped up. Billy and I were sharing a king suite with an adjoining bedroom.

"I'll see you in time for dinner," Billy said. "Get some rest, Blood."

He disappeared into the adjoining room and shut the door. I booted up my laptop and went online to check email. I sent T. Elbert an email to let him know I was out of town. I checked the market. It was down a couple hundred points but nothing to be alarmed about. There was still no other good place to park money.

I called Mary. We talked for half an hour, the highlight being her account of what she was going to do to me when I got back. Reports from the Northeast were that Lacy and Elizabeth were having a great time, including attending a Broadway matinee.

"What show?" I asked Mary.

"It's a secret," Mary said. "Lacy wants to tell both of us when she gets back."

After we said our goodbyes, I went to the vending area and got some ice, a Diet Coke, and cheese crackers. I returned to the suite and enjoyed my snack while playing Spider Solitaire on my computer. I had just finished the snack when I heard a knock on the door that led into the hallway. I looked through the peephole and saw Wolf. I opened the door, and Wolf handed me two duffel bags. One had a *Youngblood* nametag and the other a *Two-Feathers* nametag.

"Your gear," Wolf said. "Wait until after dinner to put it on. We don't want to attract attention. I suggest you wear all of it. See you at eight."

I nodded and said nothing. Wolf turned and went down the hall. I closed the door.

◆   ◆   ◆   ◆

Our deadly little band had three out-of-the-way tables for four in the hotel restaurant. Wolf, Billy, David Steele, and I sat at the most removed table. Wolf's team plus the jet pilot occupied the other two. After the food arrived, we quietly discussed the mission.

"According to our intel, the supplies arrive in a white van a half-hour or so before the copter comes in," Wolf said. "The van comes from here in Glasgow, so we'll have eyes on it and know when it leaves. Once the van arrives at the field, we'll tell the driver we have a prisoner going on the copter, so we'll unload the supplies, get as much info out of him as we can, and send him on his way."

"I'd like to be in on that conversation," I said.

"I'd like that, too," Wolf said. "There's an office in the back. I've given the airfield owner the same cover story we'll give the van driver, and he's okay with our being there. He closes at dark. I've got the keys. I rented the place for the night for five hundred dollars. He was more than happy to get it."

"Sounds good," David Steele said.

Billy nodded and said nothing.

I noticed we were just picking at our food.

Wolf noticed it, too. "We need to shut up and eat," he said. "We're going to burn a lot of calories before the night is over."

"What's the weather forecast?" David Steele asked.

"Temps in the high twenties, windy with light snow," Wolf said. "It's going to feel like ten degrees."

We finished our food at eight forty-five.

Wolf looked at me. "Ready?"

I nodded.

Loud enough for the other two table to hear, Wolf said, "Out front in fifteen minutes."

◆　　◆　　◆　　◆

Billy wasn't one to play dress-up, so I thought I might get some resistance when it came to wearing the outfit. But he said nothing. We dressed quickly. Everything was black: underwear by Under Armour, long-sleeved T-shirt, wool pants with banded knit cuffs, heavy wool socks, ankle-high boots, wool sweater, Kevlar vest, fleece-lined windbreaker big enough to fit over the vest, wool toboggan.

"You look good, Chief," I said. "How's the fit?"

"Perfect," Billy said. "My compliments to the tailor."

"Let's put the jackets and vests in the duffels," I said. "No need to put that stuff on now."

"Good idea," Billy said.

I put on my backpack, picked up the duffel, and headed out the door.

56

The night was cold, and a brisk wind was blowing light snow in swirls. Wolf was right. The temperature felt like ten degrees. We loaded into two Suburbans, six in each, and drove out of Glasgow, heading west on U.S. 2 toward Hinsdale. Wolf drove, and I rode shotgun. Billy was behind me and David Steele behind Wolf. Two of Wolf's team were in the back. The other Suburban followed.

As we made our way across the dark, cold landscape, I felt the wind buffeting the big SUV and wondered if it was too windy for the Midnight Riders' helicopter to make the trip.

"Think they'll show?" I said quietly to Wolf.

"We'll find out soon enough," he said. "We've identified their helicopter as a Bell 525. It's one of the larger midsized helicopters on today's market and should be able to handle this wind."

"I assume one of your guys can fly it."

Wolf grinned. "I sure as hell hope so."

◆   ◆   ◆   ◆

Fifteen minutes later, we left the highway and wound our way to the airfield. I made a mental note of the turns in case for some reason I had to drive back. We parked behind a one-story flat-roofed building that was obviously the office. We could not be seen from the tarmac. Floodlights on either end of the building offered the only illumination against the night, highlighting blowing snow that seemed to be getting heavier.

Wolf opened the back door and flipped a light switch. We went down a hall past an office and into a large all-purpose room. There, we found a coffee station, vending machines, a refrigerator, four dining tables with four chairs at each, and a gas-burning stove. The place was cold. Wolf flipped a switch underneath the stove, and it sprang to life. Then he adjusted a thermostat near the hall entrance.

One of Wolf's team said, "I'll make coffee."

I opened the fridge and smiled. It was well stocked with fruit, soft drinks, and juice—and also a brand-new pint carton of half-and-half.

I looked at Wolf. "Half-and-half?"

He smiled. "I read your file."

"I applaud your attention to detail," I said.

We settled in and waited for a call that the delivery truck was on the way. A digital clock on the wall read 10:08. I made myself a cup of coffee, since Wolf had gone to all the trouble of supplying me with half-and-half. *Extra caffeine isn't a bad idea*, I thought. I booted my laptop to check for Internet service, then went online and found a website for the Bell 525 helicopter that showed views of the exterior, interior, and flight deck. It was impressive. The interior had seating for sixteen, plus two crew on the flight deck. There was no mention of price, but it was obviously a big-ticket—at least seven million.

"We've got cards, if anyone's interested," somebody said.

"Anyone play bridge?" David Steele asked.

"Billy and I do," I said. Billy and I had played thousands of hands in college and become a formidable team. We still played occasionally with Mary and Maggie, us against them.

"I play," the jet pilot said.

"Let's take these two on," David Steele said to him.

Two of Wolf's men began a gin rummy game as we dealt our first hand. Wolf and one of his other men went outside to walk the grounds.

The others gathered around a large-screen TV to watch a local college basketball game.

On the first hand dealt, I opened with one no-trump, and Billy responded with two spades. I went with a bid of three no-trump, made one over-trick, and the rout was on.

◆   ◆   ◆   ◆

At eleven o'clock, Wolf's cell phone rang. He listened for a moment.

"The van is on the way," Wolf said. "The snow may slow it down some. I'm guessing it will be here in forty-five minutes."

"Good," David Steele said. "I'm tired of getting my ass kicked in bridge."

"Bad cards," I said.

"Yeah, that and the fact that you two have some kind of Jedi mind thing going."

I looked at Billy and smiled. He shrugged.

"I'm going out for some air," David Steele said.

The cards were put away. Weapons were checked. The TV was turned off. Wolf's men quietly talked among themselves. They would carry M4 automatic rifles with sound suppressors, M84 stun grenades, and tear gas, to be used as a last resort, and only on Wolf's command.

"Want an M4?" Wolf asked me.

"Never fired one," I said.

"I can give you a quick tutorial."

"I'll pass," I said. "I'd probably end up shooting myself in the foot—or worse, one of our own men."

"Probably not," Wolf said. "Billy?" he asked.

Billy shook his head and said nothing.

"I'll take one of those stun grenades," I said.

Wolf smiled and handed me one. It was about five inches long and two inches wide. I put it in a side pocket.

"One more," I said.

Wolf handed me another.

"Now, give me a quick demo," I said.

"Easy," Wolf said. "Pull the pin, squeeze the handle to pop the top, and throw. You've got about five seconds. Close your eyes, wait for the explosion, and then go after your target."

"Got it," I said, acting confident but secretly hoping I wouldn't have to use one.

"I'm going out for a few minutes, Blood," Billy said. He went down the hall and out the back door.

I could tell everyone was getting antsy with pregame excitement.

"Tell me about my file," I said to Wolf.

"You're listed as a top consultant," Wolf said. "Your file is pretty thick."

"Who has access?"

"The director and the associate deputy director. No one can read your file without permission from one of them. The associate deputy director thought I should read it, since we're working together. Relax, it's a very complimentary file."

"Maybe I'll read yours someday," I said.

"You're welcome to, but it's mostly boring stuff."

"I doubt it," I said.

The front door opened, allowing snow to blow in from outside as David Steele came back in.

"What's it doing out there?" Wolf asked.

"Mostly blowing," David Steele said. "The snow is sporadic. It's hard to tell if it's snowing or blowing."

Wolf sent two of his men back to the highway to watch for the van. Then we waited, but not for long.

57

At 11:40, Wolf's cell phone rang again.

"The van just turned off the highway," Wolf said after the call. "It should be here in five minutes. I'm killing the lights. Sit tight."

Wolf and two of his men went out the back door. We sat in darkness and waited. A few minutes later, I heard the van pull around the building and park in front. I heard the motor go quiet, heard the thud of a door shutting, then heard voices. Seconds later, the front door opened and the lights came on. A confused van driver was following Wolf, with two of Wolf's men bringing up the rear.

"Let's go to the office, and I'll explain what's going on," Wolf said to the van driver.

Wolf looked at me and nodded toward the office. I followed the procession as it went down the hall and turned left. Wolf sat behind the only desk in the office and motioned the van driver to a chair in front. I stood leaning against the doorjamb.

The van driver sat, removing his toboggan and revealing long, mostly gray hair. He was lean, maybe five-ten, with a short beard. He unzipped his ski jacket, looking nervous. Both of Wolf's men were holding M4s.

"You two, go get some coffee," Wolf said. "We're fine here."

They nodded and left, leaving the three of us.

"What's your name?" Wolf asked pleasantly. He wanted to put the man at ease.

"Willie Fron," the van driver said.

"What I tell you, Willie, is confidential," Wolf said. "You understand?"

"Yes, sir," Willie said.

"We're FBI," Wolf said, looking at me, then back to Willie. "There's been some trouble, and we're going back to the site on the helicopter that's coming in to pick up supplies. I need you to tell us how the pickup works."

"Sure," Willie said. "I come every Tuesday and Friday about this time, park out front, and come in and wait. I'm supposed to stay inside for security reasons, whatever than means. They load up and take off, then I go out, get in the van, and go home."

"How many men come?" Wolf asked.

"I don't know," Willie said. "Two at least, judging by how fast they load the helicopter."

"How do you get paid?" I asked.

"I leave a bill on the front passenger seat. When I go out and get in the van to go home, there's always an envelope with cash. They always leave a little extra," he said. "A tip, I guess."

Wolf nodded and looked at me.

"Have they ever not shown up?" I asked.

"Once or twice," Willie said. "Blizzard conditions. They'll be here tonight. This isn't much. They've got a fancy new helicopter, bigger than the last one. It'll handle this weather."

"Okay," Wolf said. "You stay here in the office until they get here and we load them up, then we'll bring your van around back and you can go. Would you like coffee?"

"Sure," Willie said. "Black."

"Wait here," Wolf said to me as he went out the office door.

I nodded. I understood. Wolf didn't want Willie left alone.

"You the owner?" I asked Willie, coming around him and sitting at the desk.

"How'd you know?" Willie said.

I shrugged. "Big order, lots of cash, late at night. You'd have to be the owner or a really trusted employee."

"Owner," Willie said proudly. "Fron's Grocery and General Store. Family owned since 1946."

Two of Wolf's men came into the office. One was carrying coffee, which he handed to Willie.

"Team leader says for you to come out front," the other man said to me.

"Nice talking with you, Willie," I said as I got up and walked out.

"You, too," he said. "I didn't catch your name."

I kept right on walking.

◆　　◆　　◆　　◆

A half-hour later, we heard the faint sound of a helicopter.

"You-all stay here while we secure the pilot and whoever else is on board," Wolf said. "As soon as that's done, one of my men will drive the van around, and Youngblood can send Willie Fron on his way with a warning to keep his mouth shut."

Two of Wolf's men were already outside. Wolf and the rest of his team went out, leaving our jet pilot, David Steele, and me in the all-purpose room. The sound grew louder as the helicopter approached. Moments later, it felt as if the helicopter were in the room with us. The building vibrated with the whir and thump of the blades. Gradually, it subsided, then stopped with a final few turns.

We waited.

I heard shouts, then a shot. Moments later, the front door opened. A blast of cold air and swirling snow preceded Wolf. He was followed by a bound and gagged prisoner being pushed into the room by one of Wolf's team.

They set the prisoner in a chair at one of the tables.

"Stay quiet," Wolf said to him.

A few minutes later, I heard the van start. Wolf looked at me. I nodded, got up, and headed toward the office. I opened the door and went in. Willie was in the middle of a hunting story and seemed disappointed to see me.

"Time for you to go," I said.

"I was just telling—"

"Now," I said firmly.

"Okay, sure," he said. He put on his ski jacket and zipped it all the way to his throat. "Nice talking with you-all," he said to Wolf's men.

"You, too," they said almost in unison.

I led Willie to the back door. "You just made your last delivery," I said.

"What?" He was incredulous, facing the realization that the gravy train had made its final run.

"We're shutting the place down," I said. "That information is top secret. If you tell anyone, you'll end up in prison. You understand me?"

"Huh? Yeah, sure," he said.

I felt sorry for him, so I added, "Now, go home and forget all about tonight, and you'll be just fine."

"It's already forgotten," he said.

Then he was out the door and into his van like he was running from a ghost. The wheels spun, the van fishtailed away from the building, and Willie disappeared into the darkness and the blowing snow.

58

The prisoner was taken to the office as I watched the van fade into the night. I heard the office door close and saw Wolf coming toward me.

"Did you put the fear of God into old Willie?"

"And then some," I said.

"Good."

"He'll talk eventually."

"I know," Wolf said. "By then, it won't matter."

"I heard a shot," I said.

Wolf nodded. "His partner didn't want to come peaceably."

"Dead?"

"Unfortunately," Wolf said.

"Sorry," I said.

"His choice."

"Yeah, I've been there."

"I know you have," Wolf said.

He turned and opened the office door, and I followed him in.

◆   ◆   ◆   ◆

The prisoner was on a stool. His hands were behind his back, cuffed with a nylon pull tie. His mouth was duct-taped. His eyes darted from Wolf to me to a team member standing guard and cradling an M4.

Wolf walked to the prisoner and pulled a knife. The prisoner's eyes went wide. Wolf cut the nylon tie and ripped the duct tape from his mouth. The sound made me flinch.

"Sit in that chair," Wolf said.

The prisoner did as he was told.

"If I don't get your full cooperation, I'll cut your throat and let you bleed out in the snow," Wolf said as he went around and sat at the desk.

It was a graphic I didn't care to dwell on.

"Do you understand?" Wolf said.

"Yes," the prisoner said.

"You're the pilot?"

"Yes."

"You help us and you can walk away from this," Wolf said. "We don't give a damn about you. Screw us in any way and you're dead. Understand?"

"Yes."

"What's the landing procedure when you return with the supplies?" Wolf asked.

"When I get close to the compound, I turn on Big Bird's lights—that's what we call her, Big Bird," he said.

Her? I wondered.

"When the lookout sees my lights, he turns on the floods and the landing-pad lights," he continued. "As soon as I'm down, I turn my lights off. We unload as quickly as possible, and I take Big Bird to the hangar."

"How do you get the helicopter inside the hangar?" I asked.

"The roof retracts. I go straight down through the roof. As soon as I'm in, I close the roof. It's all by remote."

"Is anyone in the hangar waiting for you?" I asked.

"No," he said. "It's after curfew. Everyone is in their personal quarters."

"What if you have a problem?" Wolf asked.

"I call security."

Wolf paused, thinking about his next question.

"Can I say something?" the copter pilot asked.

Wolf nodded.

"I'll help you any way I can. Hayes has gone off the deep end. Most of us want out. I'll even fly you back there. Nobody can fly that Bell like I can. I know the layout inside out, and who is where. You're not going to meet much resistance."

"Why would you do that?" Wolf asked.

"There's someone back there I care about," the pilot said.

Wolf was quiet. It was his call. I said nothing.

"What's your name?"

"Steve Dobbs," the pilot said.

"Want some coffee, Steve?" Wolf asked.

"I'd love some," he said, starting to relax.

Wolf looked at the guard. "Take him for some coffee," he said. "If he causes any trouble, shoot him."

"Glad to," the guard said.

"I won't be any trouble," Steve said.

"Go," Wolf said to his man. "And send the big cheese back here."

The guard nodded, and he and Steve Dobbs left the office.

◆   ◆   ◆   ◆

"So, do we believe him?" David Steele asked two minutes later.

"Probably," Wolf said. "It fits with what Lisa Troutman told Youngblood."

David Steele looked at me.

"I think he's telling the truth," I said.

"Do we let him fly us back?"

"Why not?" Wolf said. "I'll have my guy right beside him. If he makes a wrong move, I'll shoot him and my guy will take over."

"Okay, we need to move fast," David Steele said. "Do you have the supplies loaded?"

"Yes," Wolf said. "It may be awhile before we can get everyone out of there. We'll need to eat."

"Saddle up," David Steele said. "You leave in ten minutes. I've been ordered to stay here."

I followed Wolf into the all-purpose room.

"Ten minutes!" he shouted. "Get your asses in gear."

"When we get there, I'm staying with the Bell," I said. "Hayes or some of his men might make a run for the hangar."

"Understood," Wolf said.

"Do you have a team covering the tunnel?"

"I do," Wolf said.

"Sounds like we're all set."

"Let's hope so," Wolf said.

"The associate deputy director isn't going with us," I said.

Wolf grinned. "It's our party now."

59

Wolf handed out wireless headsets before we left the building. We gathered in a group.

"Don't turn these on before I give the signal," Wolf said. "You six, load up now." Wolf pointed to six of his team, one of whom was his second in command.

They went out the door and headed for the helicopter.

"Turn on your headsets now," Wolf said to me, Billy, Steve Dobbs, and his one remaining team member. "Keep the chatter to a minimum. You-all are on a different frequency than the others. Youngblood and I can hear everyone. Let's go."

As we started out the door, David Steele grabbed my arm and held me back. "Be careful out there," he said. "I wouldn't relish giving Mary bad news."

"I'll be fine," I said.

I took a couple of steps toward the door and stopped.

"What?" David Steele said.

"I was just thinking. That Bell 525 is an expensive bird."

"I was thinking the same thing," he said.

"The company couldn't have sold many. According to what I read online, it hasn't been out long. If we find out who bought this baby, we might have the source for the funding of the Midnight Riders."

"My thoughts exactly," David Steele said. "I'll make some calls. By the way, for what it's worth, I checked Dobbs's military record. It was clean— honorable discharge. He was a helicopter pilot in Afghanistan, probably met Hayes there. We might be able to trust him."

"Wolf promised him a free pass if he cooperates," I said.

"Your call."

"We'll see," I said, turning to leave.

"Good hunting!" David Steele yelled as I headed into the night.

◆   ◆   ◆   ◆

We loaded up, buckled up, and buttoned up. There were seats for ten of us. Two rows of seats in the back had been removed to store supplies. A double row—four seats back to back—had been left behind the two seats on the flight deck. Steve Dobbs and one of Wolf's team who was a pilot sat on the flight deck. Wolf's second in command, Billy, Wolf, and I sat directly behind the flight deck. I had a good view of the impressive four-screen instrument panel. The four seats behind us were occupied by other members of Wolf's team, two of whom were women. Wolf's final team member was on the floor in front of the supplies, which were firmly strapped down.

Wolf sat directly behind Steve Dobbs with a bayonet that looked sharp enough to carve a Thanksgiving turkey. That fact was not lost on Steve Dobbs, who said, "You won't need to use that on account of me."

"Good to know," Wolf said.

The engines revved. I felt the Bell lift off and saw the lights of the airfield diminish and then disappear as the darkness enveloped us. I expected a bumpy ride, but Big Bird handled the wind—thanks to, I suppose, the high-integrity gust alleviation and stability augmentation system I had just read about online.

"How long, Dobbs?" I heard Wolf ask in my headset.

"About an hour."

A few minutes later, I was asleep.

◆   ◆   ◆   ◆

"We're almost there," Steve Dobbs said in my headset, waking me up. "I'm turning on the lights."

"Affirmative," Wolf said.

Through the windshield, I could see a faint glow that increased by the second. Then more lights came on, and I saw the landing pad.

"Two minutes," said Steve Dobbs.

Wolf gave the sign to the team to turn on their headsets. "Two minutes," he said. "Dobbs, will the lookout come out to help you unload?"

"Affirmative," Dobbs said. "He's usually waiting when we open the door."

Wolf bent down and pulled a familiar toy out of a backpack at his feet. It was a tranquilizer pistol exactly like the one I had used on Joey Avanti back when I was working my first big case.

"I hear you know how to use one of these," he said. "Want to do the honors? It's loaded and ready to fire."

"Sure," I said, taking the pistol from Wolf.

◆ ◆ ◆ ◆

We landed. Through the blowing snow, I saw the glow from the observation deck. The door opened, and a man came out and headed for the helicopter. He wore a heavy parka, and his head was down against the wind. When he came near, Wolf opened the door.

The man saw him. "What the hell?"

I shot a dart into his right leg. He yelped, tried to pull the dart out, and collapsed.

"Go!" Wolf shouted.

Wolf's team was out of the helicopter like angry hornets. Two team members dragged the lookout back inside the observation deck.

"Good luck, Wolf," I said.

"You, too."

Then he was gone.

I looked at Billy.

"Where you go, I go," Billy said.

Mary had made sure of that, I thought.

I closed the door and secured it. "Dobbs, get us to the hangar," I said.

"Yes, sir."

As we lifted off, I noticed two sets of lights above us, no doubt the rest of the teams coming in.

60

Dobbs circled the Bell so we were directly into the wind, then pushed a button on the console. Lights came on outlining the retractable roof. Then I saw the roof below open from the center, retracting right and left, until the Bell 525 had plenty of room to set down.

Once we were down, the roof closed above us. I opened the door and peered out. The lighting inside the hangar was subdued, with lots of shadows where a person could hide. A jet was visible fifty yards away, as if it were being highlighted by floodlights. A Humvee was parked mostly in the shadows midway down the hangar near a wall. Over my headset, I could hear Wolf barking orders.

"I'm going to have a look around," Billy said. He was gone before I could say anything.

"How many ways from here to the main building?" I asked Dobbs.

"One," he said. "That way." He pointed to our right, away from the jet and the Humvee. "Look, I know you have no reason to trust me, but someone is in there I need to get to."

"A woman," I said.

Dobbs nodded. "She's the only reason I'm still here. I swear to God I won't do anything to mess up your mission. This place needs to be shut down. I'll owe you big time."

I knew he was telling the truth. I can always tell with guys. Women, not so much.

"Wolf, are you hearing this?" I said.

"It's your call, Youngblood. I'm a little busy right now," Wolf said.

"Go," I said to Dobbs.

"Dobbs, come to the mess hall," Wolf said. "I'll let my men know you're a friendly."

"On my way," Dobbs said. "Thanks, Youngblood. I owe you."

"Billy, are you hearing this?" I asked.

"I am," Billy said. "The hangar is clear."

◆   ◆   ◆   ◆

For the next fifteen minutes, I heard sounds and shouts and broken conversation that made little or no sense. Once, I thought I heard the muted burps of an M4, but I wasn't sure. At one point, Wolf said, "Hold down the chatter. It sounds like I'm in an insane asylum."

Reports were coming in of rooms being cleared and prisoners being taken to the mess hall. Things seemed to be progressing nicely. Then I started to hear reports of empty rooms on the second floor.

Billy poked his head in the Bell. "Let's go," he said. "I've got some crates set up near the door that will give us cover. Anybody comes through, we'll have them dead to rights."

As soon as we cleared the front of the helicopter, we heard the door open and close. We saw a distant silhouette—a man who looked to be carrying an assault rifle. He must have seen us because he opened fire. We ducked behind the Bell as bullets ricocheted off the glass and metal. The shooter disappeared behind the crates Billy had set up. What was supposed to be our cover was now his.

"I'll distract him," I said quietly. "Try to work your way behind him. Let me know when you're in position and I'll lob a stun grenade."

"That's a hell of a throw from here," Billy said.

"I've got two of them," I said. "I'll use the first one for cover to get closer."

Billy backed away from the Bell and into the shadows.

I lifted the mouthpiece on my headset and hollered, "That you Hayes?"

"Who wants to know?" the man yelled back.

"Don Youngblood, special consultant to the FBI," I said.

He said nothing for a moment. I wondered if he was trying to sneak up on me to get a clear shot.

"You must have a guardian angel, Youngblood!" he shouted. "You should be dead."

So they really were trying to kill me, I thought.

"Didn't work out that way!" I yelled, feeling less cocky than I sounded.

Hayes said nothing. I waited.

"Give it up, Hayes! You're not getting out of here."

"Come and get me, Youngblood!"

"Billy," I said into the headset, "I'm throwing the first grenade."

"I'm ready," Billy said.

Hayes hadn't moved, and I didn't want to wait any longer. I pulled the pin on the stun grenade, popped the top, and threw it as hard as I could. I sprinted to my right toward the shadows of the far wall as it went off. Even though I was looking away, the blinding blast nearly knocked me off my feet. I made it to the wall. Concealed by the shadows, I waited and listened.

"Nice try, Youngblood!" Hayes shouted. "I think you need more arm."

He sprayed the helicopter with a burst of bullets. When I heard him change the clip, I moved slowly down the wall. I had no idea where Billy was, but I knew he would be ready. I could see the faint outline of the crates. I estimated that I was close enough to get the second grenade all the way there.

"Second grenade in five seconds, Chief," I said through the headset.

I pulled the pin, popped the top, and threw it in a long, high arc. As soon as it went off, I sprinted toward the crates. A hail of bullets exploded from Hayes's assault rifle, but he was firing blind, unable to see a target. Then the firing stopped, and Hayes was on the ground. Billy had knocked him cold with the butt of a huge hunting knife he was carrying.

Hayes had a backpack with him. I rummaged through it, found what I was looking for, and slipped it into my own backpack.

"Wolf," I said.

"I'm here."

"We have Hayes."

"Excellent," Wolf said.

61

The mess hall was chaotic, packed with our captives, all males, who sat handcuffed with plastic ties to chairs or were sitting on the floor against the walls with their hands cuffed behind their backs. We half-pushed, half-dragged Hayes in just to show everyone the big dog was now leashed. The place went quiet.

"Wolf?" I said through my headset.

"Coming to you," Wolf said. "On your right."

I saw him turn and walk my way.

He looked at Hayes like he was roadkill. "Take him down the hall to that small office on the right," Wolf said to his second in command.

His second and another team member ushered Hayes out of the mess hall.

"Good work," Wolf said, looking from Billy to me.

"You, too," I said. "Billy did the hard stuff."

"Not true," Billy said. "Peyton Manning here made a touchdown toss with one of those stun grenades that set me up."

"You can give me the details later," Wolf said.

"Anybody killed?" I asked.

"Two of theirs," Wolf said. "It couldn't be helped."

"Did you catch anyone coming out of the escape tunnel?"

"We did," Wolf said. "That's where they lost their men. We had them trapped, and they knew it. They finally surrendered."

"Where are the women and kids?" I asked.

"We divided them up into separate rooms depending on age. They're well guarded."

"Did Dobbs make it?"

"Yeah, he's with his lady," Wolf said. "He gave us a heads-up on the best places to put the women and kids. Overall, he was very helpful."

"Have you been in touch with the associate deputy director?"

"No," Wolf said. "Protocol dictates that should be you." He removed a satellite cell phone from his right thigh pocket and handed it to me. "All you have to do is hit *Send*. Keep it. We have a few more."

He looked over his shoulder and turned back toward me with an angry look on his face.

"What?"

"I'd like to rip that banner down," Wolf said.

He pointed over his shoulder with his thumb to the far end of the mess hall, where a large banner of the Midnight Riders' logo hung— the same logo that was on their manifesto. The banner was displayed in dramatic black and red, the three daggers dripping blood, more chilling than before because of the size.

"Better not," I said. "The FBI is going to want to take pictures of all this. You can do the honors when they're finished."

"My pleasure," Wolf said.

◆　　◆　　◆　　◆

I found a quiet spot, took off my headset, and made the call.

"It's over," I said when David Steele answered. "It went about as well as it could have. We took Hayes alive. Two casualties on their side." I went on to explain the details and how we had our captives divided up.

"Good work," David Steele said. "You've done enough. Get Billy and find someone to fly you back here. Call Buckley when you can and have him come to the site with the computer forensic team. I have to call the director. The president is waiting to hear from him."

I disconnected and called Buckley.

"Special Agent Clarke," he answered, not recognizing the number.

"You can cut Lisa Troutman loose," I said. "We're done here. Tell her to keep her mouth shut and she can live happily ever after."

"Will do," Buckley said. "How did it go?"

"About as well as could be expected," I said. "Get up here with your computer forensic team. We found lots of computers. There has to be something of interest on one of them."

◆   ◆   ◆   ◆

I found Dobbs in a nearby room. He walked over to me when I came in. "How'd it go?"

"We got Hayes," I said.

"That's good to hear," he said. "I'm glad it's over."

"Get your lady and come with me," I said.

Dobbs motioned to an attractive dark-haired woman in the back. She wore camo pants and an olive-green T-shirt that fit just right. I could see why Dobbs had come back. I found Billy and motioned him to follow me. Dobbs and his lady fell in behind us as we walked toward the covered walkway connecting the main building to the hangar. It was a long walk. We made it in silence.

When we got to the Bell, Dobbs fussed like an old woman over the dings in the paint and the mushrooms on the glass. The glass was bulletproof—no big surprise.

"Forget about it," I said. "This is your last flight in Big Bird."

◆   ◆   ◆   ◆

We made the airfield at Hinsdale in an hour. Nobody said anything during the flight. The snow and wind had slacked off, and our flight was smooth. When Dobbs touched the Bell down, a committee was waiting for us. More agents had arrived to support the associate deputy director. We deboarded, and two agents took Dobbs and his lady away. I watched them go.

"You'll cut them loose when you're finished with them?" I said to David Steele.

"Was he helpful?"

"Very."

He nodded and said nothing else. Before I could pursue it further, he turned away and started giving orders to agents. I looked at Billy. He shrugged.

"I'm going inside and call Mary," I said. "You should call Maggie."

"Good idea," Billy said.

◆   ◆   ◆   ◆

The office was empty and warm. The adrenaline rush from the events of the night was wearing off. Tiredness weighed on me like a wet overcoat. My cell phone read 4:27 Rocky Mountain time, which was 6:27 Mary time. She would just be getting up, if she'd been able to sleep at all.

I speed-dialed her, and she answered on the second ring.

"Is that you, Cowboy?"

"Safe and sound," I said. "We're done here. I'll be back before the sun goes down. I'll tell you all about it."

"I've missed you."

"Good to hear. I've missed you, too. No time to talk. I've got to go."

"Safe travels," Mary said.

◆   ◆   ◆   ◆

I found David Steele in the all-purpose room. He was on his cell phone and didn't look happy.

"I'll call you right back," he said.

"What's wrong?"

"Homeland Security is hijacking the operation," he said. "A team is on the way to the camp."

"On whose authority?"

"The president's," David Steele said. "He wants the situation contained. He thinks there might be press leaks in the FBI. We'll be in charge of moving the people out."

"So let them have it," I said. "We did our job. They're just coming in and mopping up."

"That's what the director said. But they'll take all the computer hardware and won't share the information. It pisses me off. I want to know what the big target was."

I said, "Dave, maybe you don't want to know. Maybe it would scare the shit out of you to know that if we hadn't stopped this they would have hit their target, and people would have died."

He was quiet for a few moments. "Maybe you're right, Youngblood. You did good work on this, and I'll make sure it's known."

"I had help," I said. "Especially from Wolf."

He was quiet again. "It still pisses me off," he said.

"There must be a hundred laptops in that place. Who's to know if one is missing?" I pulled Hayes's laptop out of my backpack. "Like this one," I said, handing it to David Steele.

He smiled. "You probably shouldn't have done that."

"No, I really shouldn't have."

He took the laptop, then said, "Can you get home without my help?"

"Sure, if you'll get me back to the hotel."

"Take one of the Suburbans," he said. "The keys are in them. I'll be in touch."

"One more thing," I said. "I think Hayes might have had a source in the Pentagon. It's the only way I can figure he might have gotten a whiff of me. It would be nice to know who."

"I'll pass that along, but if his source is in the Pentagon he or she will be impossible to find. Too many people have access to too much information." David Steele said. "Safe travels, Youngblood."

As I was walking away to get Billy, I spotted Dobbs and his lady in a far corner sitting by themselves at a table for four. I walked over and joined them. I slid a business card across the table.

"Call me when they cut you loose," I said. "If I don't hear from you in three days, I'll start checking."

"We appreciate it," he said.

"Very much," his lady said.

I caught Billy's eye as I walked away, and he followed me out of the building.

62

While finding our way back to the Cottonwood Inn, I called Roy and asked if Jim Doak could meet Billy and me at the Glasgow airport. Luckily for us, he said yes. We slept four hours, had breakfast at the inn, and drove the Suburban to meet the Fleet Industries jet. Jim was waiting on us. Following instructions from David Steele, I left the Suburban in the short-term parking lot, unlocked with the keys under the front seat. Other agents would be flying in and would pick it up.

We landed at Tri-Cities Airport at dusk. Billy and I left Jim Doak tending to his jet and walked silently to our respective SUVs.

"Thanks for watching my back, Chief," I said.

"Wouldn't have missed it, Blood," Billy said. "Go to the lake house and get some rest. Forget about this mess. It's someone else's problem now."

I nodded. "We'll talk later."

Then I called Mary. "I'm leaving the airport," I said.

"I'll be waiting," she said. "Drive safe."

I hoped I could make it to the lake house before dark. Exhaustion rode in the passenger seat, taunting me to take a nap.

◆   ◆   ◆   ◆

Mary met me at the front door. I shut the door behind me, and we wrapped one another up and held on for what seemed like a very long time.

Finally, Mary said, "Want a glass of red wine?"

"With a straw," I said.

Mary laughed. "Go sit by the fire."

I did as I was told. A table for two was set up in front of the fireplace with cheese, crackers, and mixed nuts. Mary came back with a bottle of Molly Dooker Two Left Feet, a potent Australian red blend that will knock your socks off.

"Two glasses of this and you'll have to carry me to bed," I said.

"You just relax and enjoy," Mary said. "We'll worry about where you sleep later."

She poured the wine and toasted my return. I took a drink and thought about how good it was to be home. The last twenty-four hours had seemed like a week. I nibbled cheese and crackers while Mary fixed turkey and Swiss cheese sandwiches on Portuguese rolls.

"Tell me how it went down," Mary said.

We ate and talked. Mary did most of the talking. I ate like a farm hand. Soon after I finished, Mary decreed that it was past my bedtime. I somehow managed to make it upstairs, brush my teeth, get into my pajama bottoms and an old T-shirt, and collapse into our king-sized bed. I think I was asleep before Mary turned off the light.

63

On Sunday afternoon, a pleasant March day, Mary and I were on the observation deck at Tri-Cities Airport. I had slept late, recovering from the exhausting takedown of the Midnight Riders. Mary had fixed breakfast, and we spent the morning at the dining-room table talking about the past forty-eight hours and our future.

The afternoon was perfect for observing incoming aircraft—temperature in the mid-fifties and bright, sunny skies. We watched four flights land before the Durbinfield Financial jet floated smoothly down from the sky and kissed the runway, then began the long taxi to the private terminal. Mary and I headed down from the deck and began our five-minute walk to meet the jet and its occupants.

The pilot had just cut the engines when we arrived. The stairs opened and extended to the tarmac. Lacy came bouncing down and walked swiftly toward us.

Mary hugged her fiercely. "I missed you."

"I missed you, too," Lacy said.

Then I got a hug.

"And I missed you," she said.

"Likewise."

Elizabeth Durbinfield was close behind, smiling and watching our exchange. She greeted us, hugged Lacy goodbye, and watched as Lacy and Mary took Lacy's luggage and went toward the parking lot. There seemed to be an extra suitcase. A silent tear trickled down Elizabeth's cheek. She wiped it away.

"Was Lacy's visiting everything you hoped?" I asked.

"So much more," she said. "You and Mary have done a marvelous job with her."

"We had a lot to work with."

"Indeed," Elizabeth said. "I would be pleased if her visit turned into an annual event."

"It wouldn't surprise me if it did."

"Mary told Lacy you were away on a big case with the FBI," Elizabeth said. "How did that work out?"

"About as well as could be expected," I said.

"Will I hear about it on the news?"

"Maybe," I said. "The lid is on right now, but a lot of people were involved, so who knows? Sooner or later, there might be some leaks. And I'll bet there are a few people in Washington who'd love to take credit."

"Well, I'm glad it worked out, and I'm glad you're safe," she said. "I must go. All of you please visit sometime. I have plenty of room."

"So I hear," I said.

She laughed and then surprised me with a hug. It was then the thought popped into my head that her son would have been close to my age had he lived. I wondered if in some way I was a substitute.

"Until we meet again," Elizabeth said.

"Until then."

I watched her ascend the stairs, then gave the pilot a quick wave and headed for my ladies-in-waiting.

◆　　◆　　◆　　◆

Lacy talked almost nonstop on the ride home, a monologue spanning her entire trip that would have made Broadway proud. Every now and then, she asked for or allowed responses from Mary and me. Her energy and excitement were contagious, and I found myself wanting to make a trip back to the city and revisit some old haunts.

"Elizabeth has a huge Park Avenue apartment," Lacy said. "We spent two nights there. The view at night is unbelievable. We were chauffeured and had lunch at the Four Seasons. Have you ever been there?"

"No," Mary said.

"Many times," I said.

"Really, Don?"

"Really. Remember, I used to work in New York City."

"Right," Lacy said. "Anyway, after lunch, we went to a Broadway matinee."

"That's nice," Mary said. "I've never been to a Broadway show."

"So, guess what we saw."

"I'm not really up on what's playing on Broadway," Mary said.

"Don?" Lacy said.

"Who picked the show?" I asked.

"I did," Lacy said.

"How?"

"I read up on every show the night before. I read the reviews and looked to see how long the shows had been running."

"*Phantom of the Opera*," I said.

"Elizabeth told you," Lacy said, none too happy that I had guessed.

"Nope," I said.

"How did you know?"

"I'm a detective, remember?"

"Tell me," Lacy said.

"I do what I always do. I look at all the available information and then take my best guess."

"Based on what?"

"Well, if you read about it, then you know it's the longest-running show on Broadway, and the reviews are terrific," I said. "Plus, the storyline is intriguing and mysterious. And most important, it's my personal favorite. I've seen it twice."

"Really?" Lacy seemed pleased.

"Really."

Lacy continued her monologue through her activities of Wednesday night and into Thursday, up to the point when she and Elizabeth Durbinfield had returned to Broadway for an evening performance.

"Okay, wise one," Lacy said. "What play did I see Thursday night?"

"*Jersey Boys*," I said.

"I give up. How did you figure that one out?"

"Another guess, based on the fact you went to the Four Seasons for lunch. And you were humming one of their songs while I was putting your luggage in the back of the Pathfinder."

"Not bad," Mary said. "Not bad at all."

Lacy was winding down as we pulled in at the lake house, describing her escapades in the Museum of Natural History, her personal favorite. We got out of the Pathfinder, retrieved Lacy's luggage, and headed for the front door.

Lacy stopped and looked around. "You know," she said, "I love New York City, but I wouldn't give this up for anything."

My thoughts exactly.

64

I was in the office early Monday morning. For some reason, it seemed like I had been gone for a month. Thursday and Friday had seemed like two weeks by themselves. But I had been out only four days. I went through call slips from Gretchen and made some notes. Sarah Agnes had called again. I had completely forgotten to return her last call. I dialed her private number.

"Silverthorn." Although it was not the good sister, the voice was familiar.

"Sister Sarah, please," I said.

"The sister is out of the office today. May I take a message?"

"Regina?"

"Yes, who's this?"

"Don Youngblood."

"Oh, Mr. Youngblood," Regina Capelli said.

Regina was Carlo Vincente's granddaughter. Carlo was a semi-retired New York mob boss I had come in contact with on my first big case. I later helped Carlo out when Regina had some trouble. My solution had worked, and Carlo felt he owed me. We were not exactly friends, but we weren't enemies either—and that was a good thing.

"I still cannot thank you enough for introducing me to Silverthorn," she said. "Silverthorn is a lifesaver."

Silverthorn was a rehab facility dealing with all kinds of addictions. Regina's had been gambling. Sister Sarah was still uncertain if it was a real addiction or if Regina was acting out her rebellion against her parents.

"I'm glad I could help," I said. "How are your mother and your grandparents?"

"They're all fine," Regina said. "They're in Italy right now."

"Give them my regards," I said. "And tell Sister Sarah Agnes that I finally returned her call and I'll call again as soon as I can get off the merry-go-round I'm on."

"I'll do that," Regina said.

◆　　◆　　◆　　◆

Late that afternoon, David Steele called. Until that point, my day had been uneventful. Gretchen had come and gone, and I had turned my attention to the market and shoved the Midnight Riders to the back of my mind. I knew I owed Sheila Buckworth a final report, and I wanted to get that over with soon.

"Cherokee Investigations," I answered.

"Did you get some rest this weekend?"

"I did. How's it going, Dave?"

"It's a mess," he said. "We got all the mercenaries out of there, and we're trying to relocate the women and kids under eighteen and figure out who to charge and who not to charge. I'm glad Homeland Security is involved. They're at least carrying some of the load. Most of the kids are completely brainwashed and are going to need months, maybe even years, of therapy. Some may never recover."

"I'm glad I can walk away from it," I said. "I'm sorry you can't, Dave."

"It's depressing, Youngblood. Most of those runaways don't have anything to go back to."

"Sad situation."

"On top of all that, the president has decided to hold a press conference and take some of the credit for bringing down a significant terrorist organization."

"Imagine that," I said.

"Good PR for the party and himself," David Steele said. "He asked the director to invite the significant players in the FBI to join him on the podium. The director agreed with me that you should be there."

I laughed. "I'd rather have a root canal. Please remove me from the significant players list."

"That's what I thought you'd say," David Steele said. "I asked Wolf, and his response, although somewhat more colorful, was basically the same as yours."

"Smart guy, that Wolf."

"Well, I had to ask," David Steele said. "By the way, I just got some more DNA results back on those hair samples you picked up in the desert. One of them matched Adams, the ex-sniper."

"Not very useful now," I said. "But I guess it shows how long this thing has been going on."

"Well, thanks to Hayes's laptop, we have a pretty clear picture of the way it all came together. We took a look and then turned it over to Homeland Security. I can't share the targets, but they were significant."

"That's fine with me," I said. "I'll sleep better not knowing."

"I'll let you know when it's all put to bed, and I'll send you as much of the file as I can. You did good work on this, Youngblood."

"Thanks, Dave. A lot of people did good work. When's the press conference?"

"Wednesday, ten in the morning, on CNN."

◆　◆　◆　◆

I took a chance and called the Pentagon.

"Culpepper," the colonel answered.

"Colonel, it's Don Youngblood," I said.

"More favors, Youngblood?"

"No," I said. "This is payback. You said when it was all over you wanted to know what I was working on."

"And you're now going to tell me," he said.

"Not quite," I said. "I will tell you to watch the president's press conference Wednesday. After that, you'll probably know more than I do."

"I doubt it," Colonel Culpepper said. "But I'll watch."

"I'll call you at some point and fill in some gaps."

"Thanks, Youngblood," he said. "You can always spin and interesting yarn."

◆   ◆   ◆   ◆

That night at dinner, I was chastised about the press conference. Mary, Lacy, and I were having takeout ribs from a local barbecue joint. I ate while they talked. Jake and Junior were on standby, knowing some great-tasting rib bones were in their future.

"So you turned down an invitation to the White House," Lacy said.

"I did," I said, licking my fingers and wiping barbecue sauce off my face. Watching me eat ribs was not for the faint of heart.

"Why?" Lacy asked.

"I don't want the exposure. I prefer to fly under the radar. The fewer people who know about me, the better."

"You don't want to expose your family," Lacy said. "I can understand that. Still, you deserve credit. People should know."

"You and Mary know," I said. "That's good enough for me."

"But—"

"Lacy," Mary said. "Enough."

Lacy smiled and took another rib.

◆   ◆   ◆   ◆

Later that night, Mary and I cleaned up the kitchen. The TV was tuned to a movie channel, as it often was. Mary used the kitchen at the condo like a home office, the TV her half-watched companion.

I was loading the dishwasher, drinking wine, and observing a scene from a spy adventure movie. The scene took place in a men's room. A man walked in, set his briefcase down, and began washing his hands. A few seconds later, another man came in, set his briefcase down beside the first briefcase, and washed his hands. The briefcases looked identical. The first man finished, dried his hands, picked up the second man's briefcase, and walked out. The second man finished, dried his hands, and left with the remaining briefcase.

And then I had an epiphany.

"You've got to be kidding me," I said softly.

"What?" Mary said.

"I've got to go to the office," I said.

"Now?"

"Yes."

"Why?"

"I think I may know how Clay Carr was drugged," I said. "I'll be back soon."

◆   ◆   ◆   ◆

It took me twenty minutes to get to the office, retrieve the DVD from the top drawer of my desk, and return to the condo. Mary and I sat at the kitchen bar as I booted up my laptop and inserted the disk. I fast-forwarded to the place I wanted.

"What are you looking for?" Mary asked.

"Watch," I said.

Nothing had changed, only my perception. Clay appeared with a large drink, set it on the counter, and moved out of the frame. Someone stopped to pay for something. Then someone else moved across the frame, set his drink down, reached for something, paid, and was gone. Then Clay was back with a bag of chips. He paid, picked up his drink, and left. But this time, I paid attention to the details. I briefly saw two drinks the exact same size. Then one was gone and the other remained.

"Did you see it?" I asked Mary.

"See what?"

I reversed and replayed. "Watch Clay's drink."

Mary shook her head. "What?"

I reversed and replayed. "Watch closely. Concentrate on where he sets his drink down."

She leaned in. Clay's drink was there, then it was obscured, then it reappeared.

"It moved!" Mary said.

"Not exactly. I think whoever the other kid was took Clay's drink by mistake, and Clay got his."

"So this other kid comes in, gets a drink, and laces it with a heavy dose of sleep med. He's obviously up to no good. I'll bet he had a girlfriend waiting in the car," Mary said. "So he sets it on the counter while he gets something else, doesn't pay attention, and picks up Clay's drink by mistake."

"It's a theory," I said.

"And a damn good one," Mary said.

"Thanks to you."

"Thanks to me?"

"If you hadn't tuned in to that movie channel you love so much, I never would have made the connection."

"Glad to be of service," Mary said.

I replayed the scene another time. "Notice the jacket that kid is wearing?" I asked.

"Looks like a varsity sports jacket," she said. "I wish the damn thing were in color."

"Big kid," I said. "Probably not high school. Maybe East Tennessee State or Crockett University."

"Both out of my jurisdiction," Mary said. "You'll have to find him by yourself."

"I intend to," I said.

65

I arrived at the office later than usual the next day and checked email and read the market news. I realized I hadn't been to the diner for breakfast in over two weeks. And I hadn't seen any of my friends in more than a week. Doris was probably sending out search parties. T. Elbert was probably having a fit. Roy and Big Bob would be too busy to realize my absence.

I sent T. Elbert an email: *I've been out of town. I'll come by in the morning and get you caught up. Roy, too, if he can make it.*

I copied Roy.

I received an almost immediate reply from T. Elbert: *I'll be here.*

Then I called Sheila Buckworth and told her about the takedown of the Midnight Riders. She was subdued. I paused every now and then in my story to let her interject, but she didn't.

"That's all of it," I said when I finished.

"How many boys did they kidnap?"

"Technically, it probably wasn't kidnapping, since as far as we can tell the boys went willingly."

"Whatever," she said testily, no longer subdued. "They took vulnerable children and brainwashed them into becoming domestic terrorists. It's worse than kidnapping."

"I can't argue with that," I said, feeling her heat through the phone.

"So how many?"

"I don't know the exact count. But quite a few. I know it's little consolation, but you helped stop it."

"I appreciate your saying that," Sheila Buckworth said. "But you're the one who made it happen, and for that I'm grateful. At least I have closure and can try to move on with my life."

I had no idea what to say next. "If you ever need a private investigator again, I'd be honored to help," I finally said.

"I would most certainly call on you again if the need arises," she said, the professional woman showing through. "Please send me an invoice for your services. I must go. Thank you for calling."

I said goodbye to a dead line.

◆   ◆   ◆   ◆

I had another phone call to get out of the way. Jock Smithson was at his desk.

"It's Youngblood," I said when he answered.

"Is it over?" he asked.

"It is."

"What can you tell me?"

"Watch CNN tomorrow morning at ten," I said. "You'll figure it out."

"I'll do that," Jock said.

"Thanks for your help on this."

"Anytime," he said. "And thanks again for that lunch."

"I always try to do my best to support law enforcement."

Jock laughed. "Well, don't stop on my account."

◆   ◆   ◆   ◆

I turned my attention to the Clay Carr file. In a few minutes, I found what I was looking for: the name and number of the kid working the counter at the 7-Eleven the night of the accident. I called Lonnie Lawson's cell and got a message. I guessed he was either in class or asleep. I left a message for him to call me. Then I called Big Bob.

"Meet me at the diner," I said. "I'm buying."

"Is this business or pleasure?" the big man asked.

"Since when do you care? It's a free breakfast."

"Just askin'," he said. "I'm a busy man."

"Both," I said. "I may have another lead on the Clay Carr thing."

"In that case, I'm on my way," Big Bob said.

◆   ◆   ◆   ◆

Doris greeted me like I'd been gone for a year and asked enough questions for a feature article in the *Mountain Center Press*. Once she was satisfied that everything was okay and I was still a loyal customer, she scurried away to get two mugs and a pot of coffee.

The mugs, the coffee, and the Mountain Center chief of police arrived at the same time. Doris poured coffee, took our orders, and left us alone.

"What's this lead?" Big Bob asked. "Mary didn't say anything."

"Looks like it might be out of her jurisdiction," I said.

"So tell me."

I told him my theory. He sat silently and thought about it as we drank coffee. Our breakfast arrived.

"You might be right," he said, taking that first bite. "I like it. It fits. But finding this kid is one thing, and proving he was the cause of Clay Carr's accident is something else."

I started on my feta cheese omelet, rye toast, and home fries.

"Tell me what you've been up to," Big Bob said.

"I've been defending our country," I said.

"Doing what?"

"Watch the president's press conference tomorrow morning, then you'll know. I'm not supposed to talk about it."

Big Bob snorted. "You need to stay away from the FBI."

"Copy that," I said.

◆   ◆   ◆   ◆

By the time I returned to the office, Gretchen had arrived. She was making coffee for herself when I came in.

"How are you?" I asked.

"I'm okay," she said with no enthusiasm.

"I take it Buckley is still out of town."

"He is. What's he working on, anyway?"

"I can't talk about it," I said. "Watch the president's press conference tomorrow."

"I'll do that," Gretchen said as I headed for my office. "Lonnie Lawson returned your call," she added.

"Call and ask if he can come in sometime today," I said. "I need him to watch some of the 7-Eleven security footage."

◆　　◆　　◆　　◆

Early that afternoon, the phone rang. A few seconds later, Gretchen's voice came over the intercom: "There's a Steve Dobbs on line one."

"I'll take it," I said. "Did they cut you loose?" I asked as I picked up.

"They did," Dobbs said. "Thanks for that. I owe you big time. If you ever need a helicopter pilot, I'm your guy."

"You never know," I said. "Send me an email with your cell-phone number."

"I'll do it," he said. "Thanks again, Youngblood."

◆　　◆　　◆　　◆

Lonnie and I sat at the conference-room table watching the security footage on my laptop. He seemed thrilled to be there. It was late in the afternoon, and we were alone.

"Watch Clay's drink," I said.

Lonnie's brow wrinkled as he watched. He proved to be a quick study. "That's not Clay's drink," he said. "The other guy must have taken Clay's drink. I get it. The other guy's drink was drugged, and it led to the accident. But that will be real hard to prove, Mr. Youngblood."

"I agree. Anyway, think about the other guy. Is it possible you remember what he looked like?"

"I don't think so," Lonnie said. "I might if I saw him again."

"How about the jacket?"

"Looks like a Crockett University football jacket," he said. "When he turns, you can see a patch on the side of the sleeve. Looks like *CU* to me."

"Hang on," I said. I ran the footage again. Lonnie was right. There was something on the sleeve. It was hard to make out.

"I've seen those jackets before," Lonnie said. "I'm pretty sure it's a Crockett jacket."

"Want a cup of coffee?" I asked.

"Sure."

"Know how to use a Keurig?"

"Sure do," Lonnie said.

"Help yourself," I said. "There's a variety to choose from."

"Thanks, Mr. Youngblood."

While Lonnie brewed himself a cup of coffee, I went online and brought up the Crockett University football website. Crockett was an NCAA FCS (formerly known as Division 1-AA) powerhouse that annually made the playoffs.

Lonnie came back with his coffee and watched. I accessed the roster. It was in numerical order. I clicked on the name of the kid who wore number 1, and his picture came up with his vitals, his position, and his hometown. Number 1 was a black wide receiver from Georgia. Not our guy—our guy was white.

"Stop me if anyone looks familiar," I said, hoping this would be quick.

We sat side by side and watched the screen. I went systematically through the roster, letting Lonnie have a good, long look at the white players. I kept hearing, "No, not him," "Nope," and "Negative" to the point I almost nodded off.

"That's the dude," Lonnie said fifteen minutes later.

"You sure?"

"Positive," he said, looking at number 44, Jimmy Winstone, a six-two, 220-pound sophomore running back from Knoxville.

"How can you be sure?"

"I remember thinking at the time that he could be a running back at Crockett, and what a coincidence that he was sharing the counter with an all-state running back from Mountain Center High," Lonnie said. "It didn't click until I saw his face, but that's the guy."

"You're pre-law, right?"

"Right," he said.

"Would you swear to it in a court of law?"

Lonnie smiled. "I certainly would."

66

I was in the office the next morning by nine. I had spent an hour on T. Elbert's front porch with Roy and T. Elbert, filling them in on my latest escapades. T. Elbert had listened with excitement, demanding every detail. Roy had listened as if I should have my head examined.

Gretchen arrived promptly at ten and informed me she was recording the CNN press conference and would watch it later.

I made no response to that. Instead, I said, "I have a research project for you."

"Oh, goodie."

"It shouldn't take a crack researcher like you very long."

"No doubt." Gretchen teased me only when she was in a good mood.

"I assume Buckley is back."

She smiled demurely. "He is. Now, tell me what you need."

"I need you to find out who the head of the Crockett University Campus Police is. Get some background on him—how long he's been there, where he came from, like that."

"Is this a new case?"

"No, but it may be a lead in the Clay Carr case."

"Top priority?"

"Yes," I said.

"I'll get right on it."

◆　　◆　　◆　　◆

That afternoon, Gretchen sat across from me with a legal pad full of notes. I waited. She smiled.

"Well, what have you got?"

"The scoop," she said.

"Let's hear it."

"You realize I'm the only one in this office with the expertise to come up with all of this."

Her tease was on the fringe of insubordination, but since she had become more a younger sister than an assistant, I ignored it. "You mean you're the only one in this office with the *patience* to come up with whatever I have yet to hear," I said.

"That, too."

"So noted," I said. "Get on with it."

"William B. Savage, or Bill, is the chief of the Crockett University Campus Police. He's been there seven years. He's from Nashville, was in the Marine Corps, went to Middle Tennessee State, and graduated with a degree in criminal justice. Did you know that Crockett is the fastest-growing university in the state?"

"No, I didn't. What else?"

"Chief Savage served on the Nashville police force and the Knoxville police force before taking the job at Crockett. He has two daughters, both graduated from the University of Tennessee."

"Probably why he took the Knoxville job," I said. "Good work."

"There's more," Gretchen said. "Home address, office address, salary, religious affiliation, wife's name—"

"Okay," I interrupted. "I get it. You were thorough."

"Shoe size . . ."

I laughed. "You're the best," I said. "Now, get back to work."

◆　　◆　　◆　　◆

That night after dinner, I was forced to watch the president's press conference. Mary had recorded it and insisted the three of us watch it together. She fast-forwarded to where the president entered the room. The presidential seal was prominently displayed in front of the podium. In the background, we heard someone say, "Ladies and gentlemen, the president of the United States." Everyone stood. The president took his place at the podium and nodded, and everyone sat down. I noticed three men standing behind him. One of them was David Steele.

"This will be brief," the president said. "But I thought it important to keep the nation informed of our ongoing fight against terrorism, both at home and abroad. This past weekend, under my direction, a group of brave men and women from the FBI and Homeland Security, through their coordinated efforts, brought down a domestic terrorist group known as the Midnight Riders. This group has claimed responsibility for a number of recent bombings and had plans to do much greater damage to high-profile targets. I wanted to take the time to thank those involved and to let our nation know we are ever diligent in seeking out and stopping these kinds of threats. I am grateful for the perseverance and dedication of those involved, among them the director and associate deputy director of the FBI and the secretary of Homeland Security, who are with me today."

The president turned to acknowledge them, then turned back to the podium. "Gentlemen, thank you," he said. "Now, we'll take a few questions."

From the floor: "How many FBI personnel were involved?"

"Associate Deputy Director David Steele, who was directly involved with the operation as it unfolded, will answer questions regarding the FBI," the president said.

The president gave way as David Steele approached the podium.

"To answer your question, roughly fifty to sixty agents and one of our top consultants were involved in the takedown," David Steele said.

I groaned when I heard the words *top consultant*.

"That's you," Lacy said.

"Our little secret," I said.

Question from the floor: "Can you tell us what some of the Midnight Riders' future targets were?"

"In the interest of national security, I cannot," David Steele said. "Next question."

Question: "Who was in charge of the actual takedown?"

"I cannot give out names for security reasons," David Steele said. "But these men and women were our most experienced people, and I'm very thankful they're on our side."

Another question: "Was anyone killed during this operation?"

"Three terrorists were killed," David Steele said. "At this time, their names will remain classified. No one was killed on our side. All in all, the operation went smoothly."

David Steele sidestepped a few more questions, then gave way to the secretary of Homeland Security, whose answers were even vaguer, since Homeland Security had been the mop-up crew. The president, seeing that momentum was being lost, stepped in quickly and ended the press conference.

I turned the TV off. "Under his direction," I snorted. "What a crock. He didn't know anything until it was over."

"Top consultant," Mary teased.

"Our little secret," I said again. But I knew that wouldn't last for long.

◆　　◆　　◆　　◆

Later that night as we were getting ready for bed, I asked Mary if she had known Bill Savage when she was on the Knoxville police force.

"I know the name," she said. "I don't think I ever met him. The Knoxville PD is a big police force. It's hard to know everyone."

"I don't want to go in there cold," I said. "I'm looking for an introduction."

"Ask Big Bob, or call Liam McSwain," Mary said. "Liam should know him."

"I'll start with Big Bob. He seems to know everyone in law enforcement."

67

As it turned out, I had finally found someone in law enforcement Big Bob didn't know. So the next morning, I waited until a reasonable hour to call the Knoxville chief of police, Liam McSwain. Liam had unknowingly played a key part in putting Mary and me together.

"Donald," he said in that captivating Irish accent, "is everything okay?"

"Everything is fine, Liam. Mary, Lacy, Big Bob—we're all fine."

"Good, good."

"And how are you, Liam?"

"As fine as can be, considering I'm the chief of police of a major university city and all the crap I have to deal with," he said.

"Well, I'm not going to add to your pile," I said. "I have one question."

"Ask away."

"The chief of campus police at Crockett University is Bill Savage," I said. "I understand he came from the Knoxville PD. Do you know him?"

"Not well," Liam said. "He was here for a couple years after I arrived, then he took the Crockett job. I never had any direct dealing with him. Why do you ask?"

"I need to talk with him about a case I'm working on. I'd prefer not to go in cold. I'm looking for an introduction."

"That I can handle," Liam said. "How soon?"

"The sooner, the better."

"I'll call you back," he said.

◆　　◆　　◆　　◆

Later that morning, I called David Steele. When he picked up, I said, "Nice job of dodging those questions at the press conference."

"Somebody had to do it."

"Do I get a secret decoder ring for being a top consultant? Assuming, that is, you were referring to me."

"Yes, I was referring to you, and no, you don't get the ring until you officially join the bureau," David Steele said.

"Well, I had to ask," I said. "What's new?"

"Drugs, counterfeiting, money laundering, human trafficking—you name it, it's always something. The Midnight Riders are in my rearview mirror and fading fast."

"Well, it was more rewarding than chasing down a serial killer."

"It was that. Let me know if you get bored. I can always use you on something."

"I'll keep that in mind," I said. "For now, I have a local case I'm trying to wrap up."

"Good luck with that," David Steele said. "I've got to run. Keep in touch, Youngblood."

"I will, Dave. Stay safe."

◆　　◆　　◆　　◆

That afternoon, I was in Bill Savage's office. He sat behind his desk and looked at me with an expression that was neither friendly nor unfriendly. Savage was a stocky six feet, with dark buzz-cut hair that was showing some gray. I guessed he was on the north side of fifty, but not by much. He still looked like a marine.

"Well, this can't be good," he said. "But McSwain said you're a stand-up guy, so here we are. No need for social graces, just get to it."

"Had any trouble with a kid named Jimmy Winstone?" I asked.

The minute I said the name, the chief's face clouded over. He gazed out his window and was silent for a moment. "Running back on the football team," he said. "What's this about?"

"A dead girl."

Chief Savage sat up straighter, put his elbows on his desk, and leaned toward me. "What do you need to know?"

"Have there been any date-rape complaints involving Winstone?"

I knew by the look on his face that I'd hit pay dirt. He held up one finger, rose from his desk, and walked out of the office. A minute later, he was back. He slapped a folder on his desk and opened it. He looked up at me.

"How'd you know?"

"Tell me what you've got, and then I'll tell you why I'm asking."

"Two date-rape complaints on Jimmy," Chief Savage said. "In both cases, the girls said they must have been drugged, and then they backed off their stories and said the sex was consensual."

"You believe it?"

"Not for a minute," he said. "But there wasn't much I could do."

"When was the last one?"

He told me the date, and I did the math. It was one week after the death of Julie James.

"What did he have to say for himself?" I asked.

"That, in both instances, it was consensual, and the girls were mad that he wouldn't be exclusively with them. I won't go into all the details, but he was real cocky about it."

"Same story both times?"

"Yeah, pretty much," the chief said. "And both girls backpedaled and backed up his story."

"Paid off?"

"Maybe. Or maybe just peer pressure."

"If there's two, there's probably more," I said.

"Probably."

"How hard is it to get Ambien on campus without a prescription?"

"About as hard as getting a six-pack," he said.

"Hard to control," I said.

"Impossible."

We were quiet for a while.

"Can I have the girls' names?" I asked.

"That's confidential," Chief Savage said.

"Too bad. I might be able to really jam up Mr. Jimmy Winstone."

Chief Savage said nothing, but I could see his wheels turning. After a moment, he said, "I have to take a wiz. The restroom is down the hall. I'll be back in a few minutes."

When he left, I grabbed the file, found the names of the two complaining girls, made some notes, and put the file back.

Chief Savage returned about thirty seconds later. "Sorry about that," he said.

"Not a problem."

"Your turn," he said. "Tell me what you know."

I told him about the Clay Carr accident and the 7-Eleven security footage.

"So you can't see Jimmy's face in the footage?"

"No," I said. "But the clerk remembered him when he saw Jimmy's picture on the football website."

"You'll have a hard time proving anything."

"You never know," I said. "Justice comes in all shapes and sizes, poetic and otherwise."

"Sounds like you've got a plan," he said.

"Could be."

"I don't want to know about it."

"Know about what?"

He smiled. "Guess I'd better put this folder away. I leave it lying around, anybody could look at it."

"Wouldn't want that," I said.

68

"**F**ind out what you can on these two girls," I said to Gretchen the next morning. "They both attended CU. They may or may not still be there."

She sat in front of my desk with pad and pencil ready. "Will do."

"And call Robert Carr and ask if he can stop by this afternoon."

"Right away," Gretchen said. "Anything else?"

"That's it for now."

◆　　◆　　◆　　◆

Mary came to the office later that morning. She visited me at work so infrequently that I knew something was on her mind. We had talked the night before about what I learned at Crockett University. She had been quiet and hadn't offered any advice on what I should do.

"Gretchen is running down the two girls," I said.

"That's good."

"What's your thinking?"

"You need to cut this case loose," Mary said. "You found out what you were hired to find out. You proved the accident wasn't Clay Carr's fault, and you got some closure for the James family. Let it go."

"Jimmy Winstone needs to pay for what he did, and he needs to be stopped from doing it again."

"I don't disagree," Mary said. "But you don't have the evidence to get an arrest, and the victims seem to have moved on and are unlikely to want to get involved."

"Any ideas?"

Mary smiled.

"Tell me," I said.

So she did.

"Remind me never to get on your bad side," I said.

◆　　◆　　◆　　◆

Robert Carr was in my office soon after lunch. He sat in front of my desk with a cup of freshly brewed coffee, courtesy of Gretchen.

"How is Clay doing?"

"He seems to be doing well," Robert said. "But Clay was always a quiet kid, so you never know. He's back in school, working out, and studying more than usual. I think he just wants to put high school behind him and get to college. He still doesn't remember anything about the accident."

"At this point, he may not want to," I said.

Robert nodded. "He's also not dating. He told me he won't date again until he's in college. He really misses Julie."

"Well, he's going to be a popular kid when he gets to college. He'll meet lots of girls, and one of them is sure to knock his socks off."

"I sure hope so," Robert said. "But I'm betting you didn't invite me here just to talk about Clay."

"I wanted to tell you I've completed my investigation for the high-school class, and I'm certain that no one at Mountain Center High, or for that matter anyone in Mountain Center, was responsible for drugging Clay and Julie. I'm also sure it was accidental. The drug was not intended for Clay and Julie."

I told him how my investigation had led to the 7-Eleven footage and the switched drinks. I skirted the truth when I said I couldn't identify who had picked up Clay's drink by mistake. I didn't want him or Julie's parents aware of that yet.

He shook his head in disbelief as my story unfolded. "What's the world coming to, Don? Hasn't this generation been taught the difference between right and wrong?"

"Some obviously haven't," I said. "Are you still in touch with Julie's parents? I'd like them to know. I can tell them if you want."

"No, no," Robert said quickly. "I'll tell them. Clay sees them a lot. We're all close. They've been great to Clay."

Robert stood, and we shook hands. He turned to leave, stopped, and turned back to me.

"Are you completely finished with this?"

I smiled. "Probably not."

He nodded. "I didn't think so."

Then he was gone.

◆   ◆   ◆   ◆

As promised I called Colonel Culpepper and filled in some gaps on the Midnight Riders case. He was disappointed that I had not been mentioned on CNN.

"Then I could brag that I knew you," he said.

When I told him I thought there may be a leak at the Pentagon he laughed out loud.

"Hell, Youngblood," he said. "This place is like a sieve. No telling who Hayes might have gotten his information from."

His comment did not instill confidence in our government.

◆   ◆   ◆   ◆

My intercom buzzed at exactly four o'clock.

"Gail Fields is here," Gretchen said. "And I'm leaving."

"Send her in," I said. "See you tomorrow."

Gretchen had called Gail and asked her to come by, saying I had follow-up information on the Clay Carr story. She sat in front of my desk in one of my oversized armchairs, tape recorder and notebook at the ready. Gail was not a big woman and looked even smaller in the chair. She had short, dark hair, dark brown eyes, and a pleasant girl-next-door face.

"Are we waiting on Peggy Ann?" Gail asked.

"No," I said. "It's just you and me. Mary told me you were interested in doing an investigative piece if you found the right story."

"Definitely," she said, sitting up straighter.

"No tape recorder," I said. "No need to take notes. If you're interested, I'll give you my file, and you can ask questions later."

"Okay," Gail said. "I'm listening."

I told her about my conversation with Clay, about his drink from the 7-Eleven, about getting the security footage, and about finally discovering the drink switch.

"That was a good catch," she said.

"Better late than never. I should have caught it sooner."

"Did you identify the other person in the security footage?"

"Not right away," I said. "But with help from the 7-Eleven clerk, I was able to."

When I told her who originally had the drugged Diet Coke, her jaw dropped. I told her about my conversation with Bill Savage. Her face visibly changed at the mention of sexual assault.

"If you're willing to dig into this, I bet you'll find more young women who've been drugged by Jimmy Winstone," I said.

"Why do you think the two women chose not to pursue the matter?" Gail asked.

"I don't know. I'm guessing they were either paid off or pressured, or they decided it was just a no-win situation. You'll have to find out. They'll be more likely to talk with you than me."

"Me being a woman."

I nodded.

She was quiet.

"Another thing," I said. "You cannot use my name. You can refer to me as a source close to the investigation. If it becomes a full-fledged investigation, you can reveal me to the authorities as your source if you have to. Do not put my name in your notes. Just refer to me as your source."

"Is there an investigation?"

I smiled. "Not yet. There's just me."

I waited. She said nothing.

"You interested?"

"Damn right I'm interested," Gail Fields said. "Give me your file."

69

Exactly one week later, Gail Fields sat in the same chair in front of my desk with her notebook and my file.

"I made copies but blacked out anything that would lead back to you," she said, handing me the file.

"Was it helpful?"

"Very. We're running a story next week."

"So you did some digging and came up with some dirt."

She laughed. "A very nice metaphor," she said. "That's exactly what I did."

"Tell me all," I said.

"I saw your Keurig coffeemaker. How about a cup before we get started?"

"Sure," I said. "I should have offered. How do you take it?"

"Black."

I made coffee for both of us and then settled in to listen to Gail.

"I tracked down both girls and with some persuading got them to talk off the record. Later, both agreed I could use what they told me if I didn't use their names."

"Two victims who wish to remain anonymous," I said.

"Right," Gail said. "Anyway, girl number one transferred to UT-Knoxville. What a piece of work! She was paid off. I pretended like I already knew it, and she told me she got ten thousand dollars. She said, and I quote, 'I would have screwed him for half of that. I was just pissed that he drugged me.' She acted like it was no big deal. She said a couple of other things that were off the wall, but I'll spare you."

She paused and drank some coffee. I could tell Gail was excited.

"Girl number two quit school. She said she was threatened. She seemed like the type who could be. She lives in Morristown and is going to some other school this fall, and I quote, 'far away.' She said I could use what she told me under the same conditions as girl number one. She also gave me the name of another girl who admitted to me that she was sexually assaulted by Jimmy but was afraid to report it. She said she would testify in court if one of the other girls would."

Our coffee had turned tepid as Gail's story unfolded, so I warmed it in the microwave.

"Then I tried to talk to Jimmy Winstone," Gail said.

"He must have messed his pants."

"Quite the opposite. The smug little bastard said all the girls wanted it, and he had no further comment. The thing is, if he had said he didn't know what I was talking about, my boss would have probably said we didn't have enough to run the story."

"So that's it, then," I said.

"Not quite," Gail said. "Papa Winstone, a high-powered attorney from Knoxville, called my boss and said if we ran any story he would sue. His exact words were much more colorful, but I'll leave them to your imagination."

"And your boss said what?"

"That our sources were solid and we'd see him in court."

"Good for your boss," I said.

"But that's not all," Gail said. She was really enjoying this. "Take a big guess what happened next."

I studied her. She was smiling widely. Then a light bulb went on in my brain.

"He tried to buy you off," I said.

"Wanted to know what it would take to kill the story."

"And your boss said?"

"My boss said, 'Go to hell.'"

"Excellent," I said.

70

Our weekend was uneventful. Spring was slowly emerging. Flowers were blooming, birds were singing, the weather was getting warmer, and the lake was coming to life with the sound of motorboats drifting across the water. Rain came on Saturday, but Sunday was glorious, so we took the barge out and spent the day on the water.

The *Mountain Center Press* dropped the bomb on Monday morning. The story ran on the front page: "CU Running Back Linked to Sexual Assault Allegations." According to the story, three victims, whose names were being withheld pending further investigation, alleged they were drugged and raped by Jimmy Winstone. Dates and locations were given—late-night weekends at a cheap motel. Nameless motel clerks had identified Jimmy Winstone. Jimmy had denied the accusations by saying the sex was consensual. He was quoted by Gail Fields: "All those girls wanted it." Papa Winstone must have loved that one.

A day after the story broke, it went national. The day after that, district attorneys in two different counties subpoenaed Gail Fields's notes. Two days later, Jimmy Winstone was arrested and released on bail. That same day, he was dismissed from the Crockett University football team. Then it got worse for young Jimmy. Two more girls came forward and did not hide behind anonymity. Their names went public. When that happened, the first three girls also went public.

◆　　◆　　◆　　◆

The evening of the day the last of the girls came forward, Mary, the dogs, and I had pizza at the condo. The dogs didn't actually have pizza, but they were on high alert for any crumbs that might fall from table to floor. Occasionally, something did—accidentally, of course.

"Jimmy Winstone is in the middle of a shitstorm now," Mary said, closing the latest edition of the *Mountain Center Press*.

"He certainly is."

"No way can he avoid jail time."

"I wouldn't be too sure," I said.

"Why do you say that?"

"I had Gretchen do a little research on Winstone senior," I said. "He's well connected and very rich. Think about it. One girl has already gone on record that she would have slept with Jimmy for money. He probably could have slept with all of them if he was willing to put in the time. From the girls' standpoint, it has already happened. Why not get something out of it?"

"That would pretty much make them prostitutes," Mary said.

"Not necessarily. Sex is viewed differently today than it was when you and I were growing up. A high percentage of girls have sex before marriage and are open about it."

Mary was quiet for a while. "Okay," she said. "I'll bet you Jimmy Winstone does some jail time. If I win, I get a thousand-dollar shopping spree."

"And if I win, what do I get?"

"A night to remember," Mary said.

"That could cover a lot of territory."

"It could," Mary said.

"You're on," I said.

71

N ow that I had closed the files on the Midnight Riders case and the Clay Carr case, Mary and I turned our attention to Lacy and which college she would attend. The choice was hers alone. She had been accepted to Arizona State, George Washington University, and Penn. After online research, she decided to visit Arizona State. I reserved Fleet Industries' jet number one, and Jim Doak flew us out. Biker had also been accepted to Arizona State, and he went with us, along with his parents, who Mary said we needed to get to know, since they were Lacy's future in-laws. I wasn't sure about that, but I knew Lacy shared things with Mary that she didn't share with me, so I didn't argue. Time would tell.

We landed in Phoenix and rented two SUVs. Biker's parents wanted to do some exploring on their own with Biker after we toured the downtown campus. Mary and I were glad that we would get some alone time with Lacy.

The ASU School of Criminology and Criminal Justice was located on North Central Avenue in Phoenix; the main campus at Tempe was ten to twelve miles away. Students could go from campus to campus by light rail. We toured the downtown campus for most of the day and then split up. Lacy didn't seem to mind. Biker and his parents were staying at the Residence Inn on the Tempe campus, and we were in downtown Phoenix at the Renaissance Hotel, where I had booked a suite with an adjoining bedroom.

We had dinner in the hotel at Marston's Café. Lacy and Mary had chicken enchiladas, and I had short ribs. We ate unhurriedly and talked casually. I mostly listened.

"What did you think?" Mary asked Lacy.

"I liked what I saw and what I heard," Lacy said. "It's really different."

"And far from Mountain Center," Mary said.

"Not that far," Lacy said. "A four-hour flight or an instant cell-phone call. What do you think, Don?"

"I think it's your decision and you should take your time making it," I said.

"That's exactly what I'm going to do," Lacy said.

◆   ◆   ◆   ◆

The next day, after breakfast at the Breakfast Club, we drove to the Tempe campus. In all likelihood, if Lacy chose ASU, she would have classes on both campuses, depending on her electives. There was a lot to see at the Tempe campus. Lacy had a map and had done her research. We rendezvoused with Biker and his parents. We enjoyed the Palm Walk, a wide sidewalk lined on both sides with ancient palms, some as tall as ninety feet. We saw Cady Fountain, Danforth Chapel, and the Desert Arboretum Park, just to name a few of the sights. At the end of our day, I was whipped. Our group had dinner at a nearby restaurant, and we all turned in early.

Epilogue

At daybreak on a clear Monday, I sat on the lower deck at the lake house having my first mug of coffee. It was unusually warm for early May, and the wind that normally blew from the lake was nonexistent—a top-ten day if there ever was one. Things had been quiet recently and I was itching for another big case. I was thinking about my recent conversation with Raul Rivera. He had finally called me back a few days ago. We had talked for half an hour about nothing in particular except that he was still dating the same woman. When I had asked if a wife was in his future he was non-committal.

I heard the back door open and shut and heard footfalls coming down to the deck. Lacy sat down across from me with her own mug of coffee. She had graduated from morning soda to morning coffee, drinking it black, just like Mary.

"Good morning," I said.

"It sure is," Lacy said, sipping her coffee. I could see the steam rising from her mug.

"I'm tempted to take the barge out and forget going to the office," I said.

"I'm tempted to go with you."

"Well, then, let's do it."

"Better not," Lacy said. "But you should."

"Better not," I said.

We were quiet for a while.

"I made a decision on college," Lacy said. "I'm going to Arizona State."

"What about George Washington and Penn?"

"They're great schools, but Arizona State feels right."

"I figured ASU would be the one," I said. "It would have been my choice, too. I'm excited for you. Have you told Biker?"

"Biker is going to ASU, too, silly." She sounded just like Mary.

I laughed. "I knew that."

"Of course you did," she said. "I've got to get going. See you tomorrow. I'm staying with Hannah tonight."

She disappeared up the stairs and into the house. A minute later, I heard tires on gravel.

◆   ◆   ◆   ◆

Later that morning, I sat at my desk with my second cup of coffee—Gevalia, not Dunkin' Donuts. "Variety is the spice of life," my mother used to say. Gretchen was still an hour away from making an appearance. I was enjoying the quiet and reading with interest the main headline in the *Mountain Center Press*: "Charges Dropped against Crockett University Running Back." There was little to the story. All five complainants had dropped the charges. I knew they'd been paid off. I wondered how much.

I picked up the phone and called Rollie Ogle, a friend and lawyer specializing in divorce. Rollie had offices at the other end of my floor.

"Want to come down for a cup of coffee?" I said when he answered the phone.

"Sure," he said. "I need to make a few phone calls first, since I'm guessing you're seeking information about a certain headline in this morning's paper."

"You're too smart for your own good, Rollie," I said.

"So I've been told," Rollie said in his slow, sophisticated voice. "See you in a few minutes."

Fifteen minutes later, Rollie was enjoying his own cup of Gevalia and looking quite pleased with himself. Rollie was ten years my senior, as Southern as grits, as smart as anyone I had ever met, and as ruthless as a politician when it came to representing his clients, who were, for the most part, women. Rollie's knowledge of the law was impressive even outside his area of expertise.

"I'll bet you want to know how Jimmy Winstone slipped out of the noose," Rollie said.

"Not quite," I said. "I can pretty much guess how. What I want to know is how much."

"One hundred thousand per," Rollie smiled.

"Is that a guess or do you know for sure?"

"I made a few calls. One-hundred K was the amount. I would have gotten them much more, but a hundred thousand would probably sound like a million to them."

"Doesn't speak too well for our legal system," I said.

"Maybe not," Rollie said. "But it does spread the wealth around. Don't be too shocked, Don. This happens more than you think."

I said nothing. Rollie drank his coffee. He shared a few funny courtroom stories and then asked how I had tracked down Jimmy Winstone.

"How'd you know that?" I asked, annoyed.

"Small town, Don," Rollie said.

"I'm serious, Rollie."

"Relax," Rollie said. "Estelle saw Gail Fields leaving your office a few weeks ago."

Estelle was Rollie's version of Gretchen. She ran his office with the efficiency of a top Army Sergeant.

"I put two and two together and took a guess. Your secret's safe. I don't want to get shot."

Of course, he was kidding about getting shot.

I think.

◆   ◆   ◆   ◆

Soon after Rollie left, the phone rang. I recognized the caller ID.

"The world-famous Donald Youngblood speaking," I said.

"Mercy," she laughed. "I hope you don't always answer the phone that way."

"Of course not," I said. "I usually just say 'nationally famous.'"

"You're sounding chipper this morning," Sister Sarah Agnes said. "All is well in your world, I take it."

"I just wrapped up a couple of cases, Lacy has made a decision on college, and as soon as she graduates high school we're going to Singer Island for a couple of weeks," I said. "Things are pretty good."

"Anything exciting to report? We don't get much excitement our here in the woods."

"Lucky you."

"Explain," she said.

"I had another near-death experience," I said. "Maybe more than one."

"Tell me about them," Sarah Agnes said.

I told her about the sniper and the takedown of Colonel Hayes.

She was silent. "That Hayes fellow was right," she finally said. "You do have a guardian angel. But still, you need to find another line of work."

"So I've been told."

"But you won't."

"Probably not," I said.

"You're addicted."

"Is it treatable?"

"Maybe," Sarah Agnes said. "Want to find out?"

"No."

"I didn't think so," she said.

"Now that we've got that settled, tell me what's going on at Silverthorn."

So I spent half an hour listening to the goings-on in her addiction treatment center. She had some high-profile clients whose names she wouldn't share but that I could probably figure out if I were interested enough to do a little online research. I wasn't.

◆   ◆   ◆   ◆

The phone rang later that morning.

"Mary on line one," Gretchen announced over the intercom.

I picked up. "I thought you might call."

"Then you saw the headline in the morning paper?"

"I did."

"Looks like I lost a bet," Mary said.

"It does."

"Want to collect tonight?"

"I do," I said.

"Better rest up, Cowboy," Mary said. "It's going to be memorable."

Acknowledgments

My thanks to:

Todd Lape of Lape Designs, for another inspired jacket design.

Carolyn Sakowski and staff at John F. Blair, Publisher, for their continued efforts to introduce the Donald Youngblood Mystery Series to the masses.

Ron Lawhead, web master, for his meticulous attending to my website, www.donaldyoungbloodmysteries.com.

Buie Hancock, master potter and owner of Buie Pottery, who has given Donald Youngblood and friends a spotlight in the Gatlinburg community. Come see us when you're in town.

My wife, Tessa, proofreader supreme, who continues to amaze me with her extraordinary eye for detail.

Mary Sanchez, my publicist, who wears many hats.

Steve Kirk, my editor at John F. Blair, for his expert editing on five books and counting. Great job, as always, on this one, Steve.

Dan and Missy Saffelder, Floyd and Sarah Cook, Bill and Shirley Whisnant, Jeff and Jan Farkas, friends all, who have encouraged and supported my work.

And to all the fans of the Donald Youngblood Mystery Series who actually buy books, whether hard copy or electronic: without you, this series would not have been possible.

Author's Note

I am often asked at book signings, "Which one is your favorite?" It's a tough question. Each one is a favorite for a different reason.

Books are like children, each a unique individual. Some are easy to raise, and others are not. But they are my children, and I love them all. *Three Deuces Down* holds a special place in my heart because it was the first. I learned a lot, which made the second one, *Three Days Dead*, easier. By the time I finished the third, *Three Devils Dancing* (the hardest one to write), I thought to myself, *I can do this*. The last three have come much easier.

When I write, I take a bare-bones idea and roll with it, never quite knowing where it will take me, often afraid I cannot find my way out of the maze it had led me into. Somehow, I always find my way out, and I continue to be surprised at the process.

I wrote this book faster than the others. It was like reading a page-turner—I had to get back to my computer to see what happened next. That's the way it works. I never quite know until my fingers start typing.

Another oft-asked question: "When is the next book coming out?"

All I can tell you at this point is that I have started book seven. We'll see where it goes.

A final thought:
While researching this book, I was both surprised and depressed by how many children are reported missing each year. Statistics vary, but according to the FBI, nearly five hundred thousand children have been reported missing in each of the last two years. One in six is abducted for sex trafficking.

Keep an eye on your kids. Know where they are, who they are with and, what they are doing.

"Better to know than not to know."—T. Elbert Brown